ROLLED IN DUST

MEL A ROWE

Also by Mel A ROWE

Australian Bestselling <u>ELSIE CREEK SERIES</u>

The ART of DUST

DIAMOND in the DUST

CAKED in DUST

XMAS DUST

MUSTER in the DUST

ROLLED in DUST

WRITTEN in DUST

Standalone Stories

Avoiding the Pity Party

Unplanned Party

The Football Whisperer

USA Bestseller—Winter's Walk

Watch for more at <u>Mel A Rowe's site.</u>

COPYRIGHT

***Caveat: As a courtesy, since there may be some sparse language choices in this story that may represent an obstacle for the reader, I am offering this warning. Please note this language and cultural references are purely for fictional purposes only and not designed to offend any individual persons, culture, or religions implied.*

The Following Is Written in Australian English

I consider the ELSIE CREEK SERIES a love letter to
the unique individuals that continue to shape the
Northern Territory into a truly amazing part of
Australia.

My dad would've loved it.

1

On a sunburnt carpet of red dust, the little house clung to a rise that faced a whole load of outback nothingness. But that was insignificant compared to the overwhelming cornflower-blue sky. Que's neck ached at the impossible, endless sight of altitude.

The gravity was crushing.

It was a sky that towered over her tiny new house, exposing all its secrets under a sun that shone like a light bulb in a big blue ceiling. And with it, the wind whispered a dusty promise of a fresh new start ...

Welcome home.

Que wiped at the tears blurring her vision; her chest heavy with hope of a future, as her daughter, Billie, skipped towards the house. The little girl's laughter filled the air as her shoes crunched on the gravelly dried dirt that was a colourful mesh of soft creams, pasty greys, and a bold and rich ochre red, all perfectly contrasting with that sky.

Where did she start with all this space?

'Will we stay here forever, Momma?'

'Forever is a long time, baby.' Que swore to never make

promises of forever again. 'Let's just enjoy the moment and worry about tomorrow, tomorrow, baby.'

A chunky vintage red ute, with a meaty rumble to its engine, ambled along their dirt track, scattering dust behind it.

Red dust was everywhere. She could feel it between her fingers, leaving a layer across her skin like a diamond-fine sandpaper.

'Who's that, Momma?' Billie rushed back to grab Que's hand.

'I'm hoping that's the lady with the keys.' Her new house didn't have any security screens, no spotlights, no bars, no cameras. Just a wide wraparound verandah, and countless large windows. Except one tiny window. Why bother with a window at all?

The chunky Ford ute's doors opened and closed and two women approached.

'Hi,' the driver said. 'I'm Kat.' She tucked a loose auburn curl into her ponytail, then held out her paint-splattered hand. 'You must be Que Lawsten.'

'I am, and this is Billie.'

'I'm Billie. I'm five, and I'm going to go to a proper school soon.' Billie shook Kat's hand like a businesswoman.

Don't grow up too fast, baby.

'I have a daughter, Kaytlyn, who's almost eight,' said Kat. 'She'd love to meet you.'

'See, Momma, I've got a new friend already.'

The other woman approached. 'Hi, Billie, I'm Karen and I have a boy, Levi, the same age as you. So that means you'll have two new friends when you start school.'

The kid gave a full-wattage smile that pronounced the gap of her missing tooth. 'When do I start school, Momma? Today?'

'How about we look at the house first?' Her own house. Wow.

'These are for you.' Kat held out a set of keys.

'Here, you can do the honours, Billie.' Her daughter clutched the keys as if they were the grand prize in life. 'You did the renovations, Kat?'

'I gutted the place. It was so small and poky, I had to open it up for the view, it was in desperate need of light.' Kat stroked the side of the house like it was alive. 'But with some fresh paint and new kitchen cupboards, it came up amazing. I didn't test out the stove, or the fridge, but they seem to work.'

Que peered through the windows at the kitchen benches that begged with the potential to overcrowd them with appliances. It was like the house was all windows, with no garden, but a concrete path that led to a huge shed.

And. That. Sky.

'How come you bought this place without seeing it?' Karen asked Que.

'It was our game.' Billie's pigtails bounced as she jumped the steps to the wide verandah. 'Momma, I can roller-skate here.' Her blue eyes were as wide as chocolate-chip cookies.

'All the way around the house, baby.' It was on their wish list, along with a remote location, school, and a hospital. 'Hey, how small is the bush hospital?'

'If its anything major, they'll air vac you out of town,' replied Kat. 'The locals have a saying, *if in pain catch a plane.*'

'Let's hope that never happens.' Que knocked her knuckles across the wooden pylon that was one of many holding the verandah's roof. If one fell, would they all fall like a house of cards?

'Momma made the coolest house-hunting game everrr. She taped a map of Australia on the side of the Mighty T.'

'The what?' Karen asked.

'Our trailer's nickname.' Que pointed to the huge caravan that always had her back. 'It was originally Trailer Trash, but some of the grey nomads found the name offensive.' Que shared a soft smile at the beast that was home.

'What else did you do with your house hunting game?' Karen asked Billie.

'Momma made me wear a blindfold, and I threw a ball of sticky tape at the map, where it landed was going to be home. The Northern Territory. Here.' Billie stamped her little sneaker on the mat, and dust rose like a tiny cloud puff. 'Momma, should I take off my shoes? I don't want to dirty our new home.'

'We're good, baby. Go on, the house is all yours.'

'Aww, can I swap Billie for one of my seven boys?' Karen asked.

'Seven kids!'

'Eight. There's a little girl in the mix,' said Kat from the sidelines. 'That's why we call Karen *Supermom.*'

Billie rushed inside. Her shoes squeaked along the floorboards as she whizzed around the place like a rumbling metal ball inside a pinball machine.

'You know, you bought this the day it went on the market?' Kat said, 'I've flipped plenty of properties before, but never sold one this quick.'

'Right time, right place, I guess. What else can you tell me about the place?'

'Just that I bought it off my friend's father-in-law; he's semi-retired to Queensland. Karen, you know everything about everyone in Elsie Creek.'

'Do not.'

'Do, too. So, do tell.'

'Fine ...' Karen peeked through the open front doorway. 'I haven't been here since I was a kid. Alex's mother was friends with my mum, and Molly. Molly lives on the mango farm over there ...' Karen pointed across the expansive area that made up their driveway. 'Molly is our local hairdresser and owns the farm with her niece Verily. Verily is our softball coach. Her partner is Alex, and this was his dad Neville's house.'

'Huh.' Que had no idea who Karen was talking about. She couldn't see the neighbours' properties beyond all of that space. 'What was this farm for?' *Dirt.*

'Nothing. Neville and his son, Alex Landers, are truck drivers. They owned a few trucks, where that shed was used to drive his big trucks through it to work on the engines without unhitching his trailers.' Karen pointed to the massive open shed, with a high roof, that was big enough to park three trucks side by side. 'Neville's son, Alex, still drives trucks when he's not brewing beer or working the mangoes.'

'Verily drives them too,' said Kat. 'Don't freak out when you see their road trains, they're huge.'

From the front steps, Que couldn't see the road, hidden by scrub and tall grasses that swallowed her driveway to the outside world. But around the house it was just a lot of red dirt and spindly scrub. And that sky.

Was there such a thing as a sky phobia? Was it the opposite to claustrophobia, when feeling tiny with all this space?

Que needed to change the conversation, or they were going to hit the highway in search of some cityscape.

'What do you know about the rest of my neighbours?' A surprising question when Que had never cared about neighbours before.

'Well …' Supermom Karen took a deep breath, while Billie ricocheted around the empty house, opening windows and doors. 'Like I said, down the road towards town is Alex, Verily and Molly. They're the best.'

'Ditto to that,' said Kat. 'They've gone to visit Alex's dad in Brisbane, to do some baby shopping and a brewery tour. I'll introduce you when they return. Do you play softball? We'd love an extra player.'

'I'll have a think about it after I've settled into the neighbourhood.' Team sports or functions with friends were unheard of in Que's world. Did she dare take up the offer?

'Across the other side you have Gary and Val Cromwell,' said Karen, continuing her talking tour of the neighbours. 'Their kids, Tommy and Maddy, catch the school bus that stops right out front.'

'That's handy.'

'Oh, talking about neighbours …' Supermom Karen pointed to a large troop carrier coming up the dirt drive. 'That's Richard and Bertha Symes, they live on your left side.'

'And they're here because?'

'They've been checking out the renovations. They're really nice people,' said Kat. 'Bertha is the best baker. Can you cook?'

'Barely.' Que was barely keeping up with this conversation with a stack of neighbours' names she'd never remember. 'So everyone knows we were coming?'

Kat shook her head. 'Don't think so?'

'Er, hello ...' Supermom Karen waved her hands at Que like she was hustling some merchandise on late-night TV. 'Are you kidding me. When I first heard Kat sold this place, all I wished for was someone with children.'

'Is this the type of town no one can sneak into?' How nosy were these people?

'We get the occasional tourists on their way to Kakadu,' replied Kat, 'and they'll stop to see Karma.'

'Karma? Is that a witch doctor or a crystal carrying tarot reader?'

'The crocodile. Karma's famous, he lives at the pub.'

'A-huh?' Too many names. Too many quirks. And another round of fresh faces to meet. Should she bother to remember their names before she moved on?

Stop. Que exhaled the snark because she'd agreed to stop and be still for Billie. It was time to be civil and start making an effort— which meant meeting the neighbours.

Whipping on a smile, she approached the elderly couple climbing out of the beefy Landcruiser. 'Hello, I'm Que, I believe we're neighbours.'

'Richard and Bertha. Welcome to Elsie Creek.' Richard removed his enormous cowboy hat, before offering her a warm handshake.

'We've brought you a little something to welcome you to our

town.' Bertha held up a large wicker basket, brimming with goodies. 'Some fresh eggs, bananas, mango chutney and banana bread.'

'It's the best banana bread in the district,' said Karen.

'And my tomatoes,' said Richard, sliding on his Akubra. 'I've got a bumper crop coming on this year.'

'You didn't have to do this.' The basket was heavy, as heavy as her heart. 'Thank you so much, it's very thoughtful.' And unheard of. *Wow, what a first impression.* Que felt like she was living in some sweet telenovela, that were known for jaw-dropping bombs to drop … any minute now …

'MOMMA!'

A dog barked.

'*Billie!*' Instantly, she dumped the basket onto the verandah and ran through the front door, into the large open room with the kitchen to her right. 'Where are you? Billie?'

She raced down the central corridor, which led to the bedrooms and bathroom. It ended at a large room of windows that exposed an even grander view of the property, where Billie pointed to the outside world.

'Are you okay?' Que scooped up her daughter, holding her against her hammering chest as she searched for her escape and security blanket, the Mighty T. But her fast getaway was blocked by the entire neighbourhood thundering down the corridor louder than a herd of elephants.

Oh wait, that was the adrenalin pulsing in her throat.

'What's wrong?' Que asked Billie.

'There's a thing in that pond. And a dog.'

'Huh?' Que's fear melted away. 'What is that?'

Everyone stared through the wall of windows displaying a life-sized painting of that ginormous blue sky and olive-leafed trees that rolled like waves in the ocean. It was the open, endless outback. She'd never felt so small.

Richard slid open the glass door to the back verandah area, big enough for outdoor entertaining.

Meanwhile, Que walked backwards until she spotted the Mighty T, still attached to her four-wheel-drive, waiting like a trusty steed at the other end of the corridor. Maybe moving here was a bad idea.

'Oh, it's just Cecil,' Richard said, poking up the brim of his cowboy hat. 'And some dog. It looks young and it's lost its tail?'

'Is that doggie, okay?' Billie wriggled out of Que's hold to get to the ground.

'He looks like he could do with a decent feed, but okay, I guess. His friend there is Cecil. Now, he's the world's friendliest water buffalo. Do you want to meet him?' Richard held out his hand to Billie.

'Are you kidding? I have a dog, and a buffalo, in my backyard?' Que tightened her ponytail, desperate to get a grip.

'Cecil's doing what water buffaloes do, he's wallowing in your waterhole,' said Richard with a hearty chuckle. 'You'll need to keep your front gate shut if you don't want him to come onto your property. But I'll go check out that dog for you.'

'I wanna see,' said Billie. 'Momma said we could get a dog when we moved in. Is he ours? Can we keep him, Momma?'

'It might belong to someone else, baby. Just don't go near that water. Or that dog. Or the big black lump wallowing in that water.'

'It's only a knee-deep puddle by the looks of it,' said Richard, trotting down the back steps with Billie hot on his heels. 'It'd be the leftover from the wet season rains, or you have a boghole.'

'So, I'll have waterfront views in the wet season, huh?' Weather Que had only read about.

'Don't we all.'

'Honey,' Bertha called to her husband. 'I think you need to tell Billie about the Billabong Bunyip.'

'Good idea, luv. Come on, Billie. Cecil won't hurt you; he loves kids. And by the looks of that pup, he likes kids, too.'

Que wanted to keep Billie at her side. She always kept Billie in her line of sight, except for that one time … How was she going to cope with her baby going to school?

Yet to see the little girl take the hand of the elderly man made her tethered heart strings stretch to near breaking point. Already expanding her horizons, her baby girl was so trusting of strangers.

It was something Que had to relearn.

Taking a deep breath, she faced the three women on her back verandah. 'Can someone please explain what is a Cecil? And a Billabong Bunyip?'

'Cecil is a pet pygmy buffalo, although the men will tell you he's just short. He belongs to Esther,' said Karen. 'The kids feed him at school during lunchtime and they draw all over his back in chalk. Some days he's covered in flowers, or the new letter of the alphabet.'

'I've got stacks of chalk in the car I'll share with Billie,' said Kat. 'Look, hon, don't worry, I know exactly how you feel. Cecil scared me silly at first, but he's harmless. I used Cecil to help me propose to my husband.'

'A-huh?' Que tried to control her breathing, along with the urge to bundle up Billie and bolt for the Mighty T. But her daughter was all smiles, holding out her fingers to the muddy dog with no tail, who was cowering to meet them on the edge of the puddle.

'Cecil will easily fall in love with you if you feed him flowers and muesli bars,' continued Kat.

'As for the Billabong Bunyip,' said Bertha, a little breathless, 'it's a story we all tell the children to ensure they stay away from any of our waterways.'

'Are you okay, Bertha?' Que asked.

'Just catching my breath from that run down the corridor. I'm so unfit, and you run so fast.' Bertha patted her generous chest. 'I remember getting told about the Billabong Bunyip when I was little. I never went swimming anywhere after that. Still don't.'

'The Billabong Bunyip's scarier than crocodiles,' said Kat, with Supermom Karen nodding like a little girl with big eyes.

'Are there crocodiles in the water? We saw the warning signs at every creek crossing, which kind of sucked. There were some sweet spots we wanted to stop at.'

'Crocodiles are everywhere,' replied Kat. 'So don't go swimming anywhere unless it's a pool. You have a creek at the back.'

'I do?' Was she to expect some crocodile to bask beside the water buffalo right at her back door? Was it too late to ask for a refund?

'Which reminds me,' said Karen, turning to Bertha, 'We're organising a Mother's Day event to raise funds for a school swimming pool. I know it's two months away, but we're hoping you might bake some of your amazing banana bread?'

'Every school mum has tried for decades now, it never happens. Pools are expensive to run, and you'll need lifesavers and everything.'

'But our grants guru up at the hospital—'

'Who?'

'Jenny, head nursing sister. She's amazing for internet shopping and for finding Government grants for our region,' explained Kat.

'What did Jenny find?' Bertha asked.

Que switched off as the women continued to talk about people she didn't know.

Her daughter and Richard stood at the edge of the muddy puddle, where the short, black, shiny-nosed water buffalo sloshed his way out. He stared at them through long black lashes, chewing like a cow, with red ribbons wrapped around his curved horns like a maypole.

Billie's tiny hand patted the black sides of the buffalo, her laughter carrying across the parched soil. It was music that made Que smile. Every time.

'What do you think, Que?' Karen asked. 'Can you help with the school fundraiser?'

'I haven't even unpacked yet.' She threw her thumb back at the house she hadn't even looked at properly.

'We're doing it so we can run regular swimming classes for our little ones.' Karen pointed to the giggly child patting both the big black buffalo and mangy mutt.

Nice hustle, Karen. 'I can't bake. So, um …' Que shrugged.

'What do you do?'

'I'm a digital doodler.'

'Huh?'

'I'm a graphic designer.'

'YES!' Kat waved her arms in a hallelujah. 'Finally, my prayers have been answered. What's your specialty?'

'I design websites, logos, and merch.' Merchandise was her side hustle. 'I could donate time to do a digital design for a business. But you can't put that in a stall like you'd sell cakes.' Cake stalls and school events was a whole new world for Que.

'That's brilliant,' said Kat. 'We could raffle it off. I'll buy ten tickets.'

'Nah.' Karen swatted the air as if at a pesky fly. 'The pub does the chook raffle every Friday. We need to think bigger, because I reckon we can score other services to raise money, like Que's thing. I'm gonna hit up that snooty mine manager. Kat, you can hit up your husband about doing a car service in his mechanic's shop.'

'Kyle will be into that. We could have my brother-in-law, Jimmy, offer to play barbie king for someone's next party. JT could do a car detailing or small engine repairs like a lawnmower service. I could do a home handyman's job or an interior design consult—'

'How about a silent auction then?' butted in Que, amazed how overcrowded the house had gotten.

'A what?' Bertha asked, still catching her breath.

'People can place their bids inside a sealed box displaying the service they want to use, and the highest bid wins.' If Que was planning to stick around it'd be a great way to advertise among the locals. But then again, how much digital work did they need in this tiny outback town?

'That's brilliant,' said Kat. 'I'm going to buy you the best coffee you'll ever find in this town—once you've settled in, of course—and we can brainstorm ideas.'

'You can do the flyers,' said Karen.

'I haven't even unpacked yet.'

Then Bertha slapped a frail hand over her heart while clutching onto Que's arm. Her eyes widened as she panted for breath. Sweat broke out across her forehead, and she dropped five shades of pale in the blink of an eye.

'Bertha?'

'Can't … breathe …' She clutched her heart, collapsing to the ground. Kat and Que barely caught her from smacking her head against the concrete.

Karen squealed, flapping her hands in a panic. 'Is Bertha having a heart attack?'

Que knelt beside Bertha and felt for a pulse, but she couldn't find one. 'Call an ambulance.' Que started compressions. 'Come on …' This was not gonna happen in her new house. No way in hell.

'That could be hours, it's run by volunteers—'

'Bertha!' Richard rushed up the steps.

'We need to get to the hospital. NOW.' Que pinched Bertha's nose and forced air into her new neighbours' lungs.

'We'll go in my car.' Richard trembled, fumbling with the keys, they fell to the floor.

'I'll get the car. Karen, grab Billie.' Kat snatched up the keys and tore through the house, as Karen raced for Billie, who stood shoulder to shoulder with the buffalo and the stray dog.

In a matter of moments, they had Bertha laid down in the back of the Landcruiser. Que continued compressions, while Kat drove. Richard held Bertha's hand and Karen hugged Billie.

Que's arms ached and sweat ran down her back, as she fought to keep her neighbour alive. She wasn't a hero. She never got involved in anything, always choosing to walk away—run, more like it—but here she was, trying to save a stranger.

If this lady died, it was a bad omen in a place she hoped to call home.

Dust plumed high behind them on the track, hiding the following buffalo, leaving behind the tiny house under that big sky, with a stray dog guarding its open front door.

Welcome to the neighbourhood.

2

The blacktop glistened like a rope of liquorice stretching under the sun, where the lumpy landscape bled into the dusky pink horizon, with its familiar trees soon swallowed into hills to become microscopic fleas on the landscape.

With the wind in his face, Connor chased down the white line with only the sound of his Harley, and he flew.

This was freedom.

No cars. No people. No uniforms. No enemies.

He gunned the throttle on the bike's handlebars and the throaty pistons powered to claw closer to the tarmac, as if he'd become one with the road. It glided over the curves, the lazy dips, and smooth wide corners as if following the contours of a woman's body. This open road was a pure power shot for an adrenaline junkie.

He glanced at his side mirror, where he'd seen nothing for hours as he chased the sun. Only to arch his eyebrow at the police car.

Where did you come from?

The speedometer on his bike was hightailing it at one-eighty clicks. Gripping the throttle, he was tempted to gun for the two hundred on that open road.

Again, his eyes flickered to his mirrors for that cop car. Did he dare …

Hang on, this was cattle country, filled with cocky cowboys. So that slick highway pursuit car was probably tricked-up for speed and no doubt ready to rumble. *Dammit.*

With a hearty exhale, he eased the bike to a respectable speed, slow enough to get off and walk.

Now, would they flash the lights and pull him over? Or move along like a good little piggie?

The cop's car lights flashed blue.

Arsehole.

Connor pulled his bike to the side of the gravelly highway and turned it off, as he tried to calculate the demerit points left on his licence.

What's the big deal, anyway? They were in the middle of freaking nowhere, the only person he'd hurt would be himself.

The silence was deafening with the bike's vibration still rattling in his chest. Climbing off the bike, he pulled down the black neck gator covering his face, imprinted with the skull. He slipped off his helmet, then scratched at his buzz cut while sizing up the dude in the uniform.

The cop was a beefy bloke. His policeman's uniform outlined muscles that'd make him an even scrapper in strength, *if* they were to get hot headed, *if* the guy knew how to punch.

But Connor had to remember he wasn't in enemy territory now, just back in the Northern Territory.

'Can I help you, officer?' Then he noticed the stripes on the cop's shoulders. 'Sorry, Sergeant.'

That earned him a nod from the cop's uniform-issued cap, pulled down low on his brow, with his eyes hidden behind dark glasses. 'Got your licence on you there, mate?'

'Yeah, sure … Here.'

'Nice bike.'

'It sure is.' He glanced back at his pride and joy. Connor only had three pleasures in his life: his bike, his gun, and his bourbon. Simple.

'No freaking way. Connor Symes?' said the officer, reading Connor's licence. 'Elsie Creek's bad boy is back in town. Do I have a reason to worry?'

Connor gazed up at the sky, so much smaller on land without a sea to mirror it. After all these years, surely his reputation was buried deep beneath the dust. 'Nope. Just visiting.'

Then the cop chuckled, removing his hat and glasses. 'It's me, Marcus.'

Connor screwed up his face at his old school mate, now a man. But what made it worse he was a cop—which was impossible! 'Marcus? You're a policeman?'

'Yeah, who'd have thought.'

'The last I saw of you was when you were being chased out of town in that stolen car.' In a hail of flashing blue lights and screaming sirens, Marcus had literally booted Connor out of the car's front passenger seat to roll in the dirt. It's where he lay in the dark, helplessly watching his best mate speed down the highway with every cop car in town chasing him. Now he was a cop.

'The last I'd heard you were shipped off to sea.'

'Navy. But you … Don't they know what you did?'

Marcus shrugged beefy shoulders in a shirt that was stretched to capacity, but that wry grin was from the boy Connor remembered.

'Are you stationed at Elsie Creek, or just passing through?' Connor pointed to the patrol car. 'Nice wheels, man.'

'She flies, like you were.'

It was Connor's turn to shrug.

'Are you in town for your mum?'

'Yeah, I missed her in Adelaide.'

'I saw her at the hospital, yesterday. For someone whose been through a double bypass, she looks great. I think they're releasing her today.'

'Good.' He'd head straight for the house.

'How long are you in town for?'

'Until Mum and Dad are back on their feet.' Nothing and nowhere was permanent for Connor, not since the night he'd left this town.

'Well here, mate, consider this warning to *slow down near town* as a welcome home present.' Marcus handed back the licence to Connor.

'When did the speed limit change?'

'A few years back. The locals voted to change it for this pesky pet water buffalo who likes to wear ribbons.'

'Er, thanks.' Connor arched his eyebrow, putting his licence away. 'Hey, I'll buy you a beer and we'll catch up.'

'That'd be good. But ...' Marcus leaned in with his eyes glistening, wearing the same mischievous look Connor remembered. 'What we did as kids, goes nowhere, right?'

Connor grinned, holding his hands up to the officer as if

surrendering. 'Secrets have always been safe with me. I've never ratted out a mate, and I never will. Damn, I can't believe they made you a cop.'

'And you got accepted into the Navy. You barely passed school.'

'All those years cutting class to go pig-hunting with you didn't help.'

'What do you do in the job?' Marcus asked. 'Your dad didn't really know much.'

'Sergeant, Special Operations Command.'

'Jeez.' Marcus's nod was a sign of respect. 'You packing any of those toys they give soldiers to play with?'

The cheeky arse! 'Nope. I'm on holidays.' A working holiday if it meant hanging on the farm again.

'Enjoy your holidays then. Hey, once you've settled in, come round home and we'll have that drink. Say g'day to your parents for me.' Marcus tapped his cap's brim in a salute before opening the driver's door.

'I'll shout the bourbon while you tell me how you cheated on your Sergeant's exam.'

'Probably the same way you did. But I won't say no to a bourbon with a beer chaser.' In the sleek patrol car, Marcus spun it around to head back in the direction he'd come from.

Where did Marcus hide that cop car out here to catch speedsters?

Marcus. The boy who used to live and breathe trouble with a capital T was a cop. And Connor had been the proper partner in crime to Marcus, where they both burnt through the rule books in a town that hated them for it.

If Marcus was an officer of the law, maybe they'd forgiven Connor too?

Kicking over the Harley's engine, he slid on his helmet and scowled. In the distance, the town's roofs glistened like a tiny solar panel lost in the outback.

Fighting the temptation to swing around and ride the other way, he twisted the throttle and the bike rolled along the blacktop, where he followed that white line into town. A town he used to call home. He could just hear the old buzzards preaching, *get out your pitchforks, people, coz Connor Symes is back in town.*

3

'We have to keep him, Momma,' Billie said from her car booster seat, tightening the straps of her roller skates. 'You said if no one claimed Princess by the time the neighbours came home from the hopital—'

'Hosss-pital,' corrected Que, as she drove along Bertha and Richard's dirt driveway. 'I don't remember making that promise.' *Or the promise to keep visiting the neighbours.*

'You did, when we visited Mrs Symes and Richard—'

'Mr Symes. Come on, baby, it's a sign of respect.' And she liked Richard and Bertha.

'*He* said we should have a dog. Coz every farmer has a dog. And we have a farm. So we have to have a dog. Except we're lucky because our house came with a dog already. Princess won't leave and he follows me everywhere.'

'That's true. But it's a dog. I know nothing about dogs.'

'I'll teach you, Momma.' Billie reached over and patted Que's shoulder like she was fifty. 'Rich—Mr Symes is teaching me. And Princess listens to all my commands. And Jenny, the boss of all the nurses, said—'

'You weren't stealing paper from the hospital printer again?'

'No. Just her highlighter,' replied Billie so casually, without any remorse.

Oh great, I'm bringing up a stationery thief. The grandparents would be so proud.

'Jenny showed me a really cool site for dog obedience on the 'net, see.' Billie held up their number one babysitter, the tablet. 'He acts like he's ours, so we have to keep him.'

The dog never left, except for the vet visit where they learned Princess was still a pup of about 10 months. A dog they'd inherited that wasn't on the property description when she bought the place.

It still felt weird owning property, when Que never got attached to places or people, only Billie. So having a dog broke the rules in her game of survival.

Yet, she couldn't say no to a puppy who was all skin and bone, who was happy to sleep on the front doormat, to follow their every move through the windows. 'Do you think we should invest in one of those automatic gate openers?'

'Why, Momma? I like opening the gates.'

How long was that going to last?

Que parked her car close to her neighbours' back verandah for the concrete-loving kid to hit the pathways and do her chores. It was still unreal she was doing this when she never got involved with her neighbours.

Was this normal for country living?

Que grabbed the shopping bags from the car, as Billie's roller skates rumbled down the network of paths weaving through the vegetable gardens. 'We can't be long, Billie. Take only what we need and be quick about it.'

Wearing matching pink elbow and knee pads, Billie waved, her pink helmet disappearing behind the towering tomato bushes.

The neighbours had an amazing garden, brimming with assorted fruits and vegetables. Some Que had never heard of, but her fridge was full of plump tomatoes and the sweetest bananas she'd ever tasted. They were practically living on banana smoothies. Okay, so there were some advantages to this country living.

With arms laden with shopping bags, Que unlocked the back door and went inside. The big old house was whisper quiet.

She dumped all the goods by the fridge, shaking her head at the bags. She'd become a personal shopper and glorified house-sitter, enlisted from the day she'd arrived in this town. Is this what it meant to be neighbourly?

The quicker she unpacked, the quicker she could leave, placing the small box on the kitchen table and tucking a blue envelope beside it.

'Who the hell are you?'

Que froze, every microscopic fibre in her body on full alert at the harsh tone from the man who'd appeared from nowhere.

He filled the corridor's doorway with his hands clenched into fists. A compact network of muscles bulged on arms that came from wide shoulders. His torso narrowed down to a tight waist and hips that led down to thick thighs.

But the menacing stare was black. Cold. And full of hate.

She could feel the waves of seething hatred streaming off the guy, so much so she backed up to the door. 'I live next door.'

'In a car with interstate number plates, in a town where generations live on the same property. Bull.' He took a step closer, filling the entire room.

She couldn't breathe.

4

Connor snarled at the woman who'd woken him from his nap on the couch. 'How dare you steal from my family while my parents are still at the hospital?'

If she wasn't a female, he'd have gripped her by the throat and let his fists do the talking.

'What sort of scum steals from an elderly couple? And what's your accomplice doing out there? Stealing my dad's tools from the shed?' He'd heard wheels rumbling down the concrete paths, suggesting a trolley to cart crap to their car. 'Answer me!'

She had the look of a wallaby trapped by the glare of headlights.

Until she blinked. Then her whole demeanour changed. Damn, they were a sexy set of eyes. Violet?

'You must be Connor.'

He cocked his eyebrow at the woman, who was getting angrier at him by the second. No, the eyes were a dark blue. Her shiny hair fell like a wave of blue-black silk draped over her shoulders and down to a heavenly pert set of ... 'Get. OUT.'

'Consider it done.' She slammed a set of keys on the kitchen bench and fairly booted open the back door. 'Billie, let's go.'

'Make sure your thieving sidekick doesn't pinch what doesn't belong to you or I'll …' His eyes widened at the kid in a pink helmet and pigtails whizzing past the screen door. Not rumbling trolley wheels, but roller skates.

'Momma, I hadn't finished my chores. I don't want to upset Mr Symes, his prize tomatoes —'

'Richard and Bertha's son has finally shown up. It's his responsibility now. Get in the car, baby.' Her snarky tone was syrupy and sultry all at the same time.

She scooped up the kid in pink, strapping it into a booster seat, slamming the car door shut.

Connor stood on the back steps where she scowled at him from over her steering wheel. Only to spin her flash vehicle around in the driveway, sending a spiral of blinding red dust to engulf his parked Harley.

Bitch.

Still fired up, he headed for the fridge, hungry. But there was nothing inside, no milk, no banana bread. Nothing. Not even a beer?

He hoped his dad kept his beer in the cocky shed, or life on the farm was going to be sad.

Even after all these years of not stepping foot inside this house, he'd found the spare keys under the same aloe vera pot by the dripping drainpipe in the carport. The same veggie patch filled the backyard, brimming with tomatoes, corn, beans, and bananas that kept them in a steady supply of banana bread. His mother used to bake it daily.

He frowned at the keys on the bench with the leather tassel that held an old bullet casing. It was a standard military issue .303, left over from the war.

Connor used to have a dresser drawer full of those brass shell casings he'd scrounge along the old railway line. He'd regularly balance along the tracks with his mate Marcus, going either to or from trouble, only to turn them into what his dad called *trench art*.

As a sniper, he didn't mind tinkering with ammo while waiting to do his job. The ring on his little finger he'd made from a Winchester's primer and rim, the head stamp almost worn off a Colt 45. Ironically, it came from an antique revolver called *the Peacemaker*. He'd won it over a poker game at base camp, while on peace keeping tour that had more bullets flying in a land where it never rained, earning him a fine skill in bomb disposals.

All because of trench art. A hobby he'd turned into a career from finding some old WWII soldiers' scrap at old army posts, now lost in the Territory scrub.

As a kid, he polished those crusty brass bullet casings back to life, punching a hole into their rims to fit a tiny metal ring. Those keychains were popular Father's Day gifts that year.

Running his thumb over the bullet's brass contours, he felt the impressions along the side that spelled *Happy Father's Day*.

How did that woman get his father's keys?

He spotted the plastic bags on the table and on the floor by the fridge. Peeking inside one, he arched his eyebrow. It was full of food: milk, bread, cheese.

But what was in the pink box on the table?

Lifting the lid, it exposed a small chocolate cake with *Welcome Home Bertha* piped in white frosting across the top.

Beside it lay a blue envelope covered in a childish scribble of hearts and rainbows. He opened the hand-drawn card to read: *Welcome home Richard and Bertha, from your neighbours Billie and Que.*

The fridge engine whirred.

The clock ticked.

A bird called out to another as he stared at the simple childlike drawings covering the card that lay open on the kitchen table.

Collapsing heavily into the nearest chair, he dragged out his wallet. From within the folds, he removed a small handmade Christmas card covered in drawings from his nephew.

Inside, where the glue barely hung on, was a family photo of Connor's younger brother, Travis, with his wife Tracey and their two young children.

It was the last card they'd sent him—when they used to send him one every year.

The anger leeched out of his system, replaced by a deep sorrow. It swamped him, making his shoulders drop and his chest cave in, but he couldn't tear his eyes off the card. Glued to the seat, inside his old childhood home, trapped under the heavy burden of guilt, he couldn't swallow.

His brother had forgiven him. His parents had forgiven him. But the one person who would never forgive Connor ... was Connor himself.

5

The roll of tyres crunching along the driveway broke Connor from his misery. Was that damned woman back?

He ripped open the back door, only to blink at the harsh sunlight reflecting off the brown troopie. He recognised his parents' car from the many photos they'd sent him.

Rubbing palms over his face to control his smouldering mood, he prepared himself for the welcome home he had never imagined, because he was never meant to come back. But here he was.

His dad walked around the car, so much smaller, frailer, grey even. Richard opened the passenger door for his mother. Bertha looked the same, but also greyer, smaller, and so much older.

How long had it been since he'd been home? Ten? Twelve? Fifteen years?

'Connor?' It was still Bertha's voice.

Shoving hands into the pockets of his jeans, he kicked at a stone with his biker's boots. 'G'day, Mum.'

'Oh, my boy.'

He was soon smothered in a hug filled with that familiar fragrance of magnolia and cedarwood. Chloé. He knew it well, buying her a duty-free bottle every year for Mother's Day because he could never remember her birthday.

He was such a terrible son. He never called. Never wrote. Just sent random duty-free bottles of perfume in the mail when he'd been forced to hang out at some random airport.

Now an even bigger idiot to make the woman cry. 'Come on, Mum?'

'It's been so long, and you got so big.' Bertha bawled into his chest.

'The Navy looks after you well, son,' said Richard, patting Connor's shoulder.

'Hey, Dad.' This was awkward. Did he shake hands?

The decision was made for him when his father engulfed him with a hearty hug and a sturdy pat on the back. 'We're glad to have you back, son.'

'Only temporary. Gotta get back to base soon.' Kind of wishing he'd never left. Emotions were not a factor in his job, that was free from this kind of awkwardness.

'Let's not worry about that, now,' Bertha said, patting his cheek in a motherly fashion. 'You're here now and that's all that matters.'

'I'll get the bags. I missed you in Adelaide by only a few hours.' Effortlessly, he lugged their bags up to the house, only to slow down behind his parents' frail steps. When did they get so old?

Into the house, down the corridor to their master bedroom, where the sun shone through the sheer curtain to highlight the queen-sized bed. Everything was the same. Putting the bags down by the old dresser, he headed back to the kitchen where his parents' voices travelled down the corridor …

'Stop that, luv. You take a seat, doctor's orders.'

'I'm not helpless.'

'No, but you are precious to me. So let me look after you.' Richard kissed his wife of forty-odd years on the nose and helped her into a kitchen chair. They shared that same look of love they'd had since forever. 'We've got Connor home now to help on the farm, while I get to annoy you all day.'

There went his chances of escaping early. 'How long did the doctor say before you've recovered, Mum?'

'Oh, you know.' Bertha shrugged, pulling the cake box closer.

'Twelve weeks,' said Richard, filling up the kettle.

'Six.' Bertha peeked inside the box.

Six weeks! Was someone trying to kill him? Connor never even took holidays that long.

'Oh, what a wonderful surprise. Did you do this, Connor?' Bertha removed the cake from the box. 'Yummy, mud cake. The local bakery makes such a good one.'

'Um, no. This card came with it.' Connor sheepishly pushed the rainbow card across the table.

His mother shared the same smile he'd get for his stickmen scribbles, or those lopsided coffee mugs of clay that couldn't hold water. But she'd still treat them all like precious objects.

'Who's it from, luv?' Richard put down a set of side plates and teacups.

Connor sat like a lump of foreign lead, stuck somewhere in the void of being the little kid of the past and the man he was today. It was so surreal.

'Oh, it's from Billie and Que.' Bertha proudly showed off the card like a chick on Instagram pushing some product.

'Billie drew a picture of that dog,' Bertha said. 'Or is that Cecil?'

Richard held the card at arm's length, vacantly digging around in his shirt's top pocket and removing a set of glasses. The glasses were new.

'Oh, it's the dog.' Richard grinned, removing the glasses as he handed the card back to Bertha. 'That Billie's a good sort. We're trying to convince her mother to keep this stray dog, it's a pup. Once they washed the mud off, it was a proper blue heeler, too. A bit hyper for my liking, but it's friendly enough.'

'The dog was just there the day Que and Billie came to town. The day ...' Bertha hesitated. With her hand over her chest she took slow and deliberate breaths.

'The day, what?' Connor looked at his dad for the answer.

Richard gave his wife's shoulder a tender squeeze. 'The day I nearly lost my favourite girl.'

'But you didn't ...' Bertha stroked her husband's hand. 'I'm still here and we have Que to thank for that.'

'That girl is a quick thinker with good reflexes, ready to run in a matter of seconds.' Richard hung his hat on the hook. 'And tough, too. She kept doing those compressions on your mother, from her place all the way to the hospital in the back of the cruiser, then through to the emergency room. Que kept going even as they wheeled her on top of those hospital gurneys, and everything, like a combat medic would. She didn't stop.'

'The doctor said Que saved me.'

While Connor was the mongrel who'd scared off the family's hero. 'And you had this neighbour house sitting?'

'Caretaking while we were in Adelaide.' Richard peered out the kitchen window. 'They fed the chooks and watered the plants. They volunteered to do some shopping. Or is that you, son?' Richard peeked inside the empty fridge and then the shopping bags on the floor, pulling out a stick of butter.

Connor scrubbed at his face, too self-absorbed to even unpack. He was so out of whack with civilian life.

'What's wrong, Connor?' Bertha asked, cutting up the cake. She scooped cream from the knife, while Richard unpacked the groceries.

'I stuffed up.' Boy, did he ever. Sure, he was paid to be a prick in his day job, but not on holidays too.

'I accused this woman ...' He pointed to the cake, its rich chocolate aroma filling the room. 'She said she was a neighbour, but you would have told me if someone sold their house.' Because his mum wrote long weekly emails all about Elsie Creek.

'I'm sure I wrote about Neville Landers' house getting sold and how Kat was working on the renovations. Hold on ...' Bertha tapped on her chin. 'I don't think I sent that yet. You remember, you went to school with Neville's son, Alex, he was a few years younger than you. Alex now lives across the road at Molly's house with her niece. Verily and Alex are expecting their first child. Molly is so excited for the couple.'

Connor just shrugged at his dad. Who? What? Did he care? 'Which house got sold?'

'The one with the trucks, son. Neville's in Bris-Vegas and Alex shifted the trucks across the road. He tucks them in behind his brewery.'

'Where's the brewery?' asked the beer-and-bourbon-loving bloke.

'In the middle of Molly's mango farm. Good beer too.'

'Excuse me.' Bertha rubbed her fingers in the air between the father and son.

An old memory unfurled in his chest over a quirk that only a family shared.

'You still can't click your fingers, Mum?' Connor clicked his in unison with his father and grinned.

'Can't play the piano either, but that never stopped me from enjoying my music,' said his mother. 'But back to our new neighbours, Connor. What did you do?'

'Um, well.' He shuffled in his seat like a little boy about to 'fess up to stealing smokes from the drunk passed out behind the pub. 'I accused this …'

'Que.'

'… of breaking into the house.'

'Why? I gave Que my keys?' Richard asked.

'I was napping on the couch when I heard a car. I looked out the window and saw a car with interstate plates parked in the driveway. Then, I heard these wheels rolling down the paths and thought it was a trolley, not a kid in roller skates.' He'd thought he was protecting his parents' property.

'Que's only been here a couple of weeks,' said Richard. 'She hasn't changed over her car's registration plates yet.'

'She'll want to get onto that before Marcus catches her. He's quite strict, you know,' said Bertha. 'You remember your old friend, Marcus? He's our town's top cop. Who'd have thought it?'

'Who better to keep the peace in this town than a ratbag like Marcus.' Richard chuckled, pouring out the tea. 'Of course, your mother and I said nothing about the shenanigans you two got up to when you were boys. We could never split you pair up.'

But when they did split, they never spoke to each other again, until today. 'So, what's this Que doing with her property?'

'No idea,' said Bertha, looking at Richard, who was biting into his cake. 'But you'll have to apologise to her.'

'Why? I did nothing wrong. She didn't explain the situation.'

'Que had the keys, son.' Richard waved his hand over the table laden with goodies and said, 'She brought cake, the card, and saved your mother's life.'

Connor stared at the ceiling and sighed. It was a well-practised move, slipping into the skin of that rebellious teenager all over again. If he had ever met himself as a teenager, Connor would have probably punched the kid in his smart mouth.

He had a lot to make up for.

'What do I have to do?' His parents were always the peacekeepers with a plan, which meant that doing the right thing was usually the hardest thing to do.

How soon before he could get back to base?

6

A large cup of coffee got plonked onto the outdoor table beside Que, where she was working on her laptop.

'That's for you,' said Kat, tucking an escaping curl back into her ponytail.

'Hello, Kat, and Supermom Karen.'

'I bought the treats.' Karen unloaded a large plate of assorted pastries, before sitting opposite Que.

'Doesn't the Supermom bake?'

'Me? Never.'

'But isn't this the land of scones and home-baked delights?' Considering Karen was trying to recruit people to do a bake sale for the school. Words that were never a part of Que's vocabulary until this town.

'Why bother when we have the queen of delish dishes to do it for us. You have met our YouTube superstar, and coffee van owner, Lucy?' Karen pointed to the dark-haired woman with a gorgeous rich-coffee tone to her flawless skin.

'Are you the graphic designer Kat was telling me about?' Lucy asked.

'I pretend to be.' Que lowered the lid of her laptop. She'd been enjoying the shade of the outdoor umbrella setting, tucked away at a train station that was part of a small local museum. 'What's the coffee for, Kat?'

'I said I'd buy you one.'

'Why? When I've done nothing.'

'Come on, you bought my latest reno, and you saved the day.'

'Oh, how is your neighbour, Bertha?' Karen asked, dishing out napkins loaded with cakes and slices for everyone. They were bite-sized morsels of art made into food.

'Bertha's doing great.' Here she was, making friends, adjusting to life as a school mum.

She glanced at her watch, only one hour and seventeen-and-a-half minutes before she could pick up Billie from school. Even though Billie would prefer to catch the bus home, this mum needed an early hug.

At least she'd stopped stalking the school car park, with her own child shooing her away from the perfectly good perch under the trees. Now shifting her perch into town, she was trying to blend. Or is that pretend? 'I still haven't met my other neighbour. Molly, is it?'

'Oh, she's at the hairdressers. Verily and Alex are extending their tour of the east coast, something about doing a beer crawl for customers.'

'A-huh?' This trying to fit in was hard work. But she was trying … 'I've met Val. Kind of. We wave across the road from each other as we wait for the school bus.' Where she fought the urge to climb onboard after Billie. This separation for school was tough. She needed a new morning hobby or routine to stop her school-stalking tendencies.

'As for the rest of the neighbourhood ...' Que rolled her eyes. 'I met Bertha and Richard's son, Connor, for a whole fleeting two minutes flat. If that. It was an awesome first impression.'

The table fell silent. As in a playing-card-falling-to-the-table-in-a-shuffle kind of silent.

'Did I say something wrong?'

Kat, as per usual, shrugged. 'I don't know Connor. I only visited town in school holidays.'

'Connor's been gone for so long,' said Lucy. 'I wonder if my dad knows, yet.'

'Why? Was Connor one of the lost boys?' Kat asked Lucy.

'Um, excuse me, tourist here.' Que raised her finger in the air like she was in school, taking another peek at her watch. Should she set an alarm to not be late for that school bell? 'What's a lost boy? Is that anything to do with *Peter Pan*? Considering we live in faraway land with jumping crocodiles that'd probably eat a clock. So, who's Captain Hook?'

'My father is ...' Lucy winced.

'Is not Captain Hook. Ron is the legendary Station Hand,' finished Karen.

'Okay ...' The last local legend Que learned of was Karma. A crocodile with a gift for predicting future winners by chomping on a piece of meat. Come on, it was a fifty-fifty flip of a card's chance of winning. But it was a great con to get tourists to visit the pub. 'So he's a legend because?'

'Dad trains people to become station hands on cattle stations during a muster.'

'Your father does much more than that,' explained Kat. 'The

Station Hand is like our Gordon Ramsay, except he doesn't rescue restaurants. Ron does it for cattle stations, while teaching kids a trade in the cattle industry.'

'And the lost boys?' Que asked again, as they all looked to Lucy for the answer.

'The lost boys were bad boys. Parents would fly these teens in from all over the country to get my father to straighten them out.'

'It's like an outback bootcamp for naughty boys, cattle-station style,' explained Kat.

'You're fast becoming my interpreter, Kat. I should have you on speed dial for these things,' said Que. 'I completely get what you're saying.'

'Like I said, hon, I was in your shoes not that long ago, I can relate. So, was Connor a lost boy?'

'Connor was one of the only two boys to fail the lost boy's program,' said Lucy. 'Connor stole Dad's ute off the station, and completely disappeared with this other boy. Dad eventually got his ute back, but I'd never seen him so livid. No one had ever dared to steal from my father, who'd done so much good for so many.'

'Who was the other boy with Connor?' Kat asked over her travel mug with a tiara and tutu on it.

Lucy shrugged, taking a huge bite of her scone that gave her a cream lip. 'Dad never said.'

'What do you mean fail?' Que screwed up her nose. But she did promise to try and blend. 'Is it like a bush school that does exams?'

'The Station Hand, Dad, deemed them as boys beyond help. Going down a path that they'd either end up in jail or die,' said Lucy.

'Connor was one of those that failed.'

'I remember he was so angry with the world,' said Karen. 'Connor was a bad, bad guy. Stealing from drunks, fighting at the pub, pinching cars, and thieving property all the time. He was just terrible. And you saw him, Que?'

'For a few minutes. That was enough.' More than enough to be trapped in the same room with the man with dark eyes and a look that could kill.

'Connor must be back to help Richard until Bertha recovers. And it's about time Connor did something for his family. But be warned,' said Karen, wagging her finger, 'it's best you all steer clear of that man.'

'That's not like you, Karen.' Lucy raised her eyebrow at Karen. 'You don't have a bad word to say about anyone, except the mine's manager.'

'He's snooty—Connor is just bad. B. A. D. Big-time bad. But how is Val?'

Que grinned at Karen's swift change of topics. 'I only wave to her in the mornings, waiting for the school bus, that's it.'

'We never see Val anymore, especially when she used to organise all of these school events, and she was so brilliant at it. I've been trying to catch her, to see if she can help with Mother's Day.' And just like that, Karen controlled the conversation as she flipped open her folder. 'Seeing as how we're all here, I've got a list of things for the Mother's Day events. People are not only donating services, but we've also got furniture too.'

'Is there a furniture store in town?' Considering Que had very little.

'No. I'm donating a coffee table and this cute dresser I refurbished,' said Kat.

'Didn't that start a trend, because I've got people offering a stack of stuff to sell for this silent auction. I'm not knocking back anything. One person's hand-me-downs could be someone else's treasure.' Karen clutched her folder, and stage-whispered, 'I've been eyeing off these absolutely divine curtains that've been donated from the school principal. I can see them hanging in my house. Oh, and we're holding a friendly football match to get people to come and linger a little longer, and hopefully we'll have beer for them to do that too.'

'Good idea, Karen. Yours?' Kat asked.

'No, Samantha suggested it. She is God who knows all about men and their beer.'

'Who's God?' Que asked.

'Samantha is the publican.' Kat pointed to the mighty pub that towered over the town.

'I haven't been to the pub yet.' Que narrowed her eyes at the intermittent flow of cowboys coming and going through the hotel's main doors.

'Oh, we should do lunch,' said Kat. 'We'll organise it when Verily gets back. Which reminds me, we have a baby shower to organise for Verily. Can you do a gender reveal baby cake, Lucy?'

'I have so many ideas for that, I can't wait to start making them.'

'Good, I've got plenty of ideas for games.'

'Verily is only five months along, we have plenty of time. Can we please focus on Mother's Day first, hmm? It's only six weeks away,' Karen said, flicking her pen. 'So, Lucy, seeing as how you're besties with this organising committee, what's the best spot for your coffee van to park on the school oval?'

Again, Que half listened to names of people she didn't know, sipping on her coffee. It was a creamy caffeine shot of goodness. 'Wow, Kat, you were right.'

'Of course. Except, what for this time?'

Que eyed the simple takeaway cup. She'd gone through countless cups, but they never tasted as good as this. 'This coffee is amazing. I mean, I've had coffee, but this is superb.'

'I know,' Kat nodded in agreement.

Lucy's cheeks darkened as she meekly lowered her neck into her shoulders.

'Say *thank you*, Lucy,' said Karen like the mother she was. 'Lucy gets terribly shy over things.'

'You should take a photo of Lucy's food and share it on Instagram. What's your handle so I can follow you?' Kat pulled her mobile from her backpack.

'I don't do social media.' Or socialise. It was easier not to.

'Excuse me?'

'Um …' *Shoot.* Que scrambled for a good excuse, reminding her why she didn't keep friends. She hated lying to nice people — but she had to. 'I'm on social media for my clients. It's not a fun thing, but a work thing, so after hours I avoid it …' She was a such liar, when Que fastidiously cyber-stalked, while carefully setting up Google alerts to scream on her phone.

Connor may be a big man, but he wasn't nearly as scary as her nightmares.

7

In his dad's faded grey EH Holden ute, Connor cruised down the main dirt track. His dad had never let him drive the ute before, not that he'd wanted to as a kid, because old-school classic wasn't his style back then. But now he didn't mind the slow cruise along the firebreak, checking the boundary fence line.

He used to jump the same fence to sneak down to the neighbour's back creek to check on his cherabin pots. It was such a regular run, with his younger brother following as his shadow, Connor had built a fort one summer to keep them safe from crocodiles. Was the fort still there?

Through the side gate, then down the track a massive shed came into view, containing a large caravan with room for another five cars.

Nearby a tiny house stood on the small rise, giving it an effortless view of the outback. The house looked like a white-headed pimple that begged to be squeezed so the blemish could disappear from the landscape.

As he pulled up at the front steps a skinny blue dog bounded towards him. It was a heeler pup with a powdery white colouring, who hadn't grown into his adult coat, the signature dark blue. And no tail.

Connor unfolded from the car, and the dog cowered. Head over paws, it trembled in the red dirt.

'It's okay, mate, I like dogs.' Connor held out his hand, and the pup sniffed with his bum tucked under and back legs trembling.

But Connor was a patient man, with a healthy respect for the animal he grew up with. There'd been countless stray dogs he'd shared beef jerky with, keeping him company as a sniper in foreign lands. Switching from Navy to the SOC, he'd spent more time in deserts with the bomb dogs on his team, who were straight-up heroes, having saved his neck a few times.

The young dog finished sniffing and pressed his cold nose against Connor's open fingers, the trembling gone.

'Good, lad.' He gave the dog a pat, as its long tongue rolled in its smile.

'Can I help you?' From the far back corner of the house, a man poked back the brim of a sweat stained Akubra, as his steel-capped boots clomped along the verandah's concrete. His Bermuda shorts exposed the freckles and red-tinged hair on his legs and arms, that were deeply tanned. It was a deep farmer-tan on the man about the same age as him.

'I'm looking for Que?'

'Que's just gone to pick up Billie from school. Something about scoring a coffee in town.'

'Coffee? In this town?' Elsie Creek was strictly a tea house kind of town, where snobby old women met in the tea rooms by the train station. A place he'd never entered because some places were taboo if you were male.

'I'm here to drop this off.' Connor pulled out the cane basket from the front seat and felt like the big bad wolf selling Red Riding Hood's basket of goodies on the black market.

'You are?' The ginger asked.

'Connor. I'm from next door.'

'The boy next door, huh? I'm Mike.' His cheeky grin crunched up the myriad of freckles blending with his ginger hair, sharing a firm grip for a wiry fella. 'Your tomatoes?'

'My dad's.'

'They're amazing.' Mike held a plump tomato to the light the way a wine snob checks for sediment and colour in a glass of red wine. 'Organic?'

'You'll have to ask my old man about that one.' He then swallowed down that creepy awkwardness that had been common when he was a kid. 'Can you please tell Que, I'm sorry for yesterday. It was my mistake.'

'What did you do?' Mike's eyes narrowed at him.

'She didn't tell you?' Surely the woman would have ratted him out to her husband.

Although, the bloke wasn't wearing a wedding band. Then again, not that many men did in his line of work.

'No. But I'll ask,' said Mike.

'It was just a mix-up. No harm done.' If he said more, he'd probably cop a punch in the mouth from the ginger, and he deserved one, too.

But then he'd have to defend himself and that's when things got messy for a military man with a mean temper. 'Gotta go.'

Delivery done, apology done, so that'd make his parents happy. With any luck he wouldn't have to face Que, her husband, or anyone else in this town before he could hightail it back to base. Because he wasn't here to make friends.

8

Que spotted an old grey ute leaving her driveway. It forced a spike of fear to squirrel up her spine, as she gripped the steering wheel tighter. 'Who was that?'

'That's Mr Symes's ute, Momma,' said Billie from her booster seat in the back.

'How do you know?'

'He keeps it in the shed with the chook pellets. Covered in dust.'

'It's a cool car. Could you see me driving in that?'

'Don't be silly, Momma. Who would drive this one then?'

Que grinned, easing the tension from her shoulders, as she drove through their wide-open gate. Was she to expect a visit from the water buffalo who wore ribbons?

She parked by the house where Mike met them on the front verandah. 'What's with the basket, Goldilocks?'

'My hair colour is a finely spun ginger-red, thank you. Or are you getting colour blind in your old age? And I believe Goldilocks had locks of hair.'

'You've got hair,' said Billie, rolling across the verandah on her skates to hug Mike's waist. 'And it shines like gold in the sun. Are we having porridge for dinner?'

'No, but it'll be something to do with tomatoes. Check out these specimens.' Mike held up a huge tomato. 'They're perfect.'

'They're Mr Symes's tomatoes.' Billie poked around the basket, grabbing a big red shiny tomato and bit into it like an apple. The juice dribbled down her chin, with red seeds scattering across her cheeks. 'These are the best.'

'Were the neighbours here?' Que asked.

'Connor.'

She frowned. 'What did he want?'

'To apologise. And by that kill-look, my sweet, he must've done something to …' Mike covered Billie's ears.

'I can hear, you know.' Billie wriggled free.

'You also know the drill, baby.'

Billie rolled her eyes. 'Ugh, grown-up talk, it's soooo boring. Come on, Princess, it's skate time.' With half-eaten tomato in hand, she rolled down the path for the shed with the dog trotting beside her. Seconds later, the stereo flicked on, and her roller disco of the day had begun.

'Bring your skates out?' Que asked her best friend, Mike.

'They live in my car. But you didn't answer my question, what did this Connor do to warrant the home delivery? He's like one of those billboard pictures they'd use to advertise at gyms.'

'Connor's not that buff.' But he was certainly big enough to leave a lasting impression.

'Do I need to polish up my knuckles and go over and defend your honour.'

'Can you fight? Because we both know I have no honour.'

Mike slung his arm around her shoulders and squeezed. 'So, what gives, my sweet?'

'Nothing really. The guy made a mistake protecting his property. He thought I was breaking in.'

'Were you?'

She frowned at her best friend. 'Hey, I had the keys to the neighbours' house, and I was playing personal shopper.'

'That's a turnaround for you.'

'I know, right? Me. A personal shopper. Who knows what else I'll do out here for entertainment in this land of the laconic one-finger-waving farmer?' She gave a lazy finger salute to the horizon that curved at the edge of the world.

'Billie loves it out here. Do you?'

'Not sure.' The sky was still a worry.

'You'd want to settle in, especially after all of the work I've done, where I'm happy to report your irrigation is in, my sweet. And so is your new lawn, which is good to have as a firebreak to protect the house.'

'Great, you can visit and mow it for me.'

'Good to see you're getting with the program to finally park that van.'

'The Mighty T needed a break.'

'You could have picked a spot closer to home, in case of emergencies. You're really isolated out here.'

'You were the one who suggested I go remote.'

'I didn't think you'd take me literally.'

'Billie wanted to go to school and not do home-schooling. I must suck as a mum, because when I dropped Billie off on her first day of school, I copped this *don't cry* lecture from her. Billie didn't even shed a tear ...' But Que sat in the car park, chewing her nails, watching her only child disappear into the tiny building they called a school, thinking of excuses to break her kid out.

Her baby was growing up so fast.

She grabbed Mike's arm. 'Hey, no one followed you?'

'Of course not. I did the scenic tour of Kakadu, then went through some cattle station properties I have access to.' He patted her hand. 'You're safe out here.'

Did she dare believe it, after all these years? She wanted to.

The breeze carried Billie's out-of-tune singing of 80s rock. It made the adults cringe.

'Where did the munchkin get her bad taste in music?' Mike asked.

Que's fears softened as she smiled; her child was happy. 'Billie is obsessed with the 80s, she even asked me about a fax the other day.' Que hooked her arm through Mike's. 'Come on, let's go join the party. You can help me put up the disco lights that arrived in today's mail.' She unlocked her car boot, which was filled with assorted boxes. 'Internet shopping is very addictive.'

'And you do have a house to fill. Talking about mail ...' Mike rested his chin on the assorted boxes piled in his arms. 'I'll be leaving my car here because I've scored the mail plane back to Darwin. Care to drop me off in the morning? I'll be coming back with a truck in a few weeks.'

'Why?'

'You wanted my opinion, and told me to do what I wanted with the land, right?'

'Sure. I'm no farmer.'

'That's why I'll use this barren block as a lesson in native regeneration. It'll be a no-brainer compared to mine sites. Oh, hey, you know you have a water buffalo wallowing in your backyard boghole.'

'That's just Cecil.' She screwed her nose up. 'Do I really have a boghole?'

He nodded. 'What's a Cecil?'

'A buffalo who might become my new morning habit. First, tell me about your plans for this place. Does it involve security?'

9

'This can't be the airport,' said Que, standing beside Mike in the shade of the small office. It was overshadowed by an enormous radio tower with assorted satellite dishes hanging off it. Other than that, there was a large open hangar and a single tarmac road, with white lines on it, and nothing else.

'I've seen outback airports that are just a tin roof or a mowed strip of dirt.' Mike pointed to the far end. 'Look, it's not that remote. Hospital's there—and what the bloody hell is that?'

Their heads leaned sideways at the retro comic of a masked burglar being held back by a muscular police officer, covering an entire building's roof!

'That'd be The Long Arm of the Law, or some call it the Strong Arm of the Law. Still means the same thing,' said the grumpy guy who was weighing Mike's luggage. His grey hair matched the coveralls and the hand towel he used to dab at his crinkly brow.

'Why?' Que asked.

'That's the cop shop,' the old man said, with a whole load of gravel to his voice. He then screwed up his nose at Que with one eye shut, reminding her of Popeye. 'You a tourist?'

'I'm a visitor, although I plan to be a regular visitor. She's the local,' said Mike, nudging Que.

'Are you the sheila who bought the Landers' place?'

Que shrugged.

'Neville Landers. Truck driver. Old man to Alex who's got the brewery happenin'.'

'I believe so. You are?'

'Mickey.' He held out his grease-stained hand, leaving her no option but to shake it.

'Que.'

'I heard it was some smancy name like pool cue.'

'It's short for Quentin.'

'Still unusual. Snobby even.'

'I'm not a snob.'

'Humph, not anymore.' Mike chuckled, again nudging his elbow into her ribs.

'So, who did the roofs? Is that a peeing Dalmatian on a fire hydrant?' Que pointed to another roof as she walked further onto the airstrip.

'That'd be the fire station. There's a whole mob of 'em up there. But you'll wanna git off my strip, lady, coz the plane will be landing shortly.'

'I want to see. Do they do a tourist flight?'

'Listen, lady,' said Mickey, dabbing at his leathery brow with his cloth, 'this aint a freaking tourist town. If you want one of 'em tourist scenic flights, go visit Kakadu and get one of 'em jockey pilots to take you, coz out 'ere we're—'

A red plane flew loud and low, barely touching the tarmac,

only to roar back into the air.

'Is that a straw broom on the belly of that plane?' Que's eyes widened as big as her smile at the art in this town. Retro cartoons on roofs, now a red plane with a sparkly broom stick.

'That'd be the *Wicked Witch of the Westerly Winds* and her plane, Gertrude. Your ride back to the big smoke, mate. But she's flamin' meant to be landin' the plane, not doin' a flyby.'

Mike looked at Que, who only grinned wider.

'Aw flamin' heck, now I get why she didn't land.' Mickey scowled, jumping into his modified golf buggy. He whirled his grey towel around like a short stockwhip as he raced alongside the airstrip. 'Hee-ya! Git, you overfed pet!'

'Is he scaring off Cecil?' Mike asked Que.

Cecil, the water buffalo, lifted his head from a group of wildflowers with his white ribbons wrapped around his horns, waving in the breeze.

'I've never seen Cecil run, only mosey down the driveway or wallow in my pond.'

'Boghole.'

Que screwed up her nose. 'Can you make that boghole into a pretty pond?'

'As the guru of green, I can do anything, my sweet, except tango with water buffalos.'

They chuckled at Mickey chasing the ribbon-flapping buffalo off the tarmac to the far side of the grass.

The red plane soon landed and out stepped a pretty, petite blonde pilot.

'Hi, I'm Monet,' she said with a husky voice and sexy swagger.

'Who wanted a ride to Darwin?'

'That'd be me. Although, Que, you could talk me into staying. I'm really liking the quirky vibe of this town.' Mike pointed to Cecil, who snorted at Mickey yelling and swinging that towel around like a helicopter blade. But the buffalo gave a mellow huff and snort, then turned to waddle away with his nose in the air.

'That'd be Mickey, the Master of all things Mechanical,' said Monet. 'He has a love-hate thing going on with Cecil, but secretly he feeds him in the hangar.' The pilot removed the aviators that made her look effortlessly cool. 'Hey, are you the graphic designer, Que?'

Que nodded. 'Wow, word travels fast in this town.'

'Lucy told me. She knows I wanted to upgrade my logo and website for online bookings.'

'Sure. Here, take a card.' Mike flipped open his wallet and pulled out a card for the pilot, while speaking to Que, 'I should be on commission, you know, as your PR guy and personal gardener.'

'Don't complain. I feed you, occasionally.'

'Beer and vodka concoctions. Not food.'

'You cook better. And you're used to a big stove.'

'Your stove is buggered,' said Mike. 'Hey, Monet, do you know anyone in town who fixes stoves?'

'Ask the Retired Knights of the Round Card Table. Can't miss them, they pretend to play cards at the hardware store.'

'I know them,' said Que, ignoring Mike's raised eyebrow.

'Great, they'll know who to recommend.'

The tricked-up golf cart rolled up with Mickey sweating behind the wheel, as if he'd run some marathon. 'That flamin' buffalo is a menace, you know.'

'Cecil likes the wildflowers that grow on the sides of the tarmac. The dew collects there this time of year. The wallabies do the same,' explained Monet as she grinned at Mickey. 'Go on, admit it, you love Cecil.'

'I'm gonna fix his big black heinie and put his nose right outta joint. I've got all those fencing materials there to keep that spoiled water buffalo and the rest of the wandering livestock off my airstrip.' Mickey pointed to the piles of star pickets and fencing wire.

'You don't have a perimeter fence? At an airport.' Que had assumed it'd be standard.

'We'll be getting one. That Jenny at the hospital got us a flamin' Federal grant for one. Smart cookie, that nursing sister is. Reckons she'll keep an eye out for more coz we only got enough funding to do one side. The rest will have to be fencing wire to keep that cross-dressing, ribbon-wearing, overfed—'

'Do I have much freight to carry, Mickey? I've got a schedule to keep.' Monet tapped on her watch face.

'Just the mail bags. And this fella with carry-on luggage. Here's the sheet.'

It wasn't long before they'd loaded up, leaving Que to arch her neck up at the monstrous sky that swallowed the little red plane. It hung in the air like a toy dangling from a piece of string.

'You right there, lady?' Mickey asked with his crinkled eyes.

'Big sky.'

'You'll get used to it. You should see it in the wet season, it's the best damned fireworks display you'll ever get. Best in the world.'

'You don't say.'

'We get 'em flamin' fancy photographers and lightning

scientists visitin' every year for the show. Now, if you'll excuse me, I've got holes to dig. Don't worry 'bout your fella, Monet's the best bush pilot we've got. He'll get home safely.'

'Thanks.' She missed Mike already, would love for him to stay, but he had a job he loved and was exceptionally good at.

After a quick trip down the main street of town, she parked behind the hardware store, the biggest shop on the block, near the tiny supermarket. It sat across the road from the park that led to the train station museum and coffee van. Beyond that was the post office beside the craft shop, a hairdresser with a few other stores, all within sight of each other, with the mighty pub on the corner overshadowing them all. With only one set of lights for a pedestrian crossing, that was pretty much it for this small town.

Inside the hardware store, her eyes adjusted to the dim light as she removed her sunglasses. The temperature dropped as a cool breeze circulated by the largest ceiling fans she'd ever seen. It helped clear the aroma of cheap cigar smoke that came from the four men seated around the large card table, where ashtrays and coffee cups rested among the playing cards. They scowled from their cards, then grinned.

It was the Outback Mafia, as Kat called them from some movie she'd watched as a kid. But Que knew them as the *Retired Knights of the Round Card Table*. Billy, with his snappy suspenders, stood from the table, while the Triple Js remained seated. In coke-bottle glasses was Jeffrey, beside him sat James, then Johnny on the other side.

'Morning, gentlemen. I have a present for you.' She pulled out a small wooden box from her laptop bag.

'Where did you get these?' Billy slid one thumb along his

suspenders to lift them higher on his shoulder, before he opened the lid to show the others the box of classy cigars.

'Had a visitor who brought them in for me.'

'And what did we do to deserve this?'

'Well, besides teaching me how to play, I'm hoping you gentlemen might help me with a minor problem?' Supermom Karen may know a lot of stories about the females of this town, but these charming old fellas were walking encyclopaedias, who had all the time in the world to gossip.

Most of all, they played cards.

'Is that pesky buffalo wallowing in your yard, again?' Johnny asked with a frown. 'That mongrel ate my wife's flowers yesterday.'

'Build a fence and get over it,' grumbled James. Jeffrey chuckled, pushing his glasses higher along his nose as they inspected their cigars.

'Talking about fences,' said Billy, resuming his seat, 'that brother of mine got a grant to build a perimeter fence up at the airstrip.'

The men squinted at him while unwrapping their gifts.

'I just saw all the poles. Mickey said he was going to start digging holes today.' Que couldn't believe she actually knew who they were talking about—for once. She dropped into a seat beside Billy, laced her fingers together, then straightened her arms to let her fingers stretch and knuckles to crack. 'Is Mickey your brother?'

'Older brother,' replied Billy. 'Mickey's a confirmed bachelor with a love-hate relationship with Cecil. Really, no one wants to see Cecil get hurt, we all love him.' Billy pointed to the large open double doorway that gave a grand view of Cecil meandering down the main street. Scribbled in chalk across the black buffalo's side was *School pool needs your cash!*

Que screwed up her nose. Is that someone's form of advertising for the school's fundraiser?

The buffalo turned around to expose its other side that read, *Baked Beans & Lettuce on special in store.*

'I get it now, Cecil is the town's walking billboard.' She giggled at the absurdity of it, but now understood why they let the animal wander everywhere. Where was the owner?

'How's my mini-me?' Billy, who looked like a jazz player with his suspenders, put the stack of playing cards in front of Que. 'You deal. That way we won't cheat this round.'

'Don't mind if I do. And my Billie is great.' *Only five hours and forty-six minutes for school pick-up.*

Que grabbed the cards and started shuffling with ease. The slick feel of thin cardboard glided in her hands as she cut the deck, then did a riffle shuffle through the layers giving them a bridge bend to blend, ending with the overhand shuffle.

These cheap cards were wearing on the edges, enabling her to count with ease. But they made for a challenging backhand bridge weave, which she could do faster than a money-counting machine.

With the fancy thumb-fan throw that made her audience's eyes pop, she spotted her suits. Then with a false snap-changing cut of the deck, she had the cards stacked in her favour. Game on.

Her preference was for vinyls cards, which she'd spin to perfection listening to drunk rich men who were too busy working to enjoy their fortunes. They never caught her sly shuffles when she played for certain houses, where the house always won.

Only the true card hustlers knew, instantly folding to never sit at her table again. It was a table where bored women, dripping with diamonds and fur, waited for their partners in a place where men tugged at their neckties that matched their five-thousand-dollar suits. A place where the clink-clink of authentic clay chips matched the clink of ice in low-ball glasses as background noise.

Que couldn't be seated any further from there than in a dusty shed playing with a group of elderly gentlemen who bantered and bickered like old women. Besides being lousy cheats, they let her shuffle the cards, and they liked being useful. It was a welcoming place to spend some time, especially when she didn't want to go home to an empty house that lived under a big sky. 'I seem to have a dodgy stove.'

'What makes it dodgy?' Billie asked.

She shrugged, cutting the cards. 'My chef told me it's dodgy. The oven won't bake stuff.'

'Can you cook?' James asked.

'If opening a can or pushing the start button on a microwave is cooking, then I'm the queen of my kitchen.' She dealt out the cards with a slender flick of her fingers. 'But as I'm living in the land of scones and homemade treats and school bake sales, I don't mind learning. And apparently to bake stuff you need an oven.' Then she'd only need to bake a cake or cookies for this school fundraiser. Instead of designing the flyers, the program, the cover labels for the silent auction boxes, as well as put in a donation for her time — when she'd only been living in town a few weeks.

A large truck roared through its gears to slow down with a hiss of its brakes. In this sleepy town, it made everyone look.

'The grog truck's here,' said Johnny.

'And that's my cue. Que can take my place.' Billy winked at her as he slid on his snazzy felt fedora. 'I've got work to do. Oh, hey, before I forget, Samantha wants an upgrade on the pub's website. You keen?'

'Sure.' Que shrugged, unsure when she would get to the work that was piling up.

'Just not today, we'll be busy unloading.' He tossed his thumb back to the truck waiting to turn right for the pub on the corner.

'I'm having lunch with the ladies soon, maybe I'll meet Samantha then.' Who was she? A girl planning lunch dates with friends, playing cards where the house never won? It was unheard of.

'Great. I'll let the boss know.' Billy started to leave, only to back away from the door as two men entered. 'Oh, hello. Look at what the saltie spat out.'

'What's a saltie?' Que asked the Triple Js.

'Saltwater crocodile.'

But what made them all stop, and scowl wasn't Richard, but at his towering shadow … Connor.

Oh, shoot. Where was the nearest exit?

But Que couldn't leave. She had just dealt a hand. She never walked away from a dealt hand—that was one of the house rules when it came to playing the game. *Shoot!*

10

'You fellas remember my boy, Connor?' Richard spoke to a group of old men, seated around the card table in the hardware store, who were frowning at him.

Just like most of the local yokels did when they realised who he was. Come on, he was a kid back then. But right now, he was keen to go sit in the car and wait …

Until his attention was captured by the new neighbour, Que, seated at the old dudes' card table, wearing a clear shade of disdain in those damned sexy eyes of hers.

'Hello, Que.' The corner of his mouth twitched, but he gave no other reaction.

It matched her silent *leave me alone* vibe.

But he didn't want to leave her alone. She was the only thing worth looking at in this town—even better now he wasn't yelling at her.

'What can we do for you today, Richard?' Billy asked.

'Just getting some hinges and screws while Bertha's getting her hair done. I'm fixing the kitchen cupboards for her, while the lad works on the farm. It's really good having Connor home.' Richard patted Connor's arm.

'I'm on compassionate leave ...' But where was the compassion from the locals? He was already feeling the tines of their pitchforks digging into his spine.

'You're in the Navy, right?' Billy asked, with squinty eyes, in the same hat and suspenders as always. Back then Billy was an old grouch always shouting at them to *Get* from the back of the pub where he worked as the yardie. 'The Defence forces would've straightened out anyone. Or you broke them too?'

'Billy, my boy is a war hero with more medals than any of you mob at this table.'

'Dad, don't ...' Connor despised people getting up in his business. He also didn't deserve the kind of pride he heard in his father's tone.

'What for?' asked one of the old geezers scowling at him through the cigar smoke.

'I don't do war stories, so don't ask.' Not with the action Connor had volunteered for, where war these days was downright despicably dirty. Shame he was just so damned good at it.

He was also over the thirty thousand questions he'd copped at the supermarket and the post office. He was ready to hide back on the farm. But the view was so much better here. 'I didn't expect to find you here, Que.'

'She's been learning to play cards,' said Jeffrey. 'You play?'

'Navy boy, he'd have to,' grumbled one of the other players.

'I don't mind a game now and again. Poker?'

'Euchre,' the men replied in unison.

'Take my seat, I've gotta head to the pub,' said Billy. 'Johnny can help Richard with his shopping list.'

'Where are the Flynn brothers?' Connor's father asked.

'Helping Speedy with a stocktake in the feed store,' replied Johnny, leading his dad down the aisles of assorted tools.

'Well, okay then.' Connor dropped into the seat directly opposite Que, admiring the way the light from the open doors highlighted the blue-black shine of her hair.

And those pouty lips …

He licked his lips while staring at her lips. Perfect for kissing.

'How's the Navy treating you?' asked one of the old fellas as they settled in for a round of cards. Connor listened and commented on their banter as they played, all while he watched the woman across the table.

She had no tells, keeping her cards close to her chest. Yet, every gesture, every expression she made was as smooth and graceful the way a jet boat glides across a calm sea at daybreak. But those eyes keenly watched every microscopic gesture, aware of everything that was happening in her surrounds.

'And that's the match.' She placed her cards down and won the trick.

'Well done, partner. We've trained you well,' said James. Or was that Jeffrey who shook her hand?

'Another game?' asked the man with the coke-bottle glasses, gathering the cards.

'Not today. Gotta run.' She scooped up her laptop bag and was out the door.

That was the second time she'd fled from him.

Only this time he had to admire how her cute rear end shifted in that summer dress. With the sunlight streaming through the door, it gave the perfect shadowy outline of a curvy female figure he wanted to explore.

'Excuse me, fellas.' His chair scraped across the concrete, and he headed for the door. 'Que?'

'Yes.' She stopped on the sidewalk at the far end of the building. 'Oh, it's you.' Rolling her eyes, she turned and disappeared around the corner.

'Hey, I want to talk to you.' He gave chase. Had to. The way her hips swung in that dress, it sung to this sailor.

She went around the back towards her car, parked in the shade.

He recognised her four-wheel drive, displaying Tasmanian plates. That's a long way for someone to come and live in the middle of nowhere. Her husband must make a fortune. 'I wanted to apologise.'

'Don't bother, your mother already did that for you. Aren't you the big man getting your mother to apologise like that?' She spun around, frowning at him.

'She did what?'

'Apologised for you.'

'I said sorry to your husband.'

'My what?'

'The ginger at your house, yesterday.'

'Mike's not my husband.' She screwed her face up at him.

'Boyfriend?'

'Mike's just a friend. What's that got to do with you, anyway? Who are you to jump to so many conclusions about me? Or do you do that for everyone?'

'Nope. Just you, it seems.' This time, his lip twitched to stop the smirk. She was sexy as hell, getting angrier at him by the second.

'You judgy thing you. Is that because I'm a single mother? What else are you going to judge me for? Don't bother, I don't want to hear it. You're a military man, I'm sure you're well trained to shoot first and ask nothing later.' She unlocked the car door and opened it.

He pushed it shut on her.

'Hey!'

'Don't walk away from me when I'm trying to talk to you, here.'

She flinched, only to spin around with eyes like molten layers of velvet, as her sensual aroma washed over him, awakening a level of animality within. It was a high-spirited and deeply feminine scent, that was woody, sweet, and spicy all at the same time.

He'd sniffed around plenty of duty-free perfume counters at airports all over the world, using his favourite pick-up line on the woman staffing the counter: that he was *buying a bottle of perfume for his mother*, to make-out with them in their storerooms before his flight left.

His mother scored lots of perfume. But he'd smelled nothing as dark, rich, and intoxicatingly sexy as Que. She was unbuttoning everything inside him.

'Talking? Is that what this is? I'm sorry, I thought talking was a conversation between two people on a subject that they discussed like civil adults while respecting each other's body space. And without judgement. My first impression of you sucked and, hey, this second impression is a real doozy.'

'Hey, hang on a second, I don't judge.' Considering he was the scapegoat for all of this town's gossip.

'Yeah, you do. You called me a thief.'

Like he'd been called many times for crimes he didn't commit. 'I said I was sorry.'

'Is this your way of apologising? Pretty poor effort for someone trying to smooth over the waters, sailor. Jeez, imagine how you'd ever go at kissing and making up for it.'

'Good idea.' Grabbing her by the sides of her face and pulling her in close, he pressed his lips against hers and kissed her.

She stood frozen for a moment, until her lips parted, and it was on like a deep diver discovering the treasures of an ocean. He kissed her. Fully. Completely. And undeniably with every bit of experience he could muster.

But it went so much deeper …

It was the type of kiss you could never tell your mates about. It was a mean, dominating, punishing kiss that tasted so goddamned sweet and warm it came with loaded layers of luscious lust.

He wrapped one arm around her tiny waist, pulling her into his chest, his other hand sliding under her silky hair, he dived deeper into that kiss. It was a kiss he'd never dreamed of giving, and one he never wanted to end.

It was a kiss that a bad man should never give a good woman, because this type of kiss made them think it might mean something — when it should mean nothing.

He was not here permanently.

He was never permanently based. Anywhere.

Yet, it took everything he had — absolutely. Freaking. *Everything* — to break the connection. With his heart hammering, he forcefully swallowed down his desire.

Those perfectly pouty lips of hers were plump and so red he wanted to kiss her harder. Deeper. In another punishing kiss, a push-her-back-to-the-wall kind of kiss.

But when she opened her eyes, his stomach rolled, completely unzipping his insides as a shot of compressed lust detonated in his groin. It was a glazed after-sex look that said *I've just had the life kissed out of me.*

Damn, I did good.

Connor stroked her silky hair. He wanted to mess her hair up, to see it spread across a pillow while he explored her body. Hell, he wanted to feel the strands trickle through his fingers as he held her head in another one of those kisses, only this time skin to skin, pressed against his bare chest.

'What did you do that for?' Que murmured in a sexy, sultry tone. Her eyes hooded with low lids, it was a steamy look. All of her was a slow sensual sizzle that could easily flip a switch to crank up his inner fire.

He'd kissed the fight out of the woman, but he also wanted her fire.

'I don't know why ... because I felt like it.' He'd never given in to his impulsive animal urges so easily, but he was willing to go again.

Then something flashed in her eyes.

A sting soon followed, as she slapped him right across the cheek.

'What did you do that for?' He stepped back, rubbing his cheek as if he'd been whipped.

'Because I felt like it.' Her eyes glowed as she shoved hard against his chest. She'd completely unbalanced him in more ways than one—which was impossible for a guy like him. She had knocked him on his arse while standing!

But he'd also stuffed up. Big time.

What an idiot.

Que locked herself inside the car. 'I'm not that easy, Mister.'

She drove away as he rubbed his cheek, licking his lips that still tasted of her. Oh man, she was sweet. And the beauty was she was right next door. Game on.

11

Routines were meant to make life easier, but this morning, it was pure chaos, as Que's hair flew while pedalling the tiny pink bike along the red dirt drive. With Billie balancing on the handlebars, and Princess the dog bouncing beside them, she was probably breaking all the rules of proper parenting, because none of them were wearing a helmet.

'It's coming, Momma.' Billie pointed to the big yellow bus chugging along the road leading a rising stream of red dust.

'I'm pushing it.' This last part on her drive from the house to the road had a slight incline, making her legs burn. 'Tell them … to stop … the bus …'

'HOLD THE BUS.' Billie's voice echoed around them.

Princess barked as if shouting with Billie.

The neighbour's children, Tommy and Maddy, and their mother, Val, waved from the roadside as the bus pulled up and they arrived at the gate.

'Love you, Momma.' Billie kissed Que's cheek, then, with pigtails bouncing, her little legs raced for the bus. Que grabbed Princess to keep him at her side. 'Hello, Mrs Cromwell. Can Maddy and Tommy come over for a play date today?'

'Can we please, Mummy?' Maddy called out, with her older brother, Tommy holding the bus door open.

'Billie, bus,' said Que.

'Sorry, Momma. Bye, Momma. Bye, Princess.' Billie blew a round of kisses. She grabbed Tommy and Maddy's hands and like a conga line of children, they climbed onto the bus. The door closed, the engine roared, and it rolled down the hill towards town.

And for the first time, Que didn't feel like chasing her child onto that bus.

'We made it.' Que collapsed against the gate, while Princess chased his invisible tail.

'That was funny. Most people would drive their car,' said Val, tucking her dark brown, coarsely cut bob, behind her ears.

'By the time we'd found the keys, dashed across the paddock to the car, then loaded the bike, it was easier to just peddle.' Que chained the bike up for Billie to ride home, then removed her single-strapped backpack. 'Hi Val, it's so nice to see you on this side of the street.'

'Hi, Que. I must say, the view looks different from this side. Bigger?'

They grinned at each other.

'Have you got time to come over for a coffee?' Who was she? Asking neighbours over for coffee? But company would stop her pining for her child.

'Nah, sorry.'

'We're still on for that play date? All Billie talks about is Maddy. I feel like I know her.'

'It's the same in our household. It's Billie this and Billie that. Is it true you have a roller derby ring?'

'If you count a concrete floor in a shed that's got some fairy lights, then I guess so.'

'Sounds like fun. But we don't have any roller skates.'

'I've got heaps of spares. Come on, when was the last time you slid on a pair of skates?'

'I was a kid. I did the skateboard too.'

'How daring of you. Do you think the school will get a skate park?'

'Maybe. Although I saw Cecil the other day saying there's a school fundraiser for a pool?' Val pointed to the waddling black lump cruising along the verge, picking at wildflowers like he did at the town's airport. Cecil's coat was all clean and free from chalk scribbles or slap-happy words of want, wearing yellow ribbons today.

'Supermom Karen was hoping you'll help her with the fundraiser. She's roping in everyone.' How do you rope in a water buffalo?

Cecil was getting closer on his way to town, as part of his morning routine that Que was getting to know.

'I'll bake a cake, that'll do as my contribution,' said Val.

'Can you bake an extra one for me, so I only have to produce a cake too?'

'Can't you bake?'

'Nope. Would you teach me? I'll make the coffee, or cocktails.'

'I don't know …' Val fidgeted with her fingers as a car engine started nearby. 'Sorry, I've got to go.' She sprinted across the road like a rabbit.

'Okay, so this afternoon? Skate date? Please?' Que begged like her daughter.

'Okay, sure. Bye, Que.' Val gave a short wave, then jogged along her driveway as a red-dust-stained Hilux ute rolled to meet her. It stopped just out of sight behind a native bush covered in pink flowers.

Que looked for the water buffalo, dropping her pack to the ground to rummage through her stash of goodies. 'Cecil, I have a surprise for you.'

A man's raised voice carried from across the road, but she couldn't make out the words.

Que arched her eyebrow at the happy-go-lucky puppy, Princess, who was staring across the road, with hackles up and teeth bared, putting himself between Que and those raised voices.

'It's okay, Princess.'

The dog lowered his skinny body, growling deeper at the man shouting at Val.

'I'm going, I'm sorry,' cried Val, disappearing up the drive. The ute crunched on the gears, and its engine whined as it hit reverse, herding Val back up the drive as if chasing a load of cattle.

Que's eyes widened as a wash of heated anger rose from the pit of her belly. 'You've got to be kidding me!'

But she couldn't interfere. She never interfered. And she would never judge. Sometimes people just had bad mornings and got cranky, because that was life. Like she was running late as the lousy mother, pining for her daughter disappearing in the bus driving down the red road.

Clip-clop. Clip-clop. Sniff ... Cecil's big black nose sniffed at her ear.

'Morning, Cecil.' Goosebumps broke out across her skin as she wiped at her hair in case of buffalo drool.

'Perfect timing.' As the perfect remedy to help her focus on something else.

She unwrapped the muesli bar and held it out to the water buffalo, as Princess wagged his tailless bum, begging for a treat.

'I didn't forget you.' Que tossed the dog treat to the oversized puppy and dug around in her backpack. 'Okay, we're going to do something different today, Cecil. Just hold still and I'll give you the other half of the muesli bar when I've finished.' She'd learned this was what Kat had done to lure the animal to propose to her husband, Kyle.

But Que had other plans and began the project that had her running late this morning as she gathered the tools of her trade. When she was finished, she put her paintbrush back into the pot of chalky water and stood back to admire her walking piece of art.

Cecil says, always find a reason to smile … In perfect, easy to read, Sans Serif font. Complete with a matching yellow modern smiley face right across his rump. It was elegant. It was legible. It was tasteful. It was professional. And it was so much better than *lettuce on special*.

She even re-wrapped his yellow ribbons around his horns and added a matching bow on his long skinny tail that would have any florist nodding with approval.

'Go share your brand of love with the world, my friend.' She gave the last half of the muesli bar to Cecil and watched him waddle away.

It was perfect for this quirky town, which had art everywhere.

And for a girl who got paid to play with words, this was fun. Most of all, there was no more school morning mummy-separation anxiety or pre-school-stalking tendencies. She hoped.

Wiping her hands clean on a wipe, she repacked her backpack, slung it over her shoulder, and wandered back to her house. Princess bounced along beside her like a kangaroo, as if the earth was a doggy trampoline, with his tongue lolling around his wide smile.

'Oi!'

She jumped and Princess barked as she turned around.

'Were you daydreaming?' It was Connor, wearing a cocky grin with his arm leaning out the window of the old grey ute. It was so quiet.

'What do you want?' Where did he come from?

'Hello, mate,' said Connor, giving the dog a hearty pat.

'Traitor.' She narrowed her eyes at the pup lapping up the attention. 'What are you doing here?'

'The old fellas at the hardware store told Dad you had an issue with your oven?'

'So they sent you? Is the town that desperate for skilled labour?'

His large hand shifted the backwards cap on his head. Dark wraparound shades hid his eyes—and she just knew they were staring at her chest! 'I did some electrical work in the Navy. Can't make any promises, but I know the basics.'

'Basics don't cut it, sailor. So how about you flex those navigation skills of yours by turning around and taking a quick trip down the road and out the gate.'

'And go where?'

'Take a Loserville-left or turn right to *I don't care*, just don't let the gate hit you on your way out.'

The corner of his mouth twitched, but he gave no other reaction except to remove his shades to give her a long all-over body gaze, eating her up.

Arsehole. He'd kissed her! Which sucked because it had been so good it took her hours to recover.

'I'm here to help.'

'Don't you have some farming thing to do?'

'Your job seemed like the better offer.' He grinned.

She scowled at him with a silent-but-deadly *get lost* look.

'Hey, are you going to apologise to me?' Because there was no way she was apologising for her smart mouth. 'Tell you what, save your salty sea-dog suck up, and my time, because I don't want to hear anything except the sound of that car leaving.'

At the bottom of her verandah's steps, she turned to find him standing right behind her. For a big man, he was so stealthy.

Big, ha. He was tall, muscular, mean and lean, wearing the story of hard years in his stony eyes. They were edgy. Dangerous. And scorching hot.

Standing so close, his tight T-shirt pronounced his proud stance with each rise and fall of his chest. He was strong enough to tear her free from these steps and toss her over his shoulder caveman style.

But the curling hint of a smile and the half-rugged and yet refined cologne of woodsy spice, worn by this very masculine male, had her blushing like a schoolgirl.

Oh, come on. This was not happening. She wanted to slap herself silly. No way was she going near anything male again. No matter how hard her heart beat in his presence.

Forget the heart, it only caused trouble. *Use the head.*

'Do you usually walk away from people when they're trying to talk to you?' Connor's amused tone only irritated her.

She got to the top of her steps, taking the height advantage, and crossed her arms over her chest. 'Are you going to apologise to me?'

'Mmm …' His rumbling timbre made her want to melt. He took a step closer as she took a wary step backwards, and his lips curled at the edges. 'I apologise for making assumptions, for thinking you were a thief and …' He took another step up.

So she took a step back. 'And?'

'And for assuming your friend Mike was your husband …' Another step forward for Connor.

Another step back for her. 'And?'

'And for what?'

'Invading my body space and kissing me like that.'

'I'm not apologising for that. I wanted to do that. In fact …' As he again took a step closer, his tone deepened to a growl. 'I want to do it again.'

Her back pressed against the wall, missing her front door. 'No, you don't, sailor. You just pull up anchor and find a place to dock elsewhere.' Her outstretched hand reached along the wall for the door handle to put some desperately needed space between them.

'Not until I look at your stove.' He rested his hand on the wall right above her shoulder. 'Do I scare you?'

'Humph. No.' There were much bigger and scarier things in the world, even if she couldn't think of anything except the towering male before her. *Not fair.*

'You look worried.'

'I'm not worried.' *Liar.* 'Why? Should I be?' Her body was screaming out for this guy.

'I don't know, that's why I'm asking you?' He stepped in even closer and his warm, minty breath brushed against her cheek.

Was she worried about him, *no.*

Scared about him, *no.*

What worried her was what she'd do to him if he stayed there another second longer, because the last time he'd kissed her she'd surrendered herself completely.

But the way he looked at her, the unseen sizzle in the air intensified every millisecond.

It was lust. A whole new adult world of lust that wrapped itself around her so tightly she could hardly breathe, only increasing in depth with each breath. And all he did was narrow his eyes to drink her in from head to toe, then back to meet her eyes. His dark, smouldering eyes that belonged to a man who knew what he wanted, as a take-charge, alpha kind of guy, and she was way over her head, drowning in a hot pool of needy lust.

'Mm-hmm.' His deep voice rumbled through her spine; it had her knees weakening as he dropped his mouth a mere inch from hers.

The world stopped spinning as they stared at each other. It was as if time stood still, holding its breath …

'I give in.' She grabbed his face, pulling him towards her, and they met in a clash of lips that detonated like dynamite.

Their bodies sparked, their mouths sizzled, as their lips meshed. A groan—his? hers?—fuelled her inner fire. And she kissed him deep, hard, and for a breathtakingly long time, with her head thrumming to the frantic beat of her heart.

It was a thousand times more intense than yesterday.

'We can keep at this, or we stop now …' He spoke against her mouth with that rumble vibrating down to her quivering lower belly. 'Your call.'

He looked ready to attack.

Que hesitated. Was she ready for more from this guy? From any male?

A man like Connor could steal pieces of your heart before you consented. He'd already stolen kisses from her, drugging her common sense with his mouth.

His hands pushed her hair aside as his hot and heavy mouth dragged down her neck, as if chasing her pounding pulse.

But his fingers … Holy smokes, his fingers pressed all the right buttons across her skin. His large palms crawled hungrily over her hips, sliding down further while he punishingly kissed her mouth. Claiming her.

He was the perfect kisser.

It was madness. A sinful, overwhelming spiral of madness in the power of his kisses. She'd forgotten everything.

'I … Um … Stop … don't … want …' Her body was on fire as his lips covered hers, teasing her with his tongue as his fingers tangled in her hair.

'You're not going to slap me again, are you? Hmm …' He murmured, as his teeth scraped along her jawline, ending with his hot breath in her ear.

'No.' She barely registered speaking, losing herself. His chest pressed against hers as his lips feathered over hers. He was such a tease.

'I'm not going to be able to stop.' He pulled away, forehead lowered, and stared deeply into her eyes. It was as if he'd opened a package and could see straight past all the layers she'd built to hide the woman she was—a woman who'd never felt more desired than in this very moment.

What were the odds of ever feeling like this again?

Could this be the perfect short-term distraction to stop her mummy-separation anxiety?

'I don't want you to stop,' she said in a breathless rush. 'Just shut up and take me inside.' She found the door handle, opening it with great difficulty as his large hands clasped her buttocks and she wrapped her legs around his hips, allowing the chaos of this morning to take her.

'Good thing I follow orders ...' And his lips never left hers as he carried her inside, kicking the glass door shut behind them.

12

An alarm irritatingly beeped, forcing Connor to open his eyes, only for a soft smile to curl across his lips. Que's hair lay tousled over his bare chest like silky feathers, while his thumb traced lazy swirls over her soft fleshy thighs.

How could a hot mess of limbs be so intimate? Where this woman had invaded his psyche with her soft, feminine form; it was imprinted into his bone marrow for him to crave forever.

And let's not forget the kissing.

Kissing this female was like savouring the sweetest dessert on the planet. He had to taste her again and feed this new-found addiction, nipping at her lower lip, to then tug at it with his teeth.

She hissed out his name, 'Connor.'

'Mmm.' An overpowering supernova sizzle zapped through his nerve endings, it had his entire body drumming a beat, all because of her.

'Got to … get up.'

He lifted his head, desperate to maintain contact with her lips, but she pressed on his chest as she pushed herself off and scrambled across the floor, mere metres from the front door.

'Where are you going?'

Slipping on her dress, that he'd slip off again in a hot second, she dashed behind the kitchen's island bench and silenced the alarm. 'It's time for you to go home.'

Normally he was the first to bolt for the door, so this was new.

They'd trashed this room, which really didn't have that much furniture, just a lot of space and a 180-degree view of the countryside.

He slid on his cargo pants and climbed into his boots. 'Why is your alarm clock going off this late in the afternoon?'

'To remind me to meet my daughter at the school bus. And you will not be here.' She put the sofa cushions together.

'I get it.' He didn't know where his T-shirt was, but he found his cap. 'How long have we got?'

'Forty-five minutes. Can you, um?' She pointed to the curtain rod they'd pulled down.

They both chuckled.

'We never made it to the bedroom.'

'No ...' She exhaled the same heat he could feel.

Hell, he'd never connected with anyone like this. It had been an all-consuming lust-fest of flesh, which they'd been at all day—and he could easily go again.

'Let me.' He took the curtain rod from her, noting she was quick to pull away to avoid his touch.

Surely she wasn't suffering with the guilts over what they'd done? They were consenting adults, both single, and ... Aww crap, he wasn't permanent. Surely Que didn't want anything more than what it was—whatever this was.

'Really?' She held up her torn underwear, which she tossed in the bin, then mucked around at the sink, only to giggle. It was a sweet and sexy giggle all at the same time.

A freaking giggle that made him smirk like a goofy teenager.

Get it together, man. He shook his head, hoping to wake from the thick feel-good fog clouding his brain. At the kitchen sink he splashed cold water over his face as Que flicked on the coffee machine, which released a rich caffeine aroma.

'Coffee?' She passed him an icy water bottle she'd retrieved from her fancy new fridge.

'Yeah.' He gulped the water down in seconds, hoping to quench the fire still burning in his belly. 'I don't remember the house looking like this.'

'Kat knocked down some walls and made it look bigger by adding the windows.' She gave the house an approving nod.

There were no dust-collecting knick-knacks, no kitchen counters full of crap, and no pictures on the wall. 'Is your furniture still coming?' He nodded at the empty room, which held only a couch, a mat and a set of stools tucked under the kitchen counter. No table and chairs, not even a TV.

'We've been playing gypsy, living in a caravan for years, so I don't have much stuff.' She nodded at the shed shading her vehicle and another dusty twin-cab ute parked beside the large caravan.

That made sense. She hadn't settled in yet.

Que handed him a coffee and sat on one of the stools on the other side of the counter.

Drawn to her, he followed to sit beside her with his fingers itching to stroke down her leg, to keep her close, overcome by this need to press flesh against flesh. Again.

She sipped, looking at him over the rim of her cup with those damned violet eyes of hers. It made him gulp down the hot coffee, searing his mouth. But he felt nothing, only the need to have her again. *Down, boy.*

'What did you come here for, again?'

Oh man, did he come. 'To, um …' He scratched the back of his head, searching the modern room for answers, until his eyes landed on the outdated hunk of metal. 'The oven.'

'Oh, yeah.' She grinned, not embarrassed in the least.

He liked that. And her.

'I guess I could look at it.' He grudgingly stood before the oven, sipping his coffee.

'Good. You've got half an hour before you're out the door.' She tapped her wrist.

'No worries.'

'Good.' She took a mouthful of her coffee and headed down the corridor. 'Now you can check out the oven, while I take a shower.'

Oh boy. Didn't his groin react as his brain rolled over. 'Need help?'

'What about the stove?'

'I can come back tomorrow …' He was already stalking down the corridor of doors.

She poked her head out from an open doorway and grinned. 'Tomorrow, sure. But right now, we're on a deadline. I've got a play date with the neighbours' kids. It'll be our first one and I've got food to prepare for this party and you're not invited.'

'You make the rules, lady.' He certainly didn't play with children, only the ladies. And as a sailor on holidays, he had time to play …

13

Three small children rolled in skates across the concrete floor of the large shed with its open walls offering a panoramic view of the countryside.

Old school 80s music pumped from the speakers housed in the corners of the roof, where a bank of ceiling fans whirled along with flashing lights and a disco ball.

'We have these for you to choose from.' Que dragged a box over to Val, who was seated by a table covered in school bags; underneath lay three pairs of small shoes. 'Socks here too. All clean.'

'How did you score these?' Val asked, rummaging through the box of assorted skates.

'They were having a sale at the old skating rink, where we used to rock and roll away our Saturday nights. Developers bought the place out to make a fancy high rise.'

'I don't know about this,' said Val, hesitating. 'I don't remember how.'

'Hey, I'll be right beside you. And I bet, once you've spun around a few times, you'll get the hang of it. Easy as. Here, these will be perfect for you.'

'Thanks.' With her arms stretched out to grab the skates, her jumper's sleeve pulled back to expose wrists that were red and bruised. Val quickly tucked them away.

Que turned to face the children. 'Hey, baby, it's not a race. You keep showing off like that and no one will want to play. Help your friends, who are your guests.'

Giving the thumbs up, the kid whizzed past backwards, then spun around as if on ice to go help her friends.

Que slipped on her skates. She wanted to ask Val about the bruises, but she also didn't want to intrude. She couldn't afford to get involved in people's lives. She also didn't want to scare off Val, who seemed so timid and jumpy at everything.

With skates on, Que held her hand out to Val. 'Come on, Val, let's show these kids how it's done.'

Slowly, the adults moved from the table, with Que skating backwards, holding Val's hands as they cruised around the shed's floor.

'What are you doing with this farm?' Val asked on shaky feet.

'No idea. I don't know how to farm.'

'But you're on your own? Don't you get scared doing it all on your own?'

'I've got a dog, and Mike put in some security stuff.'

'You're very courageous in doing this on your own. I couldn't do it.' Val wobbled off-balance, then self-corrected.

'I didn't think I could either, but here I am. Beauty is, there's no guy to hassle me ...' Although she didn't mind the hassle of Connor today.

'Look at you, Mummy,' said Maddy, whizzing past, with her older brother racing with his tongue to the side as Princess bounded along on the outside.

'Show-offs,' Que said, pleased with Val's smile. 'You're doing really well, Val. Now, let's try one hand.'

'I'm not … I can't.'

'You are. See.' The small wheels rumbled under her boots as they skated slowly around the shed. 'I never learnt to skate until Billie wanted to, so if I can do it, you can too.'

'Didn't you do it as a kid?'

'No. My childhood never involved climbing trees, riding bikes, or rollerskating.' Que shared a soft smile at her daughter, who was a ball of vibrant happiness. She wanted to bottle some of that happy essence to drop into a diffuser to inhale all day long. 'I bet you had a ball as a kid growing up out here?'

'Yeah, life was so simple and full of freedom …' A memory must have flickered behind Val's eyes that brightened with her widening smile.

Each time they rolled around the shed Val grew more confident until Que was barely holding her hand. Pride filled her when Val cruised on her own. Slowly, yet awkwardly, she skated around the rink with her children helping her, as the music pumped from the speakers.

That left Que to play with Billie, where they danced in the centre on their skates. With all of them singing badly to the 80s music, even Val, time just flew.

Then a loud car horn ripped through the late afternoon air. *Beeeeeeeeeeep.*

Que turned down the music and Princess ran to stand in front of Billie to growl at the dust-stained Hilux ute with a broken headlight and dented bull bar. It waited halfway up their driveway, where the driver again punched on the horn. *Beeeeeeeeeeep.*

'Kids, it's your father,' said Val in a wide-eyed panic. 'Quickly. You know he doesn't like to be kept waiting.'

Tommy tore off his skates, scooped up his school bag and ran down the drive in his socks, while Billie helped her friend Maddy undo the laces.

'Your husband can come in if he likes.' Que told Val.

'Gary's shy, and I'm late making dinner. I was having such a wonderful time.'

'Me too. You'll have to come back again.'

'Um.' Val shrugged, pulling up her sleeves to expose dozens of old bruises all along her forearms. Her hands trembled so badly she couldn't undo the laces on her skates.

'I've got this.' Que undid the laces for Val, who tore off the skates and socks, slipping on her sandals. 'I'll see you tomorrow?'

'At the bus stop. Sure. Thanks, bye.' Val gave a limp wave. 'Come on, Maddy. You'll see your friend tomorrow.' She grabbed the little girl's hand, and they ran, not walked, not jogged, but ran at full speed to the Hilux with its engine revving impatiently. The passenger door banged shut, and it tore off in a circle, sending dust flying. It didn't slow down, whining as if stuck in second gear, down the long drive to cross the road.

How rude!

'Momma, did we do something wrong?' Billie's little hand slid into Que's.

'No. They're probably late for something.'

'Tommy said they're not allowed to talk about it, but Maddy

says their daddy is sad. And so is their mummy. Can we cheer them up?'

Whoa. Where did Que even begin with this kind of conversation? This was too heavy for a little girl, and not what she'd expected from the neighbours.

But she was also adult enough not to jump to conclusions. People had bad days.

Que crouched down to face her daughter. 'Baby, all you can do is be a good friend to Maddy.'

Billie screwed up her button nose. 'How?'

'By being kind and taking the time to listen to Maddy, that's what a friend does.' Que stood to face the empty driveway as heavy acidic dread clawed its way from the pit of her guts. 'You just let them know you're there to help them. Day or night.'

Who was she to give out advice like this because that meant getting involved for the long term?

She peeked back at the Mighty T, fully loaded and ready to hook onto the back of her car. The caravan was a security blanket, one she'd hoped to no longer need.

'Put your skates away, baby, and we'll get ready for dinner. I'll go lock the gate.'

With her back to the sunset, Que's footsteps crunched along the brittle red soil as her shadow lengthened.

She shoved the gate shut, double wrapped it with the thick chain, and exhaled at the sound of the heavy lock clicking into place. The fence line was the standard pig wire, with double strands of barbed wire running along the top. It was chest height, and jumpable if you really needed to get in. But it was her barrier to the outside world.

Across the road, the neighbour's rocky driveway was hidden by overgrown native shrubs, its fence broken, and there was no gate.

Pity their first play date ended like this, when they'd been having so much fun. But she also shouldn't jump to conclusions because every household had their dramas, and Que never shared her dramas with anyone.

Did she dare hold onto hope that this place would become a home for her tiny family to enjoy a life free from fear?

Yet again, that massive sky pushed a heavy layer of loneliness across her shoulders and chest, it was smothering.

Maybe moving here had been a bad idea.

14

'Good to see no bike riding this morning,' said Val, greeting Que at the front gate. Her children rushed to meet Billie, who was parking her bike, with the playful Princess eager for a pat.

'Morning ...' Que strolled up the lane, her pack slung over her shoulder. Unlocking the gate, she searched for her friendly neighbourhood water buffalo.

And there he was, moseying towards them with red ribbons waving off his horns.

The yellow bus overtook the beast, stopped with a hiss of its brakes, and its side door screeched open. Then it was a flurry of hugs and air kisses before the children clambered on board. The door screeched shut and its engine rumbled, as the bus rolled down the road where a watery haze hovered over the red soils, heading for town.

'Um, sorry about last night?' Val said meekly.

'Nothing to be sorry for, I had an awesome time. You did too. You couldn't fake the smile.'

'Yeah.' And there it was, that same beaming wide smile that brightened Val's eyes. It didn't hide the dull skin and dark rings, but it was an improvement. 'My children couldn't stop talking about it, and I couldn't believe how quickly they fell asleep last night.'

'Billie's the same. Me too. You?'

Val shrugged, wrapping her cardigan tighter around herself. The weather wasn't cool enough to wear wool. But then again, Que hadn't acclimatised to this kind of tropical autumn, where everything was drying out under that sapphire sky. It was a stark contrast to pale yellow grasses that punched through the red dirt.

'So how about this baking date? Bertha gave me some of her jam, so I'd love to make scones.'

'Bertha makes the best banana bread; you should ask Bertha for a lesson.'

'I'd love to, but she's still recovering.'

'Gary was telling me he'd spotted Bertha walking along the road with Richard.'

'Aww, romantic strolls.'

'Gary would never do anything like that.'

'I have no one to do that with, unless you count Princess.'

'But isn't that ginger fella your partner?'

'Mike's a mate. He'll be here next weekend.' She couldn't wait. 'His class is coming out to do a planting makeover on the block to create some wildlife regeneration thingy. You and your children are more than welcome to join us for the planting party.'

'A what?'

'Mike's a university lecturer in tropical horticulture at Charles Darwin University. He's using my property as a testing ground for planting things. He'll be proud to see I've got lawn, considering I don't garden. How could I fail, when Mike's got it all on automatic irrigation for me.'

'And you don't bake.'

'I'm such a terrible person.' Que rolled her eyes as Cecil waddled up and sniffed at her bag. 'Good morning, my friend.' Que scratched the wiry black fur of the buffalo's head, which was so soft around his ears. His dark eyes were outlined with long thick eyelashes most woman would kill for. 'Don't you worry, I've got the goods for you.'

'And that's my cue to leave. See you tomorrow, Que.'

'You too, Val.' When Que spotted a tag hanging out of the back of Val's cardigan, she automatically reached for it. 'Hold on.' Que tucked in the dress tag, in doing so it exposed a smattering of deep red bruising hidden just below Val's hairline, where the cardigan met her skin. 'It's a pet hate of mine,' said Que, calm on the outside, while inside worry churned in her belly.

'Oh, yeah. Silly me.' Val brushed her hair over her neck, pulling down her cardigan's sleeves to cover her hands.

'You know you can come over any time, you and the kids, we'd love the company.'

'I wouldn't want to bother you, working from home.' Val shied away.

'For you, I'll make an exception.' She lowered her head to meet Val's eyes. 'Any time. For anything. Just know you'd never be a problem if you ever need me. Call it the safe haven from all domestic responsibilities …'

Val frowned.

Que quickly back-pedalled, to avoid scaring her off. 'Just ask Billie, she'll tell you my motherly skills aren't the best, compared to other mothers.'

'Oh.' Val relaxed a little. 'You're doing fine.'

'Just know the invitation is there, anytime.'

'Thank you, Que.' Val gave a timid smile, rubbing her neck she peered at the colossal sky, then to the red-dirt road that led to town.

'Is there something you want to say?'

'No.' Val shook her head, with glazed eyes she blinked furiously. 'I've gotta run. So much to do.' Again, she fled across the road, only to pause on the edge of her driveway. 'Wednesday?'

'What about Wednesday?'

'Gary's out Wednesdays. I could come over for a coffee and perhaps a baking lesson then.'

Que's entire soul glowed as big and bright as the smile that grew across her face. 'Next Wednesday it is.' She waved at Val until she disappeared down her drive.

Her instincts were telling her one thing, but her head was telling her she had to be patient—she had to have proof. She also had to wait for Val.

Unfortunately, patience was never one of Que's strong suits, but she'd do it to be a friend and let Val know she was there for her. Even if it meant taking baby steps, she'd try.

But that also meant sticking her own neck out.

Yet, if she expected her daughter to do it, she should lead by example as the adult, so baby steps were good.

She whirled around and grinned at her favourite pet project of the day. 'Cecil, my darling friend, have I got the word of the day for you.'

Unzipping her bag, she pulled out a muesli bar, a paint brush and jar of paint to focus on what she loved doing most, word art. It made her forget all else around her. She didn't feel the pain or the memories that haunted her. Most of all she didn't feel the fear she'd become so used to living with it was like putting on a prickly coat to face the day.

In this small moment of time, all she saw was what stood before her, a big-butted black water buffalo.

'Off you go, my friend. Have a fabulous day.' With hand on hip and head tilted, she smiled, watching her latest work wander down the road. Today, in bold white paint, Cecil's furry rump read: *Once you choose hope, anything's possible, so said Superman.* She'd used an embellished font, to really make it pop on the walking billboard of art.

With a smile on her face, she scooped up her bag and brush, and headed up the long driveway back to the house with a clear, infinite sky stretching above her.

Could this really be that place where her past could no longer hurt her? A place to finally call home. Or was this place just another house of cards?

15

She didn't even see him, but Connor saw her. With his wrist resting on the ute's steering wheel, his eyes followed her hips, swaying in that dress up the driveway all the way to her house. She was in la-la-land.

And so was he, watching her.

And that ponytail.

A simple ponytail she'd probably slapped together without thinking. But there was nothing simple about that waterfall of black silk trailing from high on her head, down between her shoulders to the small of her waist. A waist that widened at the hips, down to that delectable tight toosh.

Toosh! Where the heck did that come from?

But the animal inside him wanted to pull on that ponytail and …

His view got cut off by Princess, bouncing like a roo in the long grass having a fat time playing in the morning dew.

Women, puppies and children together were never on his list of life's pleasures, but this morning it seemed like a fine combination to perve on through the ute's windscreen.

He engaged the ute's handbrake, climbed out, and followed

them up the driveway. The dog barked, rushing forwards with his tail-less bum wagging. Was the dog deaf to not notice him sooner?

'Morning, Princess.' He gave the dog a hearty pat, as he lapped up the attention. 'Why did you call a male dog Princess? It's a male.'

'Tell that to the little lady of the house.'

'I'm looking right at her.' And didn't he just let his eyes drink her in.

Que cocked a hand on the hip he wanted to grip, but her look said *back off*. 'Are you lost?'

Lost in those curves, hell yeah. 'I'm here to work.'

'Yeah, right! Tell me you are here to fix my oven …' She pursed those perfectly pouty lips tight in a look that made his chest burr with a growl. 'I'm serious.'

'Sure …' Best excuse on the planet. 'I might actually take the tools out of the ute this time.'

She rolled her eyes, then led the way inside. 'I'll shout the coffee while you pretend to know your way around that toolbox.'

He placed the toolbox down by the oven. 'Electric stoves are rare out here.'

'Yeah? Why?'

'We get so many blackouts with the build-up storms, it's easier to work with gas.' He peeked down the sides to the wall. 'You have the gas points in the wall ready to roll.'

She shrugged, handing him a coffee, then sat on the other side of the bench. 'Can you fix it? I'm booked in for a baking lesson.'

'Mum says you can come round home and bake there. She's always baking.' He squatted down before the oven to peer inside the enamel cavity.

'Not with your mother, with Val.'

'Who?' He peered back at her over his shoulder.

'Val, she lives across the road.'

'The Cromwells.'

'Do you know them?'

'Val was in a lower grade than me at school, I only remember her as a kid.' Connor opened the lid of his dad's toolbox and rummaged around. 'Why do you ask?'

With her bent elbow on the bench, Que rested her chin on her hand. Deep in thought, her finger traced the outline of some imaginary letters on the countertop. But her expression was serious. 'Not sure.'

'Well, something's bothering you.' He walked around the bench towards her.

'No.' She pointed her finger at him. 'Oven first. Sex second.'

'Yes, ma'am.' *What a woman.*

'Please, it's important.'

'Who knew baking was such a big thing.' He pulled the stove away from the wall to expose the back panel and unhooked it from the power source. 'How often do you bake?' The inside was spotlessly clean.

'I don't.'

'So, microwave meals and opening a jar is really your form of cooking?'

'No, I can cook, I just don't bake. But as this is the land of homemade scones and cakes, I may as well try. Can you bake?'

'Humph. How long has it not worked?'

'I don't know. Mike said it didn't work properly.'

'The not-boyfriend?'

'Mike is my best friend.'

'So, he's gay?' He hoped.

'No. Mike has girlfriends. I just wish he'd find himself a wife and not worry about me all the time.'

'So, he's into you and you've just friend-zoned him.'

She screwed her nose up. 'What's with the inquisition over Mike.'

'I don't want to tread on any toes, here.'

'Oh, I see.' As she inhaled deeply, he prepared himself for his usual set of excuses, because he didn't do permanent.

'Mike is just a mate. Yes, we were together at one time, in our late teens. It's something we grew out of, that we both know will never happen again, because we've evolved to this family support kind of love. Nothing more. He's Billie's godfather and family to me. How's your mother doing?'

She never mentioned Billie's father.

'Better than ever. Mum's dragging Dad out for walks for sunrise and sunsets. She's changed the way she cooks a lot of stuff, too. Dad's losing weight.' He chuckled, only to wipe away his smile. 'Thank you for saving her, and for taking care of the place while they were away.'

'It was nothing.' She waved her hand dismissively.

'Dad told me what you did to keep Mum alive. He said you were like a combat medic. Have you got any medical training?'

'I wanted to be a paramedic once, did all the qualification courses and everything, but hey, life happens. I like what I do now more.' She tucked her hair behind her ear and drew on the countertop with one finger.

'Okay, so why the sudden need to fix this?' He pulled out the shelves, then glanced back to grab a tool and caught Que leaning over to watch him.

'You'd make a great model for a men's clothing store, you know that.' She tasted the tip of a finger giving him a coy grin with those pouty lips. It was a hungry, sexy look.

Good thing this man was only too happy to feed her appetite.

'Are you checking me out, while my head is in this thing?'

'Although some people may call me the devil's spawn, I am human with a heartbeat.' She laughed.

Damned, wasn't it the sweetest sound he'd heard all day. It made him smile as he pulled out the oven's central coiled elements where layers of rust crumbled in his hands. 'The elements are done.'

'Can you fix it?'

'No, it's buggered. I doubt they even make parts for a stove this old.' He showed her the worn element, sprinkling rust over her clean counter. 'See? Stuffed.'

'Aww, that shoots my plans straight out of the water, sailor.'

Cheeky wench. 'You'll need a new stove.'

'Easy as. Mike can do it for me, I'll text him the deets to bring one out with him next weekend. I'm sure he'll have room to toss one of those contraptions into the back of his plant truck or some other truck passing through this town. You mentioned gas is better?' She tapped on her mobile.

'I did. But why the rush for an oven, anyway?'

'Like I said, it's for Val.'

'And …'

'You won't give up?'

'Nope.'

'Nosy thing.'

Normally, he didn't give a toss about anyone or anything, but he wanted to know all about her. 'Yep. So, tell me.' He stood square in front of her and didn't take his eyes off her, downing a mouthful of his coffee to quench his thirst.

'Because ...' Que sighed deeply. 'Val.'

'You said that before.'

'I want to make friends with her.'

'There's gotta be more to it.' Que seemed like the kind of woman who wouldn't need to try hard to make friends. She had his attention by just breathing—where he was fighting the temptation to breathe her in by covering her mouth with his.

'Because ...'

'Jeez, woman. Trying to get information out of you is like wrestling with a shark stuck in an illegal fishing net, tangled around a ship's propeller.'

'Wow, did you do that?'

'Couple of times. So, give.'

'Okay, I think Val may need help.'

'In what way?'

Que winced, with none of that brash bravado, wearing a look loaded with worry. 'Can you keep a secret?'

'Sure. Not that I talk to many people since I've been back, besides you.'

'Are we talking? I thought we only argued and then had hate-sex.'

'Hot hate-sex, honey.' *Hell yeah.* 'But I guess we are holding a conversation, so what's the secret?'

'I think, well, I don't know if I'm overreacting or reading too much into it—'

'Spit it out!'

'I think Val is being abused.' Que sat up, covering her mouth with wide eyes, as if ashamed that she'd spoken aloud.

'By who?' His frown deepened. 'How?'

'I've seen the bruises on Val's wrists.' Que wiped over her exposed arms as she explained. 'They're all over her forearms. She's got fresh ones on her neck that weren't there yesterday when we were roller-skating.'

'Do you think her husband is doing this to her?'

'I don't know. I've never met the guy. I've only seen him once when he sat on my driveway, slamming on the horn for his kids to go home. He never got out of his ute or anything.'

'Maybe he was running late for an appointment.'

'He could have driven right up to the shed to collect his family, not park fifty metres away leaning on his horn. I don't know how long he'd been sitting there watching us. It was creepy.'

A protective burr stirred inside his chest.

'Look, I don't normally run around accusing anyone of anything,' Que said. 'I've always had to have proof. Hard evidence. It's how I was brought up. However, I do have strong suspicions, but you can't say anything.'

He believed her.

But news like this could spread throughout this tiny community the way a hot wind fanned a bushfire, it could cause some serious damage to a person's reputation. He should know, having been on the receiving end of this town's gossip. Tagged the bad boy, blamed for everything—when most of the time he wasn't the one at fault. 'I've learned the hard way that you don't go pointing the finger at anyone unless you have proof. I hate gossipers, okay?' He gave a warning frown, ready to head for the door because gossip was his number one pet hate.

'Pfft,' she said dismissively. 'For the record, sailor, I've only told you, and only because you forced me. So this goes nowhere.'

'Agreed.' He gave a curt nod. 'Do you need to get involved with all of this?' Did he? Connor could easily come up with some excuse to climb back into his dad's ute and keep busy at his parents' property until it was time to head back to base.

'I'm hoping it's nothing, for Val's sake, and why I'm having baking lessons. It's the only way I can get her over here, telling her I can't cook.'

He gazed around the vacant benches that only held a coffee machine. Nothing like his mother's cluttered kitchen, full of gadgets. Worse, while his dad was fixing the cupboards, there was kitchen crap everywhere, with his mum on a spring clean. 'So pretending you can't cook is your way of getting Val over here, to befriend her? That's a lot of effort.'

'I know it is, but Val is so shy, and I like her. She's really sweet, with this wicked sense of humour hidden beneath the layers.'

'But—and I know there's a *but*, so please just say it.'

'But ...' She sighed so heavily her shoulders deflated. 'If someone is doing this to her, at least Val knows she won't be alone.'

'I'm going to ask you again, do you really want to get involved in this?'

'Somebody has to.'

'Are you sure?'

'No. Yes.' She sat tall and nodded. 'Helping your parents made Billie and I feel good, simply by doing something to help out another with no ulterior motive. It taught my daughter a valuable lesson, and it reminded me that it doesn't take much to be kind or help someone. And for someone who never gets involved,' she said, patting her chest, 'I'm actually choosing to get involved.'

Connor only got involved when orders told him to. 'But if it's nothing?'

'That's what I'm hoping for,' she said, holding up her crossed fingers. 'I really want it to be just my overactive imagination making me overthink things, because Billie and I want to make this our home. So I'm trying to play my part as a good neighbour.'

'And if there's more to Val's story?'

'She needs to know that someone's there to help her, no questions asked.'

'Fair enough.' Her motives were admirable. It's also how he lived, no questions asked. So, did he leave now and forget everything?

'Where's the lecture about keeping my nose out of other people's business?'

'Not now that you've explained.' He sat on the stool beside her and sipped his coffee. 'But do you normally go around saving the universe?'

'Never. I never bother getting to know the neighbours either, because I'm usually the first one out the door.' She tossed her thumb back to that huge caravan, where her car was parked in front of the van's front tow bar hitch, as if ready to lock and load.

'So, who usually saves you?' He asked casually, but her frown flittered.

She sat taller with chin up. 'No one. I'm fine.'

Oh, man, didn't he want to hold that chin of hers and pull her close for a kiss.

'Hey, while we're on the subject of saviours of the universe, this thing with us …' Que pointed between them.

'Yes?' Here it comes, the terms of their arrangement—if they were having an arrangement.

'It's just sex, okay.'

His lips curled as he tried to suppress his smile.

'I mean it. No strings attached. Nothing long term. No commitment. No such thing as forever. Okay?'

'Got my vote, beautiful.' He slid his arms around her delicate body, inhaling her high-spirited and deeply feminine scent. The aromatic layers suited the woman of mystery seated before him. 'Just as long as I'm out of the house before your daughter gets home. I believe that's one of the house rules.'

'Exactly. Just so you know, you are being used as a distraction for the temporary-separation anxiety I'm going through with my daughter at school, and I'm assuming you live by the cliché of the sailor with a girl in every port.'

If perfume counters at airport duty-free stores counted, *hell, yeah.*

'I know you're only in town for a visit, so we'll keep this really simple.'

'You're a girl after my own heart.' As he stood in front of her, she craned her slender neck to meet his eyes with hers. Damn they were pretty eyes.

'Hey, no heart stuff, okay? Just lust and physical, whatever this is …'

'Babe, I'll play any role you want me to play.' He chuckled, gently nuzzling her neck with only one thing on his mind. 'Reckon we'll make the bed?'

'We haven't christened the kitchen, yet.'

16

'Are you sure you and Mike aren't a thing?' Supermom Karen asked Que.

'Ditto to that,' said Kat, leaning back in an outdoor chair under the shade of a scraggly gum.

Beside them were assorted eskies and water coolers, spread around a camping table. Kat pointed to Mike working with his university students in Que's yard. 'Mike's a good-looking man, and you're single, right?'

'I am. And so is Mike. Although, he usually ends up having an affair with one of his students at least once a semester.' And it was another new group of students Mike was teaching about the fine art of planting stuff. Mike spoke of technical Latin species' names, explaining their idiosyncratic traits suitable for surviving in the outback. He was impressive to watch. Most of all, this barren patch of red dirt was getting a makeover.

'Popular guy,' said Karen, raising an eyebrow.

'Don't judge.' Kat playfully tapped Karen's knee. 'What are those students planting out here?'

'Mike says it'll be a native corridor of trees to handle the weather, regenerating this area. The bonus is it'll be a noise and dust break from the road.' Especially from the speedy dust-covered Hilux that whined as if stuck in low gear.

'Aren't you going to farm your land?'

Que shrugged. 'Richard told me they used this land for cattle and crops. Mike says the soil's been so untouched it's self-seeding in pastures or some other farm stuff.'

'Do you want to farm?'

'I'm flat out learning the intricacies of looking after a dog, that technically my five-year-old does for me.' Que grinned at Billie, working alongside Mike, planting a sapling. Beside them Princess wagged his tailless bum, digging holes with them.

Rolls of irrigation pipe sat alongside solar panels, and assorted plants in black tubing lay in her yard, which was crowded with a truck, a minibus, and Karen and Kat's cars. Their many children joined in for the day, as well as the neighbours' kids, Maddy and Tommy. But no Val.

'Hey, I saw Val the other day,' said Que. 'She's baking a cake for the school thing.'

'Oh, that's awesome.' Karen flicked open her folder. 'We have so much happening with only four weekends to go, people.'

'Mike said he'll donate some plants to sell too.'

'Does Mike do stuff outside of the university?' Karen asked. 'Farmers out here would kill for that kind of a consult if he's got skills.'

Que screwed up her nose; it was her turn to play PR for a friend. 'Mike is a horticultural guru of greenery with a specialty in tropical crops and mining site regeneration. He works alongside the CSIRO and is courted by lots of universities to be their dotty professor all over the country. Mike loves what he does, with his talents and skills in high demand, he's often called on to play the green thumb nerd.' She lowered her sunglasses and said, 'Seriously, ladies, Mike is that good when it comes to commercial gardening stuff.'

'How long have you known each other?'

'Forever. Mike is family, and just a friend, Karen.'

'A sexy friend.'

'Talking about sexy …' Kat sat forward, fanning her face. 'I saw Connor the other day at the supermarket. Holy hot tamales, Connor is seriously ripped. The T-shirt he had on was so tight, it had my sister-in-law, Nora, drooling while counting the ridges on his stomach. She swears he's got an eight pack. She also swears he's sexier than our new fire chief or top cop, Marcus.'

'How hot are your first responders?' Que asked.

'The fire chief, Jax, has these deadly inked arms on him like—'

'What was Connor doing, posing in the mirror or something?' Karen interrupted Kat.

'No. He was helping his mum carry the basket up and down the supermarket aisles. Nora was managing the deli section and that's where she asked Bertha about baking her banana bread for the Mother's Day stall. I think it was Nora's excuse to get Connor to stand still so she could perve. He's going to the fundraiser.'

'Everyone should be. Although,' Karen sighed, flicking over her charts, 'I asked Samantha to close her pub.'

'I bet she said no.' Que chuckled behind her coffee mug.

'The publican laughed in my face.'

'I would if it was my business,' said Kat, 'You can't do that to God.'

'Well, Samantha did offer a few beer kegs as a donation for the football game, but she said it'll be tricky considering schools are alcohol-free zones.'

'I told you we should have held it at the sports field,' said Kat.

'But it's for the school and should be held at the school.'

'But there's a bar on the sportsground. And the coach has got the oval looking amazing, which will be perfect for the promotional football match, where we can all sit on the grandstands.'

'Would it be too hard to change it?' Que had no clue where the sportsground was.

'But you've done the fliers already,' whined Karen, gripping her work folder.

'I can change that in a hot minute on my phone while sitting here. You haven't printed out anything yet?'

'No. But it's out in the school newsletter. We only have four weeks.'

'Plenty of time,' said Kat.

Karen frowned at Kat. 'You're supposed to be on my side. And you shouldn't be drooling at Connor. You're a married woman, and Connor's just a bad-bad man. He's a bully, a thief, a scoundrel, and Nora shouldn't be perving, either, as the Caveman's wife.'

'Whoa, Karen, lay off,' said Kat. 'We're all friends here.'

'Sorry, I'm just stressing out over this event.' Karen held up the folder as if it were made of concrete. 'I wish Val would help. She used to do this stuff so easily.'

'Maybe Val made it seem easy, when really it's a tonne of work.'

'It is. I've got all these things to organise.'

'Divvy it up,' Que suggested. 'And learn to live under the power of delegation, my friend.'

'Excuse me?'

'Nominate someone to take care of areas like car parking, food stalls, and the football match. While you play general at the top, making sure those sergeants get their soldiers together.' Huh? Had she been hanging out with Connor too much these past couple of weeks?

'Que's right, give me that list,' said Kat with her hand out, 'and we'll see who we can delegate to. Small town, shouldn't take long.'

'Just not me,' said Que, 'I don't know anybody.'

'You've done enough already, with the graphics on this.' Karen gave Que a motherly pat on the hand. 'Where is Val, if her children are here?'

Que shrugged. 'Hey, do you know Val's husband, Gary?'

'Me, no. I hardly remember Val as a kid,' said Kat. 'But Karen would.'

Karen flicked over the sheet in her folder, rummaged in her bag for a pencil, sipped her coffee, then dug deeper through the contents of her bag, again.

'Karen?' Que leaned forward to catch the woman's eye.

'I shouldn't …' Karen pursed her lips tightly.

'Shouldn't what?' Kat asked with Que nodding, hoping the normally outspoken mother would continue.

'My husband said not to.'

'Not to what?' Kat asked.

'Speak ill of anyone.'

'You call the mine manager snooty.'

'He is. That prick phones the house all the time when he's back in Sydney. It's as if he can't trust my husband to do the job that he's been doing for over ten years—'

'What has this got to do with Val's husband?' Kat asked.

Karen sank into her seat, fidgeting with her fingers in her lap. 'Gary used to live here but left with his mum when his parents' divorced. He came back when his father got cancer and tried to help him manage the farm. That's when he started dating Val. Gary sold his father's property when he married Val, but he's a lousy farmer ...'

'Are you sure that's not due to other circumstances?' Que asked. 'I'm no farmer, but from what Mike's told me people who make their living off the land have a lot to deal with.'

'Gary invested in macadamia and avocado trees that died. And don't start me on the banana spot that nearly wiped them out. So he scored a job at the mines. But Gary only lasted six months before my husband fired him for being hot-headed and fighting with a co-worker.' Karen winced. 'This is strictly between us. I don't feel right sharing this. Val's a really nice person and they're like many others who are doing it tough living on the land.'

'It's okay, Karen,' said Kat, patting her hand. 'We won't say anything.'

'I don't know anyone to tell. But I do think we need to put all of these sad stories aside and focus on the moment, by finishing the delegations for Karen then we can go and get our hands dirty in a clean way. Come on, let's go hang out with our kids and do something good for the environment and plant some trees.' Que pulled out some cotton gardening gloves from Mike's large stash of gardening gear. 'Are you in?' It had to be better than thinking about her neighbours. Not when she had the pleasure of Mike's amazing company all weekend.

Today, the sky didn't seem so big, as voices of happy people and laughing children, plus a yapping dog, filled the yard that was a part of her home. It was almost as if she were living the dream.

17

Que closed the toilet door only for the door knob to fall into her hands, with something rattling down inside the door's wooden cavity.

'No way.' Inside the toilet, she tried to re-fit the knob to the door, but it didn't work. All its internal mechanics were gone.

She tried to push in the latch with her fingernails, but it was embedded in the doorjamb.

She was trapped.

'Billie?'

Silence.

Please don't have your headphones on. 'BILLIE!'

'Yes, Momma?' Her child sounded so far away.

'Can you open the toilet door, please?' Her voice bounced off the walls in the tiniest room in the house. She opened the tiny window for air. The reinforced bars that made it their cyclone shelter were so small it was impossible for even a cat to climb out of her tiny prison.

She could hear Billie in her slippers, padding down the hallway. The door handle rattled on the other side, only to clang and bang on the corridor floor. 'It fell off, Momma.'

Que forced down her panic, laced with a touch of claustrophobia. 'Can you try to push the door open?'

'It won't move.'

'Can you get me a butter knife from the kitchen drawer?'

Billie's slippers padded back down the corridor, followed by the rattle of cutlery shifting in the drawers. She soon returned, with the pitter patter of paws now accompanying her.

'Is Princess in the house again?'

'He helped me pick the right knife, Momma. Are you making a sandwich in there?'

'No, can you pass it under the door for me?' Thinking of knife safety first with a child.

'Sure, here it comes.'

Que tried to wedge the knife in the gap between the doorjamb and strike plate, hoping to shift back the latch bolt. It was useless.

Should she try her credit card? She'd done it countless times to enter hotel rooms when her life revolved around her magic plastic.

'Hi, Momma. Princess and I can see you.' Billie's wide smile beamed through the hole, as her giggle echoed in the tiny room. 'You look funny in there, Momma.'

'Can you pick up the other door handle and push it in for me. I'll do the same?' Trapped in the smallest room in the house, surely, she could get out of it easily enough. 'Got it?'

'How's this?' Billie pushed the handle through, and Que tried to match it up. It was useless.

'Oh, come on.' She wasn't a door specialist to know what parts were missing to fix this. Sadly, the hinges were on the other side.

'Are you okay in there, Momma?'

'I'm fine, baby, I'm just thinking.'

Then the telephone rang. 'Get the phone, it's probably Mike.' This was another one of those moments she wished she'd moved closer to him.

'Hello, Billie speaking … No, Momma's locked in the toilet.'

'Who's on the phone, baby?' Que peeked through her hole to the outside world.

'It's Mrs Symes, she says hello … No, Momma's really locked in the toilet. The door handle fell off. It's so funny we have a hole in our door where I can see my momma.'

'Can you ask Mrs Symes to send some help, please, Billie?' It was hopeless, they didn't even own an axe.

Que kicked at the door. It was dangerous, leaving a little girl like this. Again, she kicked the door harder, hoping the hinges would come undone, or she'd bash a hole through it. Something.

'No, that was Momma, kicking the door. She's trying to get out …' Billie giggled as she spoke over the phone. 'No, she's really stuck in there. Oh, okay, I'll tell her … Momma?'

Settle down and breathe. 'Yes, baby.'

'Mrs Symes is sending her son, Connor, over. He said he'll finish dinner first.'

'Seriously?' That sassy sailor would.

'Oh, sorry, Mrs Symes said Connor was joking, and he's on his way … Momma? Mrs Symes wants to know if you're okay?'

'I'm fine, baby.' *Just freaking fine.* Pressing her hands against the walls on either side of her prison, she took deep breaths.

'See, Mrs Symes, Momma's just fine … Can you see her.' Billie held up the phone as if it had a camera.

'Baby, the house phone isn't a camera phone.'

'Oh, okay …' Billie held it up to her ear and listened. 'Momma? Is it okay if I keep talking with Mrs Symes until Connor gets here?'

'What a brilliant idea. Can you switch the front porch light on for Connor, but don't go outside, okay?'

'I won't, Momma.' Again, her slippers padded down the hallway.

A moist black nose poked through the hole in the door.

'Princess, you do not let that little girl out of your sight. You're on guard duty, got it?'

The dog sniffed, as if it understood. His paws tapped down the corridor to where her daughter's voice could be heard.

Que slid to the floor, hugging her knees, with no choice but to sit and wait. It was a tough lesson on patience for a woman who had none.

Head down, she listened to the outside world, focusing for a car to come down the driveway. There'd been countless times she'd feared the sound of a car pulling up, a car door closing, followed by the shake of keys in the lock, then the swishing sound of the opening door. She'd freeze for the distinct click of the lock and brace herself for the incoming nightmare.

But this was different.

How long before Connor arrived? The man she'd purposely kept hidden from her daughter.

18

onnor steered along the firebreak that ran down the fence line, then through the side gate to visit the woman who always locked her front gate on him. Only this time, she was locked in the toilet. How the heck did that happen?

Round the dark bend, the ute's spotlights sliced through the darkness where wallabies fled from around the new saplings. A tick-tick-tick came from the irrigation system as large sweeps of water cooled the air. Que had told him those new trees, her friend Mike planted a few weeks ago, were for privacy, not for produce.

The lady already lived on a big-arse block, where you couldn't see her house from the road, so how much more privacy did she need?

At the moment her place glowed with lights as he came around the bend. Its massive spotlights forced him to wince, flipping down the sun visor as he approached.

As the dog yapped inside, he grabbed the toolbox from the back of his dad's ute, then trudged up the stairs to the front door.

This time there was no stunningly sexy brunette with attitude to greet him with a mouth full of cheek.

What faced him was not what he'd expected.

She was the spitting image of her mother, with black hair in pigtails, a smattering of freckles across her button nose, and the same eyes in a lighter shade of blue. In pink pyjamas that had a unicorn on them, she tucked her teddy bear under one arm, and held the dog by the collar.

Connor knocked on the glass door.

'Who is it?' She had a tooth missing that only made her smile even more endearing. 'I can't let you in until you tell me your name. That's the rules. Momma said so and your mummy said so, see ...' She held out the phone with her eyes shining as bright as her smile.

Damn, this kid was cute—the kid he was never meant to meet.

'Billie, my name is Connor. I live next door.'

'Momma, Connor's here. Can I open the door now?'

'Yes, Billie, let him in. Thank you.' Que's voice was barely heard. She wasn't at the kitchen bench or walking down the corridor to greet him. She was nowhere.

Was Que really trapped?

A sense of urgency hit him, making him inhale deeply.

The glass door opened, and Princess was the first to greet him as he patted the dog.

'Hi, Connor. Are you here to rescue my momma?' The little girl's big eyes widened, as if the reality of the situation hit her. Just like it hit Connor.

'Absolutely. Can you show me where she is?'

'Sure.' Her teeny tiny fingers wrapped around his hand, and she dragged him down the corridor. 'Your mummy wants me to ring her back when you've saved my momma.' Bunny ears bounced on her fluffy slippers as she padded down the hallway, dragging him along, with Princess following their parade.

Damn. It really was broken.

The door handle was in pieces, leaving a gaping hole.

'Knock, knock. Are you decent in there?' Chuckling, he leant down to see his lady of the hour, on the floor hugging her knees.

'Ha-ha. Very funny, sailor. Think you can get me out of here?'

Her sarcasm only made him smile more. He got to play hero for the day, especially with a woman who was so damned independent.

The little girl tugged on his T-shirt. 'Are you going to rescue Momma? She's been in there a long time.' Her large eyes were filled with worry. It softened his hard heart.

'Want to help me?'

'Really?' And like a set of spotlights, her eyes glowed. The kid showed off every expression found in some encyclopaedia of emotions, all in the blink of an eye. He had to step back. She was so different from her mother, who was so guarded.

What happened to the single mother, who was a mystery, living in the middle of nowhere, moving all the way from Tasmania? Then there was her caravan she called the Mighty T, loaded with fuel drums and food, because they'd only raided its junk food stash the other day. Compared to the house, with barely any furniture, the van was stocked and ready to roll.

But Que never talked to him about the van or her future.

And he never asked.

Because that would mean he cared, when this was meant to be just a holiday fling. Yet, in this moment, it felt more than that.

'Billie, here, take this.' He handed the little girl a screwdriver. 'You can start unscrewing the bottom hinge like this. I'll do the top ones.'

'Awesome.' The kid nodded as if her head would bounce off.

Connor crouched down beside the little girl, who smelled of strawberries and soap, and patiently showed her how to use the screwdriver. She was just like her mother, keen to do it on her own. So while he worked on the top hinges, Billie unscrewed the bottom. 'So, you go to school, do you?'

'I do. I'm five, so I'm in first grade …' The girl happily chatted about all of her favourite things, from roller skates to 80s music. The kid knew all about Phil Collins.

Finally, he pulled the door free from its hinges, and for once Que openly wore pure gratitude, unveiling her raw vulnerability in an expression that shattered any resistance he had to her.

'Oh, Momma,' said Billie dramatically, hugging her mother on the floor. 'We rescued you.'

'Thank you, Billie. Thank you, Connor.'

Connor held out his hands and helped Que off the floor. 'Never thought I'd see the day, coming over here to rescue you.'

She rolled her eyes at him.

And for the first time in a month of them sleeping together, Connor had finally met Billie.

'So, this is the bed.' He chuckled at his reward of sharing dessert with Billie before she went to bed, then getting his grown-up dessert by finally gaining access to the inner sanctum. He smiled at the ceiling, laying on the softest set of sheets, holding Que to his bare chest where her dark hair spilled like silk across his skin.

'Mm-hmm, don't get too comfortable.'

'It's much nicer than the floor or the sofa.' They shared a soft laugh. 'So how did your baking lesson go today with Val?'

'We made scones. Mine turned into rock cakes; even the dog wouldn't eat them. So, Billie and I played soccer, smashing them all over the lawn for the wild birds and wallabies to eat.'

'Soccer?'

'Scone soccer. We couldn't stop laughing, kicking these rock-hard scones around, and we finally got Princess to fetch for us.' She rolled off to her side of the bed.

Cold without her, he rolled over to watch her. Always drawn to her, needing to touch her, to kiss her. Hell, he'd have her in bed on her back 24/7 if he could, but the woman had responsibilities, a stinking-cute responsibility in pigtails and freckles.

'So how was your mum's doctor's appointment today?'

'Good. She's in top form and on track for a full tick of approval in a few weeks. Dad's started work. Although we're meant to be harvesting hay, he makes us stop to check on Mum every hour. Is everything all right with Val?'

'Yeah.' Que rested her chin on her pillow. Even the pillows were fluffy piles of heaven. Or was that all about the woman, because her signature aroma was everywhere in this room, seducing his senses.

He reached over and traced her spine, feeling the small ridges of bumpy scars, here and there. He'd never asked what marred her beauty, after all he wore plenty of scars from the job, but Que's job wasn't like that.

'Maybe it's just my imagination over Val's domestic thing, but at least I have a regular Wednesday cooking date with her.'

He frowned. 'Every Wednesday you bake with Val?'

'Mostly coffee, depending on how much time Val has to spare, because I suck at baking. I'm never going to win any local cooking prize, that's for sure.'

'Do you think Gary knows about his wife visiting over here?'

'No.' Que answered with pure conviction. 'Val visits on Wednesdays because Gary's gone all day.'

'I bet he is.' He rolled onto his back and stared at the ceiling.

She peeked at him over her shoulder, picking up the signs of his moods. She'd make one helluva a poker player, reading people easily. Most of all, she knew how to make him smile, filling his chest full of soggy warmth. 'What am I missing, Connor?'

Did he dare tell all? Even though their conversations were brutally honest, with Que never holding back her snarky comebacks, they'd both avoided the bigger questions—especially about themselves.

But this was about the neighbours.

'Only because I know you don't spread rumours …'

'Are you being a judgy jerk again?' She narrowed those sexy eyes at him.

'No.' His palm slid over warm skin the colour of wet river sand and as exotic as a deserted tropical island that felt like home.

He frowned at the word *home*. He was not after anything permanent.

But then a flash of green jealousy scratched at the base of his neck. He had to ask...

'Hey, if you're busy playing cards on Tuesdays with the old guys at the hardware store, and baking on Wednesdays with Val, what are my days to visit as per your house rules?'

'Um, Monday, Thursday, and Fridays. Definitely not weekends with Billie around—come to think of it Tuesdays and Wednesdays too.' She frowned as his grin widened.

'So, every day of the week.' Did that make them an exclusive couple?

'Hey, you changed the subject, we were talking about the neighbours.'

'That is none of my business,' he said, rolling her gently to her back.

'But …'

'The only business I'm worried about is right here, right now, in this bed that I've finally made my way into.' He stopped all conversation, sipping and then savouring the slide of her upper lip. Satisfaction had never tasted so sweet.

Her fingers pressed into his chest and moans rose from her throat just from kissing. His heartbeat paused when her tongue swept his, and Act II had begun with a kiss that was unnervingly unique. The hunger to play and to tangle limbs grew as their lips pressed harder.

Tonight, he was in no rush. Relief and ownership flooded him, knowing she wasn't seeing anyone else, and he wanted to savour every scintillating second. She was intoxicating his bloodstream; her hot flesh and punishing kisses made up his entire universe.

With their lips flush, his kneading fingers were slow and possessive while their ravenous kiss deepened, but his inner alarms were going off all over the place. This could never last. It should never have gone on for this long.

Yet, each time, it grew more intense, deepening to levels he'd never thought possible.

She was magic, she was fire, and she was the beginning and end of everything, stretching this moment of passion into eternity. And for Connor, this was heaven.

Que was this pirate's prize he wanted to plunder, and for the first time he had all night to do it too. Why would he ever want to leave?

Well, not until morning at least.

19

A few weeks later, he couldn't believe he'd been talked into this—not that he could talk, because the kid in pigtails didn't stop talking. It was a conversation that skipped from songs to roller skates to tutus. His head was reeling while steering the ute along the firebreak's fence line to the far rear of Que's property.

'How long does your mother take to finish a job?' Connor asked Billie, in the passenger seat, swinging her little boots high off the floor. It reminded him of his little brother when he was young.

'Big jobs, looong time. Momma says the job is done when the job is done and then we celebrate and get ice cream. Do you eat ice cream?'

'Only at your house. I know your mother likes vanilla ice cream.' But there was nothing vanilla about Que, who performed torturous magic with that ice cream and his naked body! He wanted to buy the woman gallons of ice cream, but she warned him she'd throw it out, and him, because she'd get fat.

'Where are we going?'

'To check the back fence.'

'I've never been down here.' She wriggled higher to the edge of the seat, grabbing the dashboard with long slender fingers like her mother's. 'Momma says I'm not allowed to go too far. I have to see the house at all times. And, if Momma can't see me from the house, I lose my skates for a week.'

'She's only doing that to keep you safe, you know that, right?'

'I know. I heard one of them other mothers call Momma an overprotective hen because she used to sit at school and wait for me to finish.'

He'd seen flashes of the ferocious Momma bear Que was underneath, still surprised she'd agreed to let him take her kid out like this. 'It's only because Que cares for you, kid.'

'Of course she does, that's her job. Momma says so.' Billie's boots stopped swinging as her eyes widened. 'Is that a river?' Her voice rose to a squeal that made him wince.

'It's a creek.' He parked under the shade provided by a mixture of towering ghost gums and spiky-limbed pandanus.

Clambering over his seat to jump on the dirt, she stood on her tiptoes to peek at the running stream. 'Are there crocodiles in there?'

'Absolutely.'

'So why are we here?' She whispered, walking backwards.

'To check the fence, and fish for cherabin.'

'Cherries in a bin?'

'Cher-a-bin. They're a freshwater prawn, like a yabby or red claw. Have you eaten seafood before?'

She shrugged. 'Unless Uncle Mike brought it out. Momma might have.'

Connor hid his frown. He had no right to be jealous of some ginger-headed male who was Que's gardening friend and handyman.

'We'll chuck in these pots and see what's in there.'

Her little fingers wrapped around his hand. 'But what about the crocodiles? Momma and I wouldn't want you to get hurt, Connor.'

Did the sun just melt his freaking soul? 'We'll be fine. Just don't get too close to the water, and stick close to me.'

She gripped his fingers tighter as they weaved through the long grass. 'Is that our gate?'

'Yeah.' He frowned at the fallen fence line. Que had asked him to check it, worried about crocodiles ruining the backyard boghole that she kept calling a pond. *Tourist.*

'Don't crocodiles nest in grass?' The little girl's neck craned up at the long grass. From her height it would be nothing but a wall of grass.

'Come on ...' He scooped her up to sit over his shoulders. She barely weighed anything.

'I see everything from here.' Her giggle echoed, with her smile widening as a few galahs mimicked back.

'Reckon you can keep an eye out for crocodiles?' Hooking fingers through the crabbing nets, he stepped over the fallen fence line and barbed wire, following the wallaby track to the steep creek bed.

'I'll try ...'

High along the sandy bank, where the dappled shade danced with the shifting long limbed pandanus palms, he found his old fishing spot and gently off-loaded his passenger. 'Did you spot any salties, yet?'

She shaded her eyes with her hand to peer at the water like an old sailor from the crow's nest on the high seas. 'Nah. Nothing.'

'But it doesn't mean there aren't any. Now, this is how you fish for cherabin …' With his eager offsider watching, he tied bait to the mesh floor of four flimsy dilly pots. Tossing them into the creek where the water shifted over rocks, weaving around tall reeds and pink flowering wild lotus. He tied their ropes to old milk bottles that he filled with water, leaving them high on the banks.

'So, what do we do now?' Billie plonked her hands on hips just like her mother.

'We wait.'

'Oh.' She screwed her nose up, obviously not very patient. Neither was her mother.

He chuckled. 'There used to be a fort here.'

'A proper army fort? With cannons and telescoppy things? Can I see it?'

'More of a cubby house I made with my brother.' He led the way, surprised at the pitchy swell in his belly as the curiosity rose. Dry gum leaves crunched under their boots as he aimed for the tall, thick ghost gum. Its smooth pale bark was highlighted against the neighbouring African mahogany trees' dark bark that was cracked like the skin of a crocodile's back, with its large seed pods left to crackle and pop underfoot.

'I don't believe it.' He stopped and sighed.

'What?' She grabbed his hand again, half hiding behind him.

'It's still there.' Wedged in the forks of the gum tree, about six feet off the ground, were the steel poles they'd made into a floor. Fencing poles and aluminium irrigation pipe were used to build a proper fortress, not a house of twigs and sticks, but one that would last. And it looked like it had.

'How do we get up there, Connor?'

'We had a ladder in the trunk …' Holes were etched into the sturdy trunk that was perfect for little feet to climb. 'I'll go first to check it's secure.' His boot's toes barely made the rungs. He hoisted himself up to the branch as the fort's floor creaked beneath him. But it was solid.

'Can I come up?'

'Gimme a second, just checking for snakes.'

'Oh …' The little girl walked backwards, looking to flee into the grass.

What an idiot! To scare a little girl like that. Why did Que put him on babysitting duties? He wasn't ready for this.

'It's okay, Billie, there's nothing there.' He jumped down, landing beside Billie, and held out his hand. 'Come on up and see.' And when those tiny soft little fingers clutched his hand—damn, there was that soul melting feeling again.

Helping her up to the simple floor cladding, they sat with their legs dangling over the sides. 'I can't believe it's still here …' But on closer inspection, he could see someone had reinforced it with welded joints. Had his brother or the old owner done that?

'Here, this is for you.' The little girl broke him out of his daydream and wrapped a red string around his wrist.

'What's this?' He'd seen Que wearing the same.

'A friendship bracelet.'

'Why?'

'Coz you're a friend. Momma doesn't make many friends, so

you must be a special friend, and you're my friend now too. You brought me here.'

How did he answer that? 'You made this?'

'I'm not very good at the knots, but I'm learning.'

'Well, being a sailor, you learn all about knots.'

'Can you teach me?'

'Sure.' Dragging out his pocket knife, he sliced the thin rope he had tucked in his cargos, a spare he'd kept for their dilly pots. 'This is a granny knot ...' He'd never taught a kid anything, never had much inclination or opportunity before. From teaching her knots he moved on to showing her how to tie the laces on her shoes.

'I can't wait to show Momma. I'll be able to tie up my own skates soon.'

'I guess you can. Just practise.'

'Oh, I will.'

She'd probably forget this, but Connor wouldn't. He'd taught a child to tie their shoelaces and his heart pumped that little bit harder, while she re-tightened the thin red bracelet around his wrist. No one had given him a friendship bracelet because he avoided making friends.

'Is the Billabong Bunyip real?' Billie asked.

He inhaled deeply to squint at the view. Spread below them were fields of golden grasses, where the winding corridor of olive-green trees followed the meandering creek that would be a river in the wet season. He felt like a grown-up who knew the truth to Santa's story, but this was different ... 'Yeah, it's real. The Billabong Bunyip only shows up when you're on your own.'

'In this place ...' Her eyes widened as she pointed to the stream below them that sparkled like diamonds under the sun.

'You do know what the Billabong Bunyip is, don't you?'

'The boys at school say it's a make-believe monster that lives in the water.'

'The Billabong Bunyip is an ancient monster that came from the Dreamtime when this land was first created. He was an angry spirit who wanted to be a human and walk on land.'

'Can he walk on land?'

'Not far, because his body is created from the mud found on the floor of any river, or creek, waterhole or billabongs, just not the sea.'

'What about Momma's boghole?'

Oops. 'You've had Cecil in that, you're safe there.'

'So where is this bunyip?'

'Anywhere and everywhere. He's made of mud, always floating under the surface watching for any child who dares to wander to the creek on their own.'

'To do what?'

'Steal them.'

'Noooo.' She gasped. 'Why?'

'The bunyip catches children in his long claws and drags them into the water to live in the mud … Drowned.' It was the same story every parent told their children in this region. No matter the colour or culture it was a story they'd shared for centuries. 'And they say the reason the Billabong Bunyip has lived so long is because of the thousands of children's lives he's stolen.'

'What does he look like?'

'An ugly mud-dripping monster. Some say he has the snout of

a pig, yet long like a dingo's, with more teeth than a crocodile and if he's found a child his belly is big, and he waddles like a wombat. But he's got this ugly rotten-mud smell to him, you'll never forget it. You can smell him before you see him.'

She shuffled closer to him with her big eyes staring out over the creek, wrapping the rope around one finger, then the next. 'So, he's not here, because you're here.'

'Exactly. He's a sneaky, scary bully who'll only go after children who are on their own. So, promise me, Billie, you'll never come down here without a grown-up.'

'I promise,' she said with fear in her eyes. 'Does the Billabong Bunyip give grown-ups nightmares too? Like Momma.'

He wiped at the frown. 'What happens to your mother, Billie?'

'When we lived in the van, I'd hear her cry. Now we're in the house, she checks the locks on all the doors, carrying the baseball bat she keeps under her bed.' Billie shrugged, practising knots with the string.

What would scare someone as fearless as Que?

Did he need to get so involved?

His eye caught the engravings in the fort's central tree trunk. They were sturdy letters carved deep to read, *Daddy and Aiden — father and son forever.*

They sat right below the words *Connor and Travis — brothers forever.*

His heart squeezed as a layer of ice crackled and froze any goodness he had ever felt.

It made sense for his brother to visit here. Travis was always following Connor here. Even when Connor tried to avoid his little brother, Travis would show up with materials to help build their fort, like it was his entry fee. Even as a kid, Travis played engineer, finding wire, metal irrigation pipe, wood lengths for the ladders, and loads of rope he'd pluck from the back of utes parked behind the pub, to build the fort. His brother was always scrounging for fort supplies, but it was Connor who copped the blame for it.

The town gossipers had labelled Connor the thief, when all along it had been his little brother, Travis, who'd show up with tools and fishing gear as his entry fee to be a part of the club that was him and Marcus. Back then, Connor always took the blame, because he wanted to protect his brother.

Only two people knew the truth. Marcus knew everything back then, even volunteering to take the blame for Travis as well. But Connor stood tall and took the hits for his brother, so Travis could go to university, to make a life for himself as the talented engineer he came to be.

Connor scowled at the words in that damned tree trunk. They were a slam-dunk hot shot to the heart. He wanted to climb down and get back into the ute and leave this place. He struggled to concentrate on Billie's chatter as he tried to forget his past. But the memories kept rolling through his mind's eye, all about his brother.

He'd never gone to his brother's wedding.

He'd never gone to their funerals.

Wave after wave of gut-wrenching sorrow churned in his chest, squeezing his ribs in a hot metallic vice that had him struggling to breathe.

In his wallet, his brother's family photo, tucked inside a Christmas card, was burning his back pocket as guilt and grief twisted his guts like tangled barbed wire, as the word *brothers forever* blinded him.

The memories of their last day together echoed in his mind; he'd sworn to leave and never return.

Yet here he was.

He winced at the sky peeking through the thick canopy, holding his chest. These heart-gripping emotions should have been lost at sea for good. Yet, they still stung as if fresh.

He didn't deserve to be happy. He didn't deserve to be part of a family. And he certainly shouldn't be trusted with cute kids who thought the world was an amazingly safe place. He deserved desert sands and stinky alleys, with only his rifle and stray dogs for company.

He should get far away from this place, sever all ties to a life that involved fragile parents who tried to love a man who didn't deserve it. He should get away from little girls in pigtails on roller skates who called him a friend. Most of all, he should avoid the single mother with violet eyes and a sexy smile, whose kisses made him possessive, and left him craving her smiles.

It they knew who he really was, they'd run. All of them.

If the town gossipers learned his secret, it wouldn't be long before Que kicked his arse out the gate forever, so he needed to go before it all got stripped away.

He needed to go where no one knew him, so he could be who he truly was—the bad man who got paid to kill on call.

20

'Ugh, I am so done.' Que collapsed into her chair under the tent's shade, seated beside Kat, where they manned their post at the Mother's Day stall. 'How did we get talked into this?' Stuck here all morning, explaining the silent auction over and over again. She'd met so many people that all their faces blended into one. Yet, they all knew about Billie and her roller skates.

Kat lifted the lid of her small esky and removed two icy vodka cans. 'For us.'

'Tempting, but what would Supermom say?' Still unbelieving she'd volunteered to do this for Billie's sake. Retail was never Que's forte.

'Karen will want one and she deserves one for today. Your idea of the silent auction is a hit, too.'

'We haven't seen how much we've raised yet.'

The crowd of people shifted in waves of assorted hats—from cowboy hats to straw hats to baseball caps—and boots, with lots of denim. Thongs, shorts, and singlets were a second crowd favourite for fashion, celebrating their Aussie boganism loud and proud. It was a constant parade of people of all ages, waving to one group, stopping to chat to another. It was obvious the entire country town and surrounds had shown up for the school fundraiser involving bake sales and football. There was no way city schools got this sort of attention.

'So, what's this then?' Asked a man with dark curly hair and a deep tan.

Kat rolled her eyes, silently pleading for Que to do the spiel.

For someone who sucked in her retail career, Que would do her best for Billie. 'This is the silent auction for goods and services. We have car services, barbecue building, home dinner party catering, lawn mowing or was that firebreak clearing ...' She got that mixed up all the time, especially the farm stuff she knew nothing about. 'There's horse shoeing, leather work repairs for saddles and stuff. Fencing, roofing, oh and solar systems, and a sparky and plumber voucher for work too, plus stacks of household furniture.'

'What's the graphic designing for?'

'For a website upgrade or a business logo design,' said Que.

'You're the new neighbour.' The man pointed at her, while checking her up and down like everybody else did in town.

'You are?'

'Gary.'

Dammmmn. She cleared her throat, forcing a smile. 'Finally, we meet.' She held out her hand, proud it was free from any tremors.

'We do. Is that ginger bloke your partner? I'd seen him on your fence line clearing the irrigation lines on those new trees.'

'No. Just a friend.' No way was she mentioning Connor, who'd done a disappearing act after his little fishing trip with Billie, leaving them with a bucket of live freshwater prawns and some lame excuse about needing to see his mother. She hated to admit it, but Billie had done exactly what she'd hoped for—she'd scared off the big guy who Que was getting far too attached to.

Gary narrowed his dark brown eyes at her. 'So, it's true that it's just you and your daughter, Maddy's friend …' He clicked his fingers a few times as if to help him think. 'Billie. Cool name.' He then gave a lopsided boyish grin just like his son.

Val had never said anything bad about her husband, just that he wasn't into romantic sunset strolls. And there'd been no signs to further suggest any hostility within their household, just Que's overactive imagination. Even if her lower spine was tingling with suspicion, she would accuse no one of anything without hard proof. And that was a fact.

'Your kids are cool. Tommy is an absolute sweetheart the way he cares for his little sister. That boy is going to break some hearts when he gets older.'

Gary's grin grew as his chest rose with pride. 'Thank you,' he said with a series of short sharp nods. 'No one tells us anything good like that, not in this town. I mean, Val and I try our best, and she's a bloody good mother …'

'Is Val here today?'

'Nah. She's not well. Pity, Val would've loved this. She loved running these school fundraising events, or parents' meetings or some other charity … Shame none of them mob she worked so hard for ever give anything back. But Tommy dropped off the cakes and stuff Val baked for this event.' His smile disappeared as he rubbed the back of his neck, frowning at the football players running on the oval. 'How well do you know Val?'

'Only from the bus stop. We wave to each other across the road, and that skate date.' She was such a liar.

'Yeah, kids slept like logs that night. You could hear them snoring through the walls.'

She forced herself to chuckle with him. 'Is there anything you'd like to bid for? Just write down what you think is a fair price, fold it up, and put it into the box. Easy as.'

'The old ute could do with a service.' Gary scribbled on the paper, folded it over a few times, then slid it into the box. 'Nice to meet you, Que. See ya round the neighbourhood sometime.'

'No worries, Gary.'

Gary smiled, giving a friendly nod, nothing like the monster she'd imagined. He sauntered away to shake hands and slap backs with other men who all wore the same deep tan, drinking beer and watching football.

Had it truly been all in her imagination?

'It's sad Val can't be here. It's meant to be for Mother's Day. She shouldn't miss this.' Que plonked down in her seat next to Kat and sipped her can.

'And just what do you two think you're doing?' It was Supermom Karen, with a straw hat and clipboard in hand. 'Here, give me that.' She snatched Kat's can and nearly drank it dry. 'I'm never doing this again. Ever. Next time I come up with one of these crazy ideas, I expect you pair to talk me down. Remember this moment.'

'Oh, I will,' said Que, giggling behind her can. 'Take a seat, you look like you deserve it.'

'I will.' She plonked onto the esky, looking like a little girl barely peeking over the tabletop. 'We had a great day. I hope we've raised enough.'

'Do you know how much?'

'Not a clue, but the day is not over yet. For the footy half-time races, I've delegated some people to decide the winners of the silent auction, so you're hereby both free from your auctioneer duties.' She reached for Que's can and drank deeply.

A loud siren blared across the grounds, followed by the whistle of the football umpires and the players jogged off the field.

'Half-time, ladies. I hope you've got your running shoes on.' Karen bounced to her tiny feet and up-ended the can, drinking it dry as a group of men and women showed up at the tent and she was back in charge like a mini-general, organising them to count the bids.

The voice over the loudspeaker called out: *'Can we have all of the mothers in the middle of the oval for the Mother's Day relay.'*

'Can I skip this bit?' Que asked.

'Ditto, on what she said,' said Kat, slinging her thumb at Que.

'It's an Elsie Creek tradition,' barked out Karen.

Kat and Que shrugged at each other.

'Normally they hold it on the Friday at the school, where we have a Mother's Day brunch, but it's here this year. So come on, let's go.' The little woman grabbed their hands, dragging them out to the chaotic middle of the oval where children were busily running around looking for their mothers.

A little boy ran past who Que recognised. It was Val's eldest. 'Hey, Tommy, is your mother here today?'

He shook his head slowly, the smile disappearing from his face.

'How come? It's Mother's Day. Val wouldn't miss this.' Gary

may have answered her question already, but he didn't say what was wrong with Val.

'The bees got her. All over her face, too.' Tommy waved a hand outlining his sweaty face. 'Mum's all bruised and swollen with this huge fat lip. She reckons she's allergic to bees. Dad had to burn the nest and everything. Are you racing with anyone?' he asked, hopeful.

What the—stay calm. 'I'm supposed to be. Got any tips?'

'Yeah.' Tommy nodded, pulling up his little jeans as he swaggered towards her. 'Use Billie like a broomstick to stab at the balloons like a sword. Dad told Mum to do that last year and we killed them in seconds.'

'Good tip. Anything else?'

'Tell Billie to put her thumb on the egg in the egg and spoon race. Coz she's so little, they'll let her get away with it. Good luck, we'll be watching.' Tommy waved, then raced off with his friends.

'Momma? Where are you?'

'Over here, Billie.' It was their first public school event. Both Kat and Karen had told her to loosen her apron strings and let Billie play with her friends. Boy, did Billie play! Her face was covered in face paint that highlighted her big smile, with a stained shirt, dirty knees, and her shorts hidden by a bouncy bright-blue tutu. 'Where did the tutu come from?'

'I was wondering when that was going to happen.' Kat stood beside them with her own daughter wearing the same-coloured tutu. Both mother and daughter's auburn curls shone like a rich fire. 'I've just been told I have to buy roller skates for school now, because that's the latest trend in town.'

'Are you saying my kid's a trendsetter?' Que grinned as she

was dragged to the middle of the field, where women and children lined up to wrap a scarf around their ankles, preparing for the three-legged race.

'What do we do?' Que asked her friends. Oh wow, she had friends. Female friends that is, because she'd always had Mike.

'You race to every station, where there's a task you have to complete,' said Kat, getting tied up to her daughter, Kaytlyn.

Karen rushed past, with an entire tribe of boys following. 'I'm only one mum, boys, it's Levi's turn this year.' She squeezed herself in between Kat and Que along with her blond boy who was a little taller than Billie.

'Karen, what do we do?' Que asked.

'From here to the first table is the three-legged race, you'll know what to do when you get there. They change it up every year, but it's the sprint for the finish line, that I do remember. So, shoes off, unless you can run.'

'Did you get all that?' Que asked Billie, peering at their boots. 'I can run in these, you?'

Billie nodded. 'Momma, this is our first race.'

'So it is.' It was a Mother's Day she'd never forget, copping a messy brekkie of raw egg on bread, crunching eggshells on the kitchen floor that had been licked clean by the dog. But she had a handmade card and photo calendar that sat pride of place on their fridge for Mother's Day.

The buzz in her chest grew as the adrenalin rose, spreading from the women and children around her. But it was bigger than that. It came from the community, from those in the grandstands, all pulling together for this event to build a pool for the school. Even those who didn't have children had turned up. She'd never seen anything like this.

The locals were not rich. There was no one tossing their Black Amex around or handing out business cards to have someone call their assistants. The people in this outback town donated goods and services to provide for their community. For a woman who never got involved, this community spirit was addictive.

'We've got this, baby.' She slung her arm around her little trooper, who clung to her mother's waist. 'It'll be like roller-skating, in unison.'

A woman wearing thongs with footy socks flip-flopped towards them. Her long thick plait swung like a donkey's tail, and a yellow duckbill visor shaded her eyes. The outfit was completed with glow-in-the-dark board shorts and a navy flannel shirt. She blew her whistle long and loud, then silenced them all with a scary scowl.

'What is that?' Que whispered to Kat and Karen.

'That's our softball coach.'

'And you want me to join your team?' The coach was scary with a capital S.

'RIGHT, YOU RASCALLY WOMBATS, AND YOU MOTHERS, ARE WE READY TO HIT THE GROUND RUNNING?'

21

'Come on, Connor, come watch this,' his mother said, pointing through the crowds to the footy oval.

Connor would rather hang at home and drink beer than be at this freaking fundraiser. But his parents had insisted. He had to drive his mother in so she could deliver her cakes for the bake sale. His father had driven in earlier to help the other men put up tents. And none of them had a kid at the school.

But it wasn't his parents that irritated him, it was everyone else.

From the second he'd climbed out of his dad's old ute to help his mother out, he felt the locals talking about him. Even as he walked past, the gossipers of this town frowned, no doubt sharpening their imaginary pitchfork tines to aim for his back. If only one of the arseholes had the guts to say something to his face, he'd sort 'em out.

But he was stuck here because it was Mother's Day. His first one in well over fifteen years, and he didn't even have a gift for his mum. His parents had been in the kitchen for days cooking for this event, and somehow, he'd completely forgotten what day it was.

He was such a lousy son.

'Come on, Connor.' Bertha grabbed his hand to drag him through the crowds like she'd done all morning, to go to this tent, that tent, buy this, get that. He'd managed to avoid Que, barely, by offering to take his mother's haul to his dad's car.

'Remember when we used to do this?' Bertha said with a wide smile and shiny eyes, pointing to the group of women and children in the centre field.

Bugger. How could he forget the Mother's Day race, that was normally held at the school?

How soon before he could bolt from this crowd of locals? Some he recognised from school, now adults. But many others were scowling at him.

Having been through war zones where foreigners would try and kill him on a daily basis, he didn't give a toss what people thought of him. He wasn't here to make friends, so they could bloody well think what they wanted of him. Their opinions were nothing but dust slipping off his bullet-proof hide. Impenetrable.

Only one face in the crowd made him grin. His old partner in crime, the town's top cop in full uniform. With a radio clipped to his belt, Marcus gave a curt nod of his cap as he approached.

'Remember this, officer?' Connor said to Marcus in his blue uniform that showed off his beefy arms.

In their shared childhood they'd been fiercely competitive over this very event. Yet, the same event ended up turning the warring boys into partners.

'Don't remind me,' said Marcus. 'How are you, Bertha?' He kissed her cheek. 'You look well.'

'I'm magnificent, thank you. Oh, look, it's Que and Billie.'

Bertha pointed to the middle of the field.

Oh, man … Even though she was well over fifty metres away in a field among twenty other mothers with their children, all he saw was Que. He swallowed at the sight of her, as a gaping black hole grew in his chest. No matter how much air he sucked in, he couldn't fill the space enough for him to breathe. He missed her.

When he shouldn't.

He'd purposely distanced himself these past few days, after fishing with Billie. But he was still wearing the red band the kid had wrapped around his wrist that he kept as a cruel reminder.

He'd also been prepared for Que's phone calls, for her visits, for something, but he got nothing. Instead, it was complete radio silence from the neighbours.

But there she was, in the middle of the field, wearing a dazzling smile across those luscious lips. It was obvious Que didn't need him, and he'd been nothing to her.

Exactly as they'd agreed. A short-term fling, with no emotional attachment. There was *no such thing as forever* with Que.

'So that's the new woman, huh?' Marcus nodded in Que's direction. 'Being your neighbour, I'm guessing you know her.'

'I do.' *Did.*

'Good. Tell her to get her vehicle's plates transferred over. She's got two weeks left before I fine her.'

'Are you serious? Since when were you such a stickler for rules?' When Marcus and Connor were once all about breaking them.

'It's my job, mate.'

Some woman—or man—in a yellow cap, wearing thongs, socks, and glow-in-the-dark board shorts, blew a whistle. Connor tilted his head. 'What is that?'

'Agnes is the softball coach. Remember her?'

'Nope. Oh, wait, didn't we let out her pigs one year to run a derby down the main street of town?'

Marcus gave a low chuckle. 'Agnes sold the farm, lives here as the caretaker and manages the Dusty Dingoes softball team. But we will never ever tell her we painted her pigs.'

'Your secrets are safe with me, officer.' Connor grinned back at his mate. 'What about that woman with the gnomes? Nasty Nancy.'

'Gone. Sold up and went to live with her daughter in Queensland. And all those gnomes got scattered to the outback desert in a lawn sale.'

'So who painted your station's roof? Is that meant to be the Strong Arm of the Law. That's gotta be your arm, right?'

Marcus gave a coy grin. 'You haven't been back long enough to know all my secrets.'

And Connor never told war stories.

But there was one name they both never mentioned … the *Station Hand.* The man who wanted them strung by their necks to leave them hanging from a tree. 'Have you seen him?'

'Yeah, he's here, over by the horse yards. You haven't spoken to him yet?'

Connor barely shrugged. 'What do you want me to say?' Because he'd always back his mate's alibi.

Marcus patted his back. 'Why don't you bring over that bourbon like you promised me and we'll make something up?' The men chuckled.

'If I wasn't booked as my mother's date to this event, believe me, I'd be pouring. But it'll happen soon.' He wouldn't mind a drink with Marcus before he left.

'READY …' hollered the softball coach, Agnes. The women and children stood in a line along the grass, as the crowd behind them hushed. 'STEADY … SET … GO!'

It began with a three-legged race. Some teams tripped at the start, some had their mother's just pick up their kid and run. The older kids with their mothers found their stride and hit the lead.

But what had Connor arching an eyebrow were Que and Billie in complete unison, steady in their stride.

'Oh look! I've seen those two do that on their skates in the shed,' said Bertha.

'I heard the new kids' craze is roller skates,' said Marcus, cleaning his sunglasses on his shirt before putting them back on. 'Maybe they'll finally ditch the tutus for a while.'

'What's up with all these kids in tutus?' Connor asked. They were everywhere, in all sizes and colours, for both boys and girls.

'They're the Dusty Dingoes' cheerleaders,' replied Bertha, 'considering most of the mothers are the softball players.'

Que and Billie raced to the first table, where they untied their restraints, climbed into the large hessian sacks, and jumped to the next table. Mothers and their children fell all over the place, but Que and Billie kept at their steady place.

The next table was bean tossing, where they had to throw cloth bags filled with beans to hit the target. Que slung back and *bam*, she hit the triangle of three empty tin cans set like bowling pins. All of them fell from her first throw.

'Good shot,' said Marcus.

Connor nodded, impressed with the woman.

Then the mother and daughter team were retying the scarf around their ankles, to resume the next section of the three-legged race to the next table. There were five long tables set in a circle, over fifty metres apart, in the centre of the football field where they had to make their way back to the starting line.

'They're in fourth position. *Go Que and Billie,*' called out Bertha with her fist raised but her other hand covering her heart.

'Careful, Mum. We don't want you exerting yourself.'

'But it's so exciting. Que and Billie might win this?'

'There's more to do yet, Mum.'

'I remember it wasn't that easy,' said Marcus, 'but that mother makes it look easy. She single?'

Connor cleared his throat, barely keeping his frown in check. Like a freaking caveman his growl started from his lower gut, wanting to claim the lady as his own. *Settle down, man.*

Marcus chuckled, adjusting his police cap.

'You prick.' His mate had done that on purpose, to bait him. Just like old times.

'Don't worry, mate. I've got enough on my plate to bother. But I might take a crack after you've left town.'

Connor was counting down the minutes on the doctor's all-clear to pack his bags, climb back onto his bike, and hit the highway.

The crowd roared. The front contenders, an older boy and his mother fell in the three-legged race, which put Billie and Que in third place.

At the next table, it was the balloon popping, and with gusto Billie jumped with both feet together, as her mother lifted her up and used the kid like a battering ram.

'There's my girls.' His chest filled with pride for the mother and daughter team.

'Now why didn't we use that technique when we did this?' Marcus said.

'Because our mothers couldn't lift us.'

Que and Billie had burst their six balloons, bang, bang, bang, one after the other and swiftly moved onto the egg and spoon race. They were much slower with Que talking to Billie, no doubt with words of encouragement, as they glided across the grass as if roller-skating.

But other contenders were catching up. Fast. Putting them back to sixth place.

They got to the last table and Que didn't hesitate, tossing Billie over her shoulder to sprint for the final checkpoint. There, she left the child standing on a crate, then ran for the laundry baskets filled with clothes. She grabbed a string of feathers, ran back to Billie, who swung it around her neck like a scarf.

He had to chuckle at Billie the kid, in her pigtails, face paint and a blue tutu. While Que bolted back to the basket for a large slouchy hat, dressing up the child.

'If I remember correctly, you boys made us mothers sit while you dressed us up,' said Bertha to the grown men.

'She's got some speed on her,' said Marcus.

'You should have seen Que tear down her corridor the day she arrived,' said Bertha. 'One minute, we're all standing out front talking. Then Billie screams, and Que instantly drops everything and runs. She looked like she was ready to pack up her van and leave, the way she held onto her child that day. It was only Cecil, so no harm.'

'You don't say,' Marcus said, giving Connor a side-glance. 'A single mother moving from Tasmania to the middle of nowhere on the other side of the country … What's her story, Connor?'

Connor shrugged. He didn't know much as there were plenty of unanswered questions that Que avoided, with the many more he never asked. 'I know Que studied to be a paramedic, but then she found her love for graphics.'

'It's obvious the lady can react under pressure, considering what she did with your mother,' said Marcus. 'The hospital would love a paramedic on staff, even part-time. If she can drive a caravan, the ambulance would be easy for her.'

'You'll have to speak to Que about that, not me.' Connor couldn't get involved.

'Maybe I will, when I warn Que to switch her car's rego plates over to the Territory.'

The dress-up part of the race was over, with Billie jumping onto her mother's back and they ran full pelt across the field. It was a sprint for the finish with Que and Billie coming in third place.

'They did so well.' Bertha clapped and cheered with the rest of the grandstand.

Both mother and daughter hugged each other, wearing matching smiles. It had Connor dragging out his phone, to zoom in and take a photo of the moment. He'd send it to Que, or he'd keep it hidden in his phone's gallery with all of the others, as a memory of his time with her.

Que and Billie were a family, and Connor wasn't worthy of a family. Que deserved better, for her sake and for Billie's.

But damn, he missed her like a dozen bullet holes had gone and shredded his heart, leaving him empty.

22

Que wove her way through the gathered crowds towards the bar. 'Two lemonades and three vodka and limes ...' She felt him before she saw him, inhaling his familiar aroma. 'Can you grab a beer for my mate too, please?' Jeez, didn't she sound country!

'Make that a lite, I'm driving,' Connor said to the barmaid over her shoulder. Just his deep voice and hot breath near her ear unleashed an army of feelgood goosebumps charging up her neck. 'Are you driving?'

'I got a lift in with Kat to help set up. Have you got room for two more when you leave?'

'Sure. Hey, congrats on third place in the race,' Connor said, grabbing his beer. 'Shouldn't I be shouting you a drink?'

'The lift home's enough.' Her eyes widened at the cop coming up alongside. *Crap.*

But Connor hooked his arm around her back, holding her in place. 'Relax, he's a mate of mine.'

She swallowed down the lump in her throat, while pushing away the tension, choosing to trust Connor. Even though she missed him, distance had been just what she needed.

Connor would head back to sea in a matter of weeks, so she couldn't afford to get attached to him. It was good his cut-and-run routine was happening now, giving her time to prepare Billie who'd gotten way too attached to the big friend these past few weeks since the bathroom door incident.

'Marcus, this is Que, my neighbour.'

Just the neighbour, huh? She gave a sly grin to Connor, the edges of his lips barely giving it away. But she'd been with him enough to know his tells. Like he knew hers, obviously.

'Hi, Marcus.' She could've picked her jaw up off the floor. The cop was hot. Now she understood what the women were on about … If this was what the cop looked like, how hot was the fire chief she'd heard so much about.

'Hey, Que.' Marcus' large hand enveloped hers. 'Welcome to town.'

'Thanks, Sergeant.'

'You recognise ranks?'

Que shrugged. She wasn't going to tell him she was used to cops knocking on her door at all hours, wanting to speak to her parents. Or that they'd bring her home to face the parents.

'Connor was telling me you wanted to be a paramedic.'

The big mouth. 'I did, a long time ago.'

'Our local hospital is always looking for volunteers to drive the ambo,' said the very well built, mouth-watering, hot cop.

She had to look away.

'After what you did for Bertha,' Marcus said, 'I'm sure the hospital will be happy to take you on board.'

She paid for her drinks and scooped up her cans. 'Can I get

over this volunteering thing I did today? I might think about it once I've settled in.' And away from all of these powerful men. Not one, but two of them. But Connor was hotter, and stronger, and sexier, and … *leaving.*

'So you're staying for a while?' Marcus asked.

'I hope to, sure.'

As the officer stepped in closer, she stepped back, but Connor tucked her in closer to his side. She felt safe there. But shouldn't.

'Marcus is going to play cop and tell you off about your car's number plates,' muttered Connor.

'There's plenty of registration left on my car.'

'You'll need to transfer them over to Northern Territory plates,' said Marcus.

'Oh?' She hadn't thought of that. 'How much time do I have?'

'Two weeks.'

A lot could happen in two weeks. Look at what she'd accomplished in just eight weeks in this town. She looked at Connor for help. How did she talk her way out of this one?

'I'll take Que to Kyle's for a rego check,' replied Connor. 'Her car will pass with ease.'

'Good. You can download the paperwork online, bring it to the station with a copy of your current registration papers and Kyle's report, and I'll switch over your licence, too.'

'Driver's licence?' No. No. No. It's why she kept on the move, to avoid paperwork.

'Yeah.' Marcus gave her a curt nod, but his eyes saw more.

'Are you worried about your demerit points?' Connor asked, giving her shoulders a gentle squeeze. 'Hey, Marcus, do we get fresh demerit points if we transfer our licences over?'

'Why? How many have you got left riding that Harley of yours?'

Connor shrugged.

Que needed time to think. 'I'll get on to that paperwork, thanks, Marcus. If you'll excuse me, I've got some friends who are probably making voodoo dolls of me because I've taken forever with their drinks.' Calm on the outside, inside, Que's tummy was in a flustering twirl. She hadn't thought about her licence, or her vehicle's registration.

It's why she never stopped long, and why she never made friends, because she didn't want to answer questions. She'd sworn to Billie and Mike that they'd stay, but Que couldn't afford the luxury of settling in and staying, because she'd had it all ripped away from her before.

Or could she finally truly stay?

Okay, switching registrations over was easy enough. The vehicle, the van, and the house weren't in her name. Nothing was in her name.

But the name on her driver's licence was a whole other story.

23

'Here we go, ladies. Sorry, I got distracted.' In the most inconvenient way, but Que needed time to think—preferably sober. She handed out the drink cans and passed the soft drink to Billie. 'You drink water after this, okay?'

'Thanks, Momma. Can I stay at Kaytlyn's house tonight? Puhleese, pretty please?' Both little girls began pleading.

'When did this happen?' Que asked Karen and Kat, seated on one side of their tent, watching the final count for the silent auctions.

'The two girls conspired between themselves while you were talking to Marcus,' said Kat. 'How do you like our top cop?'

'He's … Phew …' *Good looking, and nosy, and clever.* Que knew a smart police officer when she met one.

She plonked into her chair, watching Connor and Marcus talk like old friends, while people nearby frowned, walking around the pair of men. *What was that all about? Did everyone else feel the same way about Connor like Karen did?*

'So, Momma? Can we?'

'Go on, mother,' urged Kat. 'We've got tomorrow off, so for me it's purely for my own selfish reasons. The girls can amuse themselves, while my husband and I get a sleep-in. My Aunty Bea's keen. She lives with us and does the weekend breakfasts. It's a sweet deal.'

'When was the last time Billie had a sleepover?' Karen asked.

'Um, never. Unless you count Mike.'

'Oh, girl, you are so overdue.' Kat playfully slapped Que's knee. 'Consider this your Mother's Day present. You can pay me back next year.'

If Que was still here next year. 'Okay, Billie, you can have a sleepover.'

'Yaaaay.' As if riding a sugar-rush, the kid raised her can in the air to dance on her toes in some ballerina rain dance in her dirty tutu.

'You two girls, hold hands while Kaytlyn finds her father. Kyle's doing a run home with his brother to put away the barbecues,' said Kat. 'You girls can play in the tree house, while I stay here and hang with my girls for a bit.'

'Bye, Momma. Luv you, Momma.' With a squeezing hug around Que's neck her baby was gone. Just like that.

Que didn't know how to react. It took weeks to get over her motherly separation anxiety, how was she going to cope with this?

'Drink up, my friend,' said Karen. 'You're gonna be kid free.'

'RIGHT, KAREN, YOU'RE RUNNING THIS SHOW. HERE'S YOUR LIST OF AUCTION WINNERS,' said Agnes, the scary coach. 'YOU GONNA DO THE ANNOUNCIN'?'

'Now I've sat down, I'm never going to get up again. My poor husband may just have to carry me to the car.' She kicked off her shoes and lifted her legs onto the spare chair and glanced over the list. 'I'll post the names in the school newsletter at the end of the week and do the ring around then. Thanks, coach, and to the rest of you, too.'

'Did you bid for the massage?' Que asked.

'I should have,' replied Karen, as the three women settled back in their chairs with the football match starting its last quarter. 'Yes! I got those curtains; they'll look amazing in my house.'

'Who got my tables and chairs?' Kat leaned over to peek at the list. 'Cool. Rigsy did.'

'Who?' Que shrugged.

'Rigsy. Sweet guy. He's engaged to one of the Muster Sisters. They're living in their shed while building their dream home, so they'll need furniture. Like you do.' Kat held out the page to Que. 'Check out who won your graphic design gig.'

She arched her eyebrow at the name.

'Why would Connor bid for your work?' Kat asked, tucking her auburn curls into her hair tie.

Que only shrugged. When and how did Connor sneak in a bid, when she'd been stuck here most of the day?

'Connor bid two grand,' said Karen with a frown 'It's the largest bid of the entire auction. Can Connor afford that?'

'I have no idea.' About that, or why he bid at all, especially when he'd given her the cold shoulder these past few days.

Her stomach rolled over as a layer of guilt gripped her shoulders. She'd set him up with Billie, testing him in hope he'd leave. Which he'd done. So why was she sulking?

'Any idea how much we raised, Karen?' Que had to deflect their questions because she didn't have answers.

'It'll be a few days for the final tally. The beer tent is still operating, and people will have to pay to collect their auction prizes.'

What sort of prize was Connor thinking of, bidding two thousand for a two-hundred-dollar job? 'You really must want this pool.'

'Sweetie, we live in the land of eternal summer, where we can't go swimming in any of our natural waterways because of crocodiles. I'd rather my children swim in a safe environment where we can watch them, while they learn to swim properly.'

'Agreed.'

'Anyway, I saw you getting all cosy with Connor over there.' Karen wriggled her finger at Que like a worm. 'I've warned you about him. He's a bad man. I doubt he'll pay for this bid, it's too much. I don't think we can accept it.'

'Why not? Connor's money is as good as anyone's. He adores Billie.' The two had bonded so swiftly in only a few weeks. Was that why he did it?

'But he's a bad man.'

'Is he?' Que's neck hairs bristled defensively. She'd been with him long enough to know the difference, but she'd never told them she'd been spending time with Connor. 'What did Connor ever do to you? Or anyone? All I heard was that Connor was a troublemaker as a kid. Weren't we all ratbags when younger? I know I was.'

'Ditto to that one.' Kat waved her arm. 'Karen, you've got seven boys. You said so yourself, they're no angels.'

'And Connor hasn't been here for over fifteen years,' said Que. 'So, I'm guessing there's some bad blood between you two.'

Karen screwed up her nose. She'd been the most vocal against Connor from the beginning, and Que liked Karen. And Connor.

Although with Connor, it may be way too much.

'Karen …' Kat said, muscling into the conversation. 'Connor's come all this way to help Bertha and Richard, who are an amazing couple. And Connor was talking to Marcus like a friend before. People change …'

'Karen, why are you so anti-Connor?' Que asked.

'Fine.' Karen huffed, crossing her legs at the ankles. 'I had this crush on Connor all the way through school. It got worse when he worked on my father's property one mango season.' She took a sip of her can, staring at her hands. 'I was practically stalking the guy.'

Que raised her hand and grinned. 'I'm the school stalker.'

'You grew out of it. You should have seen me with my daughter at childcare. But back to this …' Kat pointed at Karen. 'Did you say anything to Connor about how you felt?'

'Yes. I blurted it out one day when I was thirteen and kissed him!' Karen screwed up her face, peeked around the empty tent, then leaned in closer. 'I threw myself at him, clinging to his neck and everything.' She hid her glowing red face in her hands. 'Of course, he pushed me away, asking me what the hell I was thinking.'

'You're blushing.' Kat pulled Karen's fingers away, exposing her tomato-red complexion.

'It gets worse. I told him I loved him too.'

Kat and Que sat back, lips pursed, holding their laughter.

'What did Connor do?' Que asked.

'Connor told me I was too young to know the difference. He said he wasn't interested and told me he wasn't any good for anyone.' Karen shifted in her seat with her whole demeanour softening. 'I'd never been so humiliated. I was determined to get my revenge.'

'How?' Que asked.

'By blaming Connor for damaging a bin of mangoes, so my parents would fire him. I don't know why he worked for us, when he should have been helping on his parents' farm ...' Karen leaned over and whispered, 'I can't believe I set him up. It was me who did the damage, and he was innocent, but he still got fired.'

Que tried to swallow down her own guilt for setting up Connor, and for using him as her way to stop her school-stalking separation syndrome. But he knew he was being used as her distraction, she'd told him so.

'It's really silly now, if I think about it,' continued Karen. 'Connor left town soon after that. I should tell my parents the truth, and apologise to Connor, too.'

'What do you mean left?' Que asked.

'He got scooped up by the Station Hand, but Connor ruined his chances there too ...'

'Is that why people don't like Connor?' Que asked the two women.

'They remember how angry he was, and many accused him of thieving,' replied Karen. 'But the final straw was for upsetting the Station Hand, who everyone respects.'

'Let me get this straight, because Connor didn't want to be some cowboy, everyone hates him for it?'

'Connor failed the Lost Boys program.'

'One program, when there's an entire world of programs out there. If Connor is as bad as this town makes him out to be, he wouldn't be in the Navy with his rank and responsibilities.' Que sat back, realising she cared way too much for the man, defending his honour like this. 'Are you saying this whole town is against Connor for something he did as a kid?'

Kat, who'd only visited during the summer holidays, shrugged. But Karen, who knew everyone's business, was quiet.

'No wonder Connor didn't want to stick around. Why would he? Where is this town's forgiving community spirit now?'

'Any idea how long Connor is in town for?' Kat asked.

'He's taken a leave of absence until Bertha and Richard get back on their feet.' And Bertha was getting stronger every day.

'You know, Connor was always the fighting rebel back then. He was really angry at the world ...' Karen pointed to the beer tent. 'Maybe he still is.'

'Karen, Connor is not what you think he is. Considering you set him up, imagine how many other people made Connor their scapegoat for other things, too?' Que scooped up her bag and headed for Connor.

'I'll call you later about picking up Billie tomorrow,' said Kat.

'Sure. Thanks.' Que gave a limp wave as she left the tent with the gloss from these so-called good townsfolk disappearing. Surely, they didn't hold a grudge over a man who'd done wrong as a kid.

But as she approached the tent, angry voices rose.

'You're a wanker who should've stayed lost at sea!' A man yelled at Connor, while being held back by two men.

'Don't go there, Zach,' said Connor calmly, while obviously poised, ready to defend himself. Other men gathered around them, all scowling at Connor.

What did Connor do, for these people to be so openly hostile towards him like this?

Que should have run the other way, but instead, she did the most daring thing ever and clutched Connor's clenched fist. Wincing with her heart in her throat, she prayed for the right reaction.

Connor whirled around with dark eyes full of anger. 'What are you doing?'

She swallowed down raw fear that was like razor blades, giving his hand a gentle squeeze. 'I'm ready for that lift home now.'

In the blink of an eye his anger was diffused. He exhaled heavily. 'Sure, let's go.' Connor gave her a slight smile, as he casually slung his arm around her shoulders.

'Where are you going, chicken? Get back here,' called out Zach.

Connor stopped and frowned over his shoulder.

'Who would you rather play with, sailor? Me, or that idiot behind you? Especially when I'm going to be home all alone.' Was her small house, which copped the brunt of a ginormous sun, really a home? Was this town worthy of being a home for the pair of them?

But her house was a place without judgment and once again Connor would be the perfect distraction to keep her company while Billie was away.

'I'll shout you a drink.' She needed one for what she'd done. What happened to her rules of survival—being the first to walk away?

Would Connor walk away from the guy goading him to fight?

'Mmm …' Connor's face remained neutral, but his eyes slowly roamed all over her body. She felt naked under that stare. 'Looks like I got a much better offer than to play with you, Zach.' He delicately kissed Que's cheek and they walked out arm in arm, leaving plenty of stunned faces behind them.

24

Connor steered his dad's ute towards Que's house with his other hand resting on Que's thigh. Her perfume filled the car. He'd been missing that aroma, and her. 'Are you using me as a distraction to stop your separation anxiety again?'

'Of course. This is my first sleepover and I needed something to amuse me.'

He grinned. The woman was brutal. Did he dare ask why she froze up with Marcus earlier?

'Hey, what are the bees like out here?'

'Bees?' Conversations with this woman were so random.

'You know? Bees, yellow and black, makers of honey with the nasty stingers.'

'You're talking European bees. We don't have them up here, they can't handle the heat and their hives melt. We've got plenty of bush bees, which are smaller than flies.'

'Do people get face-swelling allergic reactions to these native bees?'

'No, they don't sting. But wasp bites cause swelling, and we've got plenty of those out here. Nasty buggers. Marcus and I made a killing out of it one year as kids, pedalling our bikes around town, lighting up fly spray cans to burn their nests. It paid for our motorbikes.'

'How entrepreneurial of you.'

'Why do you ask?'

'You know …'

He gave her thigh a squeeze. 'I ask, you answer. Not that hard, right?'

It was unlike any relationship he'd ever had, both of them skirting the edges of all conversations that involved their pasts and the future. Connor had plenty to be ashamed of, but what did Que have to hide?

'Why the question about the bees?' He turned into her driveway.

Que faced the neighbour's direction as she spoke. 'Val didn't come to the fundraiser today, but she baked cakes for it. Her boy, Tommy, told me her face was all swollen and bruised from bee stings. Who'd want to bake when you're wounded? And what mother would miss the Mother's Day events, when both Val and I were looking forward to this event. But then, with you saying it could be a wasp's nest, could Tommy have confused bees with wasps? Or is there something else going on?'

Whoa. He pulled on the handbrake at the closed gate.

'Let's not talk about this now …' She got out of the car, unlocked the heavy chain, pushed it open, then waited for him to roll the ute forward.

He watched Que in the side mirror as she locked it. She was gorgeous, especially with the way the low sun caught her dark hair.

But he also spotted the worry she tried to conceal.

'I'm getting one of those automatic gate openers,' she said, jumping into her seat. He drove towards the small house with the enormous view where Princess guarded the front door. That blue dog never strayed.

'G'day, mate.' The dog was ecstatic to see Connor again, with his wriggly tail-less rump and wide smile.

'Come and check out my new outdoor lounge area.' Through the front door, she kicked off her shoes, then down the corridor, past her office with its walls of windows. She unlocked the back glass doors and pulled them back like a theatre curtain to reveal the sunset spread across the outback.

'Nice. When did this come in?' He pointed to the deep comfy outdoor lounge. It matched the new outdoor kitchen and bar set up on her spacious back verandah.

'The other day. Mike spotted it on special and put it on the truck for me.' She opened the fridge and grabbed two beers. Handing him one, she all but fell into the cushions of the couch, put her feet on the wicker coffee table and stared at an uninterrupted view that rolled on forever.

But he'd rather look at the woman.

Seated beside her, he took a deep mouthful of his beer. It was time they talked. 'Are you going to ask me what we were arguing about in the bar earlier?'

'You'll talk about it if you want to.'

If she didn't ask, he wouldn't have to share. But this time, he did. 'Aren't you even curious?'

'Of course, I am. You know it won't go anywhere; I know you

hate gossip.'

'Yeah, I trust you.' The words rolled off his tongue, unlocking something deep within his soul. He trusted her. And for a man who trusted no one—let alone himself—it hit home. 'I think we'll be creating enough gossip after tonight.'

'Ah, yes, our dramatic exit.' She giggled behind her bottle. 'Joys of living in a small town, right?'

'You really don't care what people think, do you?'

'There's only a few whose opinions matter to me.' She then peered at him sideways. 'I heard a lot of talk about you, today.'

He frowned. 'Yeah, like what?'

'Supermom Karen Kimble was telling me she caused the damage to some mangoes that got you fired before you left town. She set you up.'

He stared at his beer bottle, trying to find that memory, but he heard fire in her voice. It's what he called her Momma-bear tone when she got protective over her daughter. Was Que being protective over him?

'I couldn't believe she was badmouthing you, calling you this bad man, when she was the one who'd set you up. How many other people blamed you for things you didn't do?'

'It happened all the time.' He took a deep pull of his beer. 'People only remember what they want to remember.' He'd become some myth neighbours used for spreading stories. 'Who are you talking about?'

'Karen Kimble, Supermom of seven boys and one girl. She used to stalk you when she was thirteen while you worked at her parents' mango farm, she said she kissed you.'

His eyes rolled up to the ceiling. 'I remember … Every time I turned around there she was. Then she suddenly launched herself at me, with this sticky strawberry lipstick stuff too.' He screwed his face up.

Que laughed. 'Karen's actually embarrassed about it all now, but she did say she was going to apologise, so she should.'

'It was a long time ago. Why bother?' That was actually the day that led to his fateful last night at home. 'But I want to tell you about tonight's argument before you hear about it in some edited gossip's version, because it started off with Zach making some smart-arse comment about you?'

'Oh really? Is that because I knocked him back when he asked me out earlier?'

'I didn't know that.' He frowned. After what they'd done in town today, it should keep those dogs back for a bit.

'Were you protecting my honour? Me, a woman who has none. You're quite chivalrous under that extremely toned exterior.' She poked his chest, with her words purring over her plump lips.

'Zach called you a few unsavoury things I won't repeat, and claimed you got the farm by conning the money out of Billie's father.'

'What?' She sat up with a scowl. 'I get nothing from Billie's father. Nothing. It's my money.'

'I know you work hard.' Que worked long hours for some big-name clients. If they called, she'd drop everything—it's how he'd got sucked into babysitting Billie.

'Sounds like someone was picking an argument.'

'Zach was itching for a fight. He would've had one too, if his mates hadn't held him back.' He clenched his fist; he could've easily done some damage, and when he was angry he rarely had the power to stop himself, which was a lethal combination when out of control.

But he'd found control, in an instant, just by Que holding his hand.

'What did he have a go at you for?' Her tone was laced with concern.

'A few things …' Where did he start? 'Zach's sister, Tracey, married my brother, Travis.'

'I didn't know you have a brother.'

'*Had*. Zach gave me a hard time about not going to the funerals of my brother and his family. Travis, his sister, our niece, and nephew.' Connor dragged his wallet out and grabbed the worn Christmas card, passing it to Que.

She opened the card to reveal the last family photo inside.

'They were in a lethal car accident a few years ago. The reason I …' He inhaled deeply, with his thumb brushing down the beer bottle's condensation. 'I didn't go to their funeral because I was laid up in hospital, recovering from a landmine discharge. I was on the roof of a nearby building that partially collapsed from the explosion.'

Her gasp sent a bucket of chills over his skin.

'I'm all right.' He clasped her thigh, as if to calm them both down. It was the first time he'd ever mentioned his job to her. And Que never asked.

Besides Bertha and Richard, no one openly feared for him, not like this.

'Honestly, I never wanted to come back to this town.' Her palm covered his hand, to lace their fingers together. Again, she gave the tiniest of gestures, a simple squeeze that soothed him some, allowing another chunk of his inner shields to fall away.

'My brother wanted me to be best man at his wedding, but I couldn't. I didn't want to do it …' His throat was raw as if he'd swallowed a load of gravel. 'He wasn't really my brother.'

'You're adopted?'

'I found out when I was sixteen, getting the paperwork for my driver's licence. I'm adopted, but Travis was Richard and Bertha's biological son. He came along two years after they adopted me.'

'I've heard of that happening.'

'Our family was living proof of it.'

'How did it make you feel finding out you were adopted?'

'Ticked. Off.' He scowled at the distant sun sinking on the horizon. 'It started this sibling rivalry between us, so Richard and Bertha offered to help me find my biological parents.'

'Did you find them?'

His shoulders slumped as he traced the intricate pattern of her soft skin on the back of her hand. 'I never met them, but I found out about them. My birth mother was only sixteen. She gave me up for adoption because … because …' He swallowed down razor blades and fire as he spilled his greatest secret. 'She'd been raped.'

Que remained calm and perfectly still. Again, she gave his hand a gentle squeeze.

But it did nothing for the layers of shame, guilt, and grief overpowering him. He'd told no one about this, yet he couldn't stop. 'It gets worse …' He looked at her in hope she'd say stop, but those damned sexy eyes of hers were clear and focused.

He rose to his feet and paced the verandah like a caged lion, trying to tamp down this overwhelming need to confess the ugliness of his heritage. 'My biological father was convicted for the rape and is now serving a double life sentence for murder.'

Que sat and listened.

Connor paced and talked.

He'd had the mandatory regulation shrink visits and never mentioned this, yet the woman who sat listening made him want to spill everything. To think he'd been such a judgy prick to her in the beginning.

'You get it, don't you? I'm scum from some terrible seed, I'm someone who was never meant to be. Born with a tonne of bad blood, I get paid to spill blood, which means I shouldn't even be near you or Billie.'

'Hey. Stop that!' Even though he towered over her, she stood in his path and blocked him from a quick exit, her stare steady and unflinching. 'I know how much Richard and Bertha care about you, they've only seen you as their son. In the hospital, all they talked about was you, the way a mother and father talk about their child. They're very proud of you.'

'No one knows about this but them, my brother and Marcus. Now you. Can you imagine what the gossips in this town would say?'

'Hey …' She cupped his cheek and made him face her. 'It's just me standing here.'

'Fine, ask me something. Anything.' They may as well rip off this Band-Aid.

'This guy tonight, how did he push your buttons? It wasn't just about me.'

'Zach went on about how I never helped my family out.' He brushed fingers through hair that had gotten long since he'd been on holidays. 'For the past fifteen years, I paid the mortgage on the farm, until there was none. Then, every time I'd receive a tour bonus, I'd drop the money into their account to buy something extra, materials, machinery, whatever. I owed them.'

'What do you mean, owed them?'

'They fed me, put me through school, so I owed them for sixteen years of food and board.'

'Connor …' She grabbed his hands. '*No.* That's what family—well most families—do for their children.'

'I didn't need the money. I had everything supplied to me in the Navy. I even paid for Travis's family's funerals. All of them were under the family policy I had for the farm.'

'See, you still saw them as family.'

'No. It was guilt over what I was, for what I'd done.'

'How? Did you rape anyone? Kill anyone?'

'I'm a special ops sniper,' he said, punching the centre of his chest. 'They don't unleash this dog and my team unless it's a fight to the death.'

'That's different. Serving your country is honourable.'

'Is it?' He glowered at the ground, where long shadows stretched from the dying sunset. 'As a teen, I struggled a lot with the adoption, and how I came to be. I believed I was bad.'

She frowned at him.

He held his hand up to silence her. He needed to finish this. 'I was always scrapping for fights at school. After school. Hell, I earned cash in the illegal fights they used to hold in the creek bed at the end of your property.'

Her eyebrows shot up, staring out at her large landfall.

'Don't worry, Marcus would've shut that down the day he started the job.'

'You two were tight?'

'Tighter than I ever was with my brother—my adopted brother.' He then slowly shook his heavy head. 'That kid … Travis used to follow me around like a shadow.'

'Like Billie does on her skates.'

'Yeah …' He even managed a small smile as his thumb flicked at the red braided friendship bracelet wrapped around his wrist. That kid in skates and pigtails got to him. And so did her mother.

Pity he was about to scare the woman off for good.

'I couldn't work on the farm at home anymore,' he said, tossing his thumb towards his parents' place. 'By rights, I had no claim to it. Everything should've gone to Travis.'

'Is that why you worked on other people's farms? Like Karen's family?'

'Yeah.'

'Where I come from, there's two sides to every story.' She gave a soft shrug, then leaned her shoulder against one of the verandah's supporting poles.

He did the same on the opposite pole. Even though he didn't like the distance between them, it's what they needed. Distance. 'When I got fired from the Karen's Mango Farm, I got drunk, and Travis and I got into an argument. It was vicious, with Travis saying I was nothing like him and his parents, my adoptive parents. That I was just like my rapist, murdering father. I punched him over it, too. The only problem was, I lost it and kept punching.'

He stared at his fists with his head hanging low, as the burden of shame strapped heavily across his shoulders. 'When Mum came to pull me off Travis, I was swinging so wildly I'd punched her too.'

Que inhaled, short and sharp.

He couldn't even look at her. 'I didn't mean to. I'd never meant to hurt her. I was so mortified by what I'd done, I ran to the house, packed my bag, and left that night. Only the freaking Station Hand showed up before I even made it out of town … Then life went to hell from there.'

Hell was a land of dust storms under a sweltering outback sun following a herd of stinky cattle, sleeping on thin swags on cold dirt, drinking over-sugared black-leaf billy tea and eating chunks of damper with jam. Being forced to hustle on horseback from dusk to dawn, at the crack of a stock whip, in clothes stiff with sweat and dirt. It was a nightmare world of sunburn, snakes, and sticky black flies, following the watery haze stretch across the horizon that made the world of dust shine. It had been months of pure hell.

Until Marcus came up with a plan and Connor scored a set a car keys. Together they scrounged for jerry cans of fuel and pushed a stolen ute under the midnight stars to get far enough away from their stock camp, before starting that engine in their long journey back to civilisation.

It ended with them separating. Marcus headed south in that stolen ute, while Connor went north for Darwin where he scored work on some prawn trawlers until he got accepted into the Navy to live a life on the sea. Only to end up in war-torn lands of rubble and sand, that were nothing compared to his time with the Station Hand.

He lifted his heavy head to stare at the first stars barely breaking through … Back in the place where his story began.

And she never said a word.

But she didn't walk away either.

'I'm still disgusted with myself for punching my mother. It scared me to think how far I would have gone if Bertha hadn't stepped in, I could have killed Travis.'

Then when he peered at her, his stomach dropped at the silent tears staining her cheeks.

'That's why I never came back, and why I don't wipe myself out with alcohol. But I've also never walked away from a fight— which made me perfect for my job—until tonight. You helped me walk away, for the first time ever.'

In a few steps, Que crossed the distance between them and wrapped her arms around his shoulders. He tasted her tears as their lips brushed, he burrowed his face in that safe space between her neck and shoulder.

He clung to her, as the load of suffering and shame he'd been silently carrying finally lifted, all in the comforting arms of a woman. He was tired of carrying a mountain of self-blame. It kept his heart locked in a vault of black granite that a sledgehammer wouldn't dent.

But that vault was now smashed to smithereens in a crumbling explosion bigger than any landmine, all by looking into her violet eyes.

Connor had never felt more exposed in his life. 'Are you going to kick me out now?'

'No. But I'll tell you a story that might make you want to leave afterwards …' She held out her hand to him. 'But only if you think you can handle it?'

25

They nestled side by side on the outdoor couch as the crickets chirped in time to the dog snoring on the back doorstep. Twilight filled the outback skies, where darkness arrived in coloured layers, displaying that fine balance between light and dark.

She could see Connor was wrestling with his dark side too.

Que was no angel either …

'Once upon a time, there was the honourable Mr Reginald M and his lovely wife, the esteemed honourable justice Mrs Hazel M,' she said, rolling her eyes at Connor.

'They sound fancy.'

'Oh, they were. Highly intellectual lawyers with a blue-blood reputation in society. Mr M was a magistrate. His wife, Mrs M had the honourable appointment as a high court judge, where the official tick of approval for that position only came from the Prime Minister of that time.'

'Top dogs, huh?'

'You bet. Cops were forever crawling up the magistrate's butt to issue their warrants, and lawyers were constantly couriering invitations to dinner parties. They had their lives perfectly planned for holidays abroad, summer houses on the coast, specific fundraising galas to attend to strategically grow their careers, and an adult son as their golden boy to carry on the family name. He was a junior partner in their family-owned law firm. Everything they did as a family was all about public opinion, to show how perfect they were to the world.'

'No one's perfect.'

'They came close, because their life was golden, until Mrs M thought she was having menopause problems, discovering too late she was pregnant … with me.'

'Sheesh.' Connor took a deep mouthful of his beer.

'Did you know my name is all about the law these people lived and breathed?'

'Que Lawsten?'

'My first name was after Quentin Bryce, who was a family friend and later Australia's first female Governor-General. My middle name is Astraia, which is the name of the Greek goddess of justice and innocence.'

'Fancy.'

'Imagine my surprise, given all the effort they'd put into my name, to find out that the woman had actually wanted me terminated.'

Connor crinkled his brow. 'You're kidding?'

'Mummy dearest told me to my face many times. At fifty-seven, when she gave birth to me, Mrs M did not want to raise a child. So, I lived with my much older brother and his new wife, until they had their own children. Only to discover that my *mother* wasn't actually my mother, but my sister-in-law. And she didn't want me anymore, not when they had their own children coming, so they gave me back.'

'Are you serious?'

'It was such a confusing time for me, being abandoned by those I thought were my parents, not knowing who to call mother, father, aunty or uncle. So, they shipped me off to boarding school at the tender age of five. The same age my daughter is now.' Que's throat was so dry, she swallowed mouthful after mouthful of her beer.

The gentleman he was, Connor grabbed a fresh round. 'Go on.'

'They sent me away because I interfered with their lifestyle and wasn't part of their plans. On weekends I'd hang at the school. If I was lucky, I'd get invited to stay with other boarding students' families who were from the country, which gave me some amazing memories.'

'Which is why you moved to the rural area now?'

'Yes.' *And no*. It was too much to share in one day. It was best to just stick to one story at a time … 'Anyway, my parents were never around. They never bothered to show up for parent–teacher conferences, sending some snot-nosed intern who was more interested in sucking up to my parents than doing anything for me.'

'Where were they?'

'In the halls of the courthouse having some deep debate over constitutional law, or discussing the latest news headlines at their yacht club or summer house. Basically, they were too busy with their own lifestyles to bother with me.'

'Their loss.'

'No, they saw me as their shame.' She playfully nudged Connor's shoulder and said, 'You may have been clueless about your shameful heritage until your mid-teens, but I was pretty much made to feel ashamed for being born.

Connor frowned.

'Then, when I turned sweet sixteen, my father retired as the Chief Magistrate, so the government threw him a party. It was the who's who of the legal world, from lawyers, prosecutors, and police superintendents, and I got drunk because it was my birthday too, but my parents had forgotten all about that.'

'You didn't? Underage drinking, with all of those lawmakers in the room?'

'I completely wiped myself out and threw up everywhere. And you know what?'

'What?'

'My parents actually noticed me for a change!' She giggled. 'Lighten up, it was funny.'

'That would've hurt.'

She shrugged. 'I was home because I'd been expelled from school number five.'

'What for?'

'I was running an in-house casino. I was a great croupier; the house always won. Oh, and of course skipping classes all the time because I worked nights.'

'My picture of you as the perfect mummy is …'

'I never said I was perfect. Or even good.' She grinned at him. 'I was a poor little rich girl with a platinum card. I had everything a kid could ever want, materialistically, except the mere acknowledgement of my existence. But I soon learnt that the only way I got any sort of attention from my parents was by getting their legal attention through my rebellious actions. And boy, didn't the cops learn to love me.'

'What happened?'

'Um, let's see… There were charges of drunk and disorderly, illegal gambling, driving while under the influence without a licence, it goes on … Dad or Mum or my brother managed to get all of my charges dropped, so I have a spotlessly clean record, just a very tawdry past.'

He scratched the back of his head. 'I thought I was bad.'

'We all have a little trouble in our blood. But hey, settle in, sailor, it's just about to get good.' She swallowed another load of amber bubbles for Dutch courage, but he needed to hear this. 'With no school, I got shipped off to this penthouse apartment on the Sydney waterfront that my parents kept for guests. So, while they tried to deal with the inconvenient shame I caused them, I got rewarded with a monthly allowance and a new sports car. And I didn't even have my car licence then.'

'I'm guessing you cleaned up your act?'

'Baby, I partied hard.'

'For how long?'

'Until I was eighteen. The second I was of age they evicted me from the penthouse and cut off my allowance. By then, I didn't care. They had emotionally cut me off all my life, and I was in complete and total self-destruct mode. You'd know that phase.'

'I do. The Navy snapped me out of it. You?'

'I ended up at Mike's place.'

'Mike, the ginger guy …' He pointed to the lush lawn that grew around the house.

'Who you thought was my husband.'

'But he's your best friend?'

'Back then, he wasn't. I'd been couch surfing with all my party friends in Sydney and then somehow ended up on Mike's couch in Adelaide, which was the beginning of a terrible relationship.'

Connor arched an eyebrow at her. 'Right? Big party.'

'I never remembered how I got there, but in the beginning Mike and I were bad for each other. I'm surprised he didn't get booted out of university that first year, because we shared the same vices.'

'He passed, right?'

'How could he not. Mike's a horticultural genius who scored some scholarship to become the professor he is now. But back then I felt guilty for nearly ruining his chances of a decent life. He was a good guy until he met me.'

'So, you were a ...'

She hid her face, feeling the shame she'd caused Mike. 'I was such a bad influence for Mike. So, we agreed to clean up our acts, together. While Mike studied, I got my first job, working in the towel-folding section in this huge industrial, commercial laundry, to pay the bills.'

'You're kidding.'

'It was the only work I could get. After being expelled from five different schools, my grades sucked. With my smart mouth, I wasn't any good at customer relations. The laundry was gross, but it could have been worse. Other people there had to deal with all that icky bloody surgery stuff that comes from the hospital.' Yet she'd behaved today at the silent auction. Maybe she was finally growing up.

'So how long were you there for?'

'Nearly three months, until I scored a job at a casino. Where, like you with the military life, the casino chain supplied me with practically everything to work as their high-rollers croupier. I got to transfer from casino to casino, interstate and overseas. I even spent some time on cruise ships and at island resorts, because when people are on holiday, they love to play cards.'

'I've seen you shuffle cards. Do you stack the deck?'

'God, no. That would have got me fired. But there was no need because the house always wins,' she said with a wry grin. 'It was good money, and the tips from high rollers were insane. It truly opened my eyes watching the rich from the other side of the table. And I could reinvent myself. I healed and found *me* and then, when Billie came along, I folded up my cards. Mike encouraged me to take a course at his university, something that would be useful. He even paid for it. And that's where I found my love for graphic design, and turned it into a job that helped pay for our travelling lifestyle.'

'You love being a digital doodler.'

She smiled at her job nickname. 'I do.'

'And you're good at it.'

She shrugged.

'So, I'm guessing from there, you saved enough to play the property game with Billie and ended up here?' Connor asked.

'Yes.' *And no.* She didn't dare tell all. 'Last year my brother tracked me down, to tell me our parents had been killed in an accident. He still owns the legal firm and was the executor of their wills. This property is paid for with the inheritance I didn't know I had. I honestly thought my parents had cut me off forever, but ...'

She waved her hand to the scenery that was a gift.

She then narrowed her eyes at him. 'So, the point of my story is: you may have only had a few years as a rebel, but I've lived most of my life as one, when I came from such outstanding pillars of society. So stop thinking your heritage makes you who you are, because I believe everyone is their own person, and your destiny is what you choose.'

'But ...'

'I'm not done, Mister.' She then poked his arm. 'You had something I used to wish for *every day* as a kid. You had the love of the most amazing couple, a mother and father, who took you in as their own child. You had parental love, and for a long time you had an idyllic upbringing. You are the product of that upbringing. The circumstances of your birth have nothing to do with the person you are now, any more than mine have to do with who I am.'

She stood from the couch. 'All I can do is learn from my mistakes. And there were plenty of them, but they're all mine, that I take full responsibility for them. But I'm also learning from the mistakes my parents made, to try and do the best I can for my daughter, but also in how I treat myself. That's why I don't care what everyone else says about me. Only those who truly know who I am have the right to judge me.'

She leaned down and this time she gently stabbed the centre of his chest and held her finger there. 'You deserve to give yourself a break, Connor, by believing in yourself. No one can do that for you, only you can. But you should know your parents believe in you, Billie believes in you, and I believe in you. You're a good person, or I would have never let you into our yard. I would have chased you off with the baseball bat I keep under my bed.'

She stepped back, crossing her arms over her chest. 'I could've gone down some terrible and scary paths, but I didn't. And you could've done the same, but you didn't either. Connor, you should be proud of who you are, and of your adoptive family. They truly love you for who you are, and they don't care where you came from.'

She took a casual sip of her beer, realising it was empty. 'You can go home now, unless you want to stay and have another beer and explain why you bid two thousand dollars for me to work for you, when you don't have a kid at that school?' She was ready for him to leave anytime, but she also knew he wasn't in town forever. And for a girl who was always ready to run, this time of being still she'd allow—but she couldn't share all her secrets with him.

Connor stood before her, that tall wall of muscle and male with his dark eyes searching hers.

She wasn't sorry or ashamed of her past, it moulded her into who she was today. A much better person, she hoped. She could only try and improve for herself and for her daughter's sake.

But did Connor still want to tango with this bad girl with a past?

He pressed his lips against hers, warm, soft, and forgiving. Then he pulled back. 'I'd like to stick around for that beer. I hear you're home alone, so we can discuss the job I want you to do. All night long.'

Their smiles pressed against each other, as the air sizzled. No more conversation was needed. It was time for these survivors to feel the pleasure that would help release them from the pain of their pasts.

26

'I'm going over there today,' announced Que from behind the kitchen counter, as she took a sip of her coffee, then resumed making Billie's lunch.

'Where?' Connor asked, seated on the other side of the kitchen bench, finishing breakfast.

She leaned over and whispered, 'Over to the Cromwell's. But only if I don't see Val at the bus stop this morning.'

'Why?'

'It's Wednesday and Gary's not home.' She tucked the sandwich into Billie's lunch box, along with stacks of snacks, adding double for Billie the kid to split with her besties, Maddy and Tommy. All at the request of her daughter, who wanted to share with her friends, making her a proud momma.

Connor reached across the counter to hold her in place. 'Why are you worried? And don't say you aren't, because you're wearing that determined look on your face that pretty much says *get outta the way, I'm doing this.*'

She grinned at the guy who wasn't meant to be here. Maybe he could talk her out of this. 'I haven't seen Val since Friday afternoon. That's five days, Connor. Val's always been at the gate to watch her children go to school, but she wasn't there yesterday, and poor Tommy told me she looks sick.'

'Hmmm … If Val had an allergy to the wasp stings it should have cleared up by now. If it was wasps.'

'Tommy said it was definitely bees, not wasps. He swears he knows the difference. Yet, his description was—' She peeked over her shoulder and listened for Billie in her room getting ready for school.

Connor came around the counter to stand in front of her. 'Go on?'

'Tommy said his mother's got black eyes, and a swollen face. I checked it out on the net last night and you're right, the Territory's native bees are harmless. So, if Val needs medical treatment, I'll drive her to the clinic. Easy as.' Yet it didn't feel easy.

'When did Tommy tell you this?'

'While we were waiting for the school bus. He's only eight and told me to keep it a secret too, but he's worried.' She frowned at the ground, trying to calm the worry clawing around in her stomach. 'I should have played nosy neighbour yesterday.' But they'd been indulging in a long weekend.

'Momma, I'm ready to get my hair brushed. Unless you want to do it, Connor?' Billie rushed down the hallway with brush in hand.

'I'll leave that to your mother, thanks.' Connor put his hands up, while backing away from the small child carrying a loaded hairbrush.

'Shoes, Billie,' Que said. 'I'll be right down there. Need help with the laces?'

'No, Momma, Connor showed me how.' The kid's voice carried down the corridor.

Connor grinned with pride behind his coffee cup. 'When are you going over to the Cromwell's?'

'As soon as I wave the kids off at the school bus this morning. If Val's not there, I'm going straight over. That way, if she needs treatment, we can be in and back before Gary notices anything.' She took a deep breath, forcing down the repulsive blend of fear and worry. It was a potent combination she knew only too well. 'I'm hoping it's my imagination, and all is well. Right?'

'I'm coming with you.'

'No. You'll probably scare her off.'

Connor gently held her wrist to stop her walking away. 'No, I won't. I'll sit in the car and wait, because I'm not letting you go over there on your own.'

'So, you're worried too?'

'Now that you've explained your reasons, yeah. I'll just play back up. I'm trained in that.'

'Cool.' Not cool, because Connor was supposed to talk her out of this, not volunteer to help. 'Did they train you to do the breakfast dishes too?'

'Nice try.'

'Let me get Billie ready and then we'll see if Val's at the bus stop this morning. If not, we'll take it from there.' She swivelled back and gave him a quick kiss on the cheek, because whenever their lips met, that dangerously delicious erogenous zone ignited their passion. 'Thanks for wanting to help.' Connor didn't need to get involved and Mike was hours away, but she was willing to do this on her own if she had to.

Under a clear morning sky, the bus stopped at the roadside with a hiss of brakes. The side door squealed open, and the two little girls kissed Que's cheeks and eagerly climbed on the bus. No doubt those extra snacks Que had stashed in Billie's lunchbox would be devoured before they hit town.

Que waved at them with Princess the dog, and Cecil the stocky water buffalo wearing pink ribbons standing on either side. But no Val. 'Tommy, is your mum okay?'

With his head low, he kicked at a stone, dragging his feet towards the bus door. 'She's all purple and yellow in the face, and really sad.'

'Want me to go see her today?'

'Could you?' His head lifted with eyes widening.

'Absolutely. Here, take this too.' She handed him a fifty dollar note. 'For the school tuck shop. I think today is a good day for ice cream, but I'll want you to buy lunch for the girls, too, okay?'

'I will.' Gone was the worry, replaced by a big grin as he hugged her, then climbed onto the bus. 'Oh, and you might wanna leave Princess home, coz our dogs, Bundy and Cola, might get rough with him.'

'Thanks.' She waved at the three children, their smiley faces shining through the windows. The school bus door swished shut, the gears clunked, and the gravel popped and crunched under the large tyres as it rolled down the red road towards town. It kicked up some dust, which floated with the slight breeze to fall on the neighbour's driveway, vacant without Val.

Cecil sniffed at her hair, making Que duck to avoid any buffalo drool.

'Sorry, Cecil, we won't be painting our word of the day, today.' It had become a school-day tradition.

Ha. For a woman who never made habits, or traditions, she had acquired a few. One that allowed her to befriend a big black beast, learning all his soft spots. Cecil loved the tickle behind his ear that made him croon with a fat lower lip and rolled eyes. He'd raise his head and stretch out his neck whenever she'd scratch between his shoulder blades or massage the bend of his lower back—that was his favourite.

She also learned where to not paint her words of the day, because Cecil apparently liked the taste of her paint. She'd been making it herself, so as to not upset his skin, and it was giving his coat an all-over gloss. She was spoiling the animal, and she'd never met its owner.

'Here's your treat, Cecil, your favourite one with extra nuts.' Yes, she knew the eating preferences of a water buffalo. If anyone told her she'd be doing this a few months ago, she'd laugh in their face.

She then shook her head at the dog she was never meant to own, begging for attention. 'Princess, you'll get your treat at the house.'

She ripped open the muesli bar packaging and held the treat in her open palm. The buffalo sniffed and sighed, his velvety lips barely touching her skin as he accepted his morning treat. His big black eyes widened, fluttering his long lashes at her as if to say *thanks*, before wandering off down the road while chewing like a cow. The buffalo may look like a daunting creature with his wide horns and solid build, but Que knew he really was a big softy.

Leaving the gate wide open, she ran up her driveway, with Princess racing ahead in some fun game.

But it didn't feel like fun.

She still had a chance to reshuffle the deck. She could choose to leave the playing cards on the table and not deal the next hand, because Que never walked away from a game when the cards were dealt. So, did she dare take a seat at the table and play the next hand in life? Especially if it meant reliving her greatest fear, one that no woman should ever have to live through.

27

onnor watched as Que led Billie on her tiny bike heading for the road to catch the bus. The pup bounced like a wallaby through the scrub that ran alongside their dirt drive.

As they walked out of sight, he reached for the phone, dialling the number he'd known forever. Normally, he'd be taking the side track to start work on the farm, but not today.

'Hello?'

'Mum, it's Connor. Is Dad with you?'

'Yes, dear, we're still eating breakfast.'

'Er, yeah ...' He could just picture the couple, carrying on like newlyweds. His father was reluctant to leave the house in case something happened to Bertha while he was out in the fields. 'Can you put the phone on speaker?'

'Sure ... What's wrong, Connor?'

'Um ...' Connor gulped down the last of his coffee and started stacking the dishwasher. Yes, he was becoming domesticated. 'I won't be coming in this morning, for work.'

'What's wrong, son?' His father's voice was loaded with recognisable worry.

'I'm only telling you this because I trust you guys ...' His parents had always had his back, even at his worst as a kid. 'Que's going to visit Val ...' And he explained all he knew about Val's situation. 'So, I'm going to help Que today.'

'That's good, son.' Connor could picture his dad nodding at the phone. 'If you or Que need anything from us, you just have to call. Your mother and I will help any way we can.'

Which they had, every time he got into trouble. Oh man, wasn't this a turnaround of events. 'I'd appreciate it if you didn't say anything to anyone else, because we have no proof, just suspicions.' Que was switched on over legalities. Damn, she was smart, sexy, and sassy all at the same time.

'We won't. You can count on us,' Bertha said, 'we never spread rumours.' Yet his parents had copped a lot of crap over his juvenile actions.

And for the first time he uttered the words, 'I'm sorry.'

Clearing his throat, which was being shredded by a line of green ants, again he said, 'I'm sorry.'

'For what, son.'

'For what I did to you both over the years. Mum, I'm sorry about that night, I never meant to hit you, or get so carried away punching Travis. I'm sorry for always being an arse to Travis, for not being his best man at his wedding and for not being there for you both when they died. I'm sorry for not coming back sooner, and I'm sorry for being the arsehole of a kid you both had to defend.'

Connor never had to see the long-term repercussions his parents faced in this town for what he'd done. He'd gotten off easy by leaving. 'I'm sorry I caused you both so much pain. And I'm so very sorry for being such a rotten kid.'

'But you're forgetting the pride and joy you brought into our world too, Connor.' Bertha's strained voice wavered as his father sniffed in the background. 'We were so proud when you got into the Navy. To see you graduate, the postcards you sent us, and you paid our mortgage, which gave us the pure luxury of a stress-free lifestyle. We always knew you were a good person. You were kind and patient with your little brother, teaching him to ride his bike, fishing, or how to kick a footy. You always defended Travis, even when we knew he was the one stealing from people to build your fort.'

'H-h-how did you know?'

'Travis told us, after you left. He felt so bad for what he'd done to upset you, and for letting you take the blame for his stealing. He tried to make up for it, correcting people if anyone ever mentioned you as a thief. We knew you weren't a thief, and Travis said he owed you ...'

Connor wasn't expecting this town to forgive or forget, because he'd done plenty of wrong things too. 'You didn't tell Travis I paid his university fees?'

His mother's silence was his answer.

'Son ...' his father croaked, then heavily sniffed. 'We've always been proud of you. And, you know that key chain you made for me for Father's Day, the one with the bullet, your trench art? Every day I see it, son, I think of you ...'

Connor winced, rubbing his forehead.

'If you're looking for our forgiveness, you've always had it, son. We're so glad to have you home again, because life is too precious to waste time being sad over the past, isn't it, luv?'

'Yes.' Now his mother was sniffling.

'Thank you, both of you, for not giving up on me.' He'd never made it easy on them.

'We'll always be here for you, son. Always.'

When he spotted Que racing around the bend. 'I've got to go. Que's coming back.'

'Connor?'

'Yes, Mum?'

'Trust Que. She's got good instincts. If she says something is wrong, it probably is.'

'I agree. Que knows there's more to this, she's the one who spotted the signs ...' Que also spoke with a deeper understanding of this situation, and that bothered him more. It's why he wasn't leaving her alone today.

Que could read people and she was a helluva card player, kicking his butt in their friendly games on the back verandah, watching the sunsets. He was going to buy her a proper card table for that back verandah as a gift for all she'd done for him. Did he have time to find her one before he returned to base? Would she accept it?

'I'll keep you posted.' He disconnected the call with a heavy heart, not expecting so much from one phone call. But ever since he'd spilled all to Que, releasing all his inner demons, he felt better. As Que said, you can only do so much with the hand you're dealt in a game and that's by playing one card at a time. And he'd needed to repair that bridge with his parents.

Que leaped up the verandah steps, strode through the front door and headed straight for the fridge. 'Val didn't show up.'

Damn, it was show time.

Que rummaged through her freezer, putting meat bones into a plastic bag, then ripped flowers from her vase, wrapping them in paper.

'What are you doing?'

'These are get-well flowers for Val. The bones are for their dogs, I hope they're friendly.' Que whistled for Princess at the front door and fed him a bone. 'Thanks for cleaning up the breakfast stuff.'

He was becoming domesticated, never leaving grocery bags unpacked by the fridge again. How much he'd changed away from base.

'Did Tommy mention his mother this morning?' Connor asked.

'He said Val's still not well.' She slung her bag over her shoulder and grabbed her car keys. 'Do you still want to come with me?'

'Absolutely.'

'We'll take my car. It's got more muscle than your dad's, and it's got this massive bull bar to knock down fences and gates if needed.'

'Have you ever done that?'

'No. Here, you drive. I hope I'm just being an over-reacting, nosy neighbour.'

Connor hoped for the same.

Connor slowly drove down the lumpy laneway full of dirt rivets and rocks, crowded with overgrown natives that gave way to the Cromwell's homestead. He hadn't been here since he was a kid.

'It looks deserted.' Tall weeds grew through a rusty tractor.

Assorted fences and holding yards were broken, and the hay shed's roof had collapsed on one corner. It resembled a ghost town, not a home. 'It never used to look like this when Val's parents were alive.'

'I've never been here.'

The front door was blocked with an overgrown shrub and piles of broken beer bottles. 'We'll go round the back, it leads directly to the kitchen. There's the dogs.' He pointed at two skinny cattle dogs lying by wooden kennels under a tree. 'I'll put them on the chain before you get out of the car.' Que was clueless when it came to canines, what with Princess being her first dog.

He parked near the dogs, who stood warily.

'Easy, fellas, we're just visiting.' Connor tossed them a bone each. They happily lay by their kennels with tails wagging, clasping their feast between their teeth as he clipped on their chains. They could do with another twenty feeds.

'Okay, they're happy.' Connor opened the passenger door for Que. She stood holding her flowers, staring at the house. The side gutter was barely hanging on, sheets of wall panelling were cracked, some of the eaves were broken, with paint peeling in patches.

The shed creaked as the morning breeze carried dried leaves from dying trees.

But not even a bird chirped.

Nothing.

'Do you think she's home?'

'Tommy said she was.' Que took a deep shaky breath.

He grabbed her hand and gently squeezed it, his plans of staying in the car forgotten. 'I'll be right beside you.'

'Thank you.'

He'd do anything for the lady. They made a good team.

The parched soil crunched with each step to the back of the house, where assorted dead weeds crowded the vegetable patch, poking through the fallen walls of the chook pen. The Hills Hoist leaned to one side, holding an old blanket.

Up the cracked concrete path to the back steps, they approached the backdoor, torn clean off the hinges. Its bottom all smashed in.

'Put on a happy face,' murmured Que. She took another deep breath and pasted on a smile. 'Knock. Knock,' she said through the screen door. 'Hello, Val. It's me Que. I heard you weren't well—'

'No! You can't come in,' said Val in a panic, her voice so distant.

'Quick, hide against the wall. I don't want to scare her,' she whispered to Connor.

He flattened his back against the house. Que had a point. He was a mean-looking man with a crappy reputation.

But Que never saw him that way, except in the beginning and due to his own actions. They'd certainly come a long way in their short time together, even if they weren't technically a couple.

'I've brought some flowers to cheer you up.' Que put her hand on the screen door.

Every instinct made him want to stop her. 'Don't …'

'I'm sorry, I'm not well. You'll have to leave.' Val's voice was shaky, timid even.

'Like hell I will,' Que muttered under her breath, opening the screen door. 'Sorry Val, did you say something? I can't quite make out what you said?' She walked inside, leaving Connor ready for anything. He hated this. He did not want that woman out of his sight, because in the pit of his iron guts, he could feel that something was terribly wrong.

28

'*Yoo-hoo*, it's the neighbour from hell,' called out Que, calm on the outside, inside she was a ball of nerves. 'Where are you, Val?' She stepped into the kitchen as the screen door eerily creaked shut behind her.

Connor nodded at her from the outside. She was relieved he was there.

'Val?' She peered around the poky kitchen where a worn dining table rested against the wall. Another door stood off its hinges, with kitchen cupboards the same.

Gaping holes were scattered across the walls. Fist-sized holes at shoulder height and boot-sized holes at kicking height stood next to badly patched areas. They were everywhere. 'Val?'

'No, don't come in. Go away.'

Fighting her own fear and a screaming urge to run back to Connor, Que entered the shadows of the hallway to find Val pressed up against the wall.

Her heart dropped to the pit of her stomach, she had to force herself not to rush to her friend. 'I brought you some flowers.'

'Go away. You can't be here.' Val crumpled to her knees, hiding her face in her hands as her tears splashed on the floorboards.

'I'm not going anywhere.' Que crouched down to put a tender hand on Val's arm.

Val flinched from the bruising on her arm, exposing her face. Her beautiful face, swollen, her nose broken, teeth were missing, and a massive bruise spread across her jawline. 'Go away.' Val whimpered, with pure misery etched into her broken frame, as her tears fell in a steady stream.

'I'm not going anywhere. I'm your friend, and I'm so sorry for not being here sooner.' Que pulled the poor battered woman to her chest and let Val cry in her arms for some time.

'How about I put the kettle on,' suggested Que when the tears had subsided. 'I'll make us a cup of coffee because I'm lousy at making tea. Come on.' She helped Val limp through to the kitchen, where she gingerly sat as if on a thousand razor blades.

'Val, Connor's here. He's waiting just outside.'

'Why?' Val gasped as her body trembled.

Que patted Val's hands, the only place that wasn't obviously bruised. 'Because Connor was worried about you, too. We're only here to help, okay? Trust me, please.'

It was barely a nod from the poor woman at the kitchen table.

Que put on the kettle and went out the back door to find her hero, looking at her with pure open concern. 'You can come in.'

'Is she okay?'

'No, she's a mess. That's bastard, he's—I wish I'd done something sooner.' She cupped her face, desperate to hold back her tears.

'Hey, we're here now.' He rubbed her shoulders, holding her close, when she shouldn't be finding comfort in the man, she did.

'Come in but go easy, I don't want to spook her.' She grabbed his hand and led him to the kitchen table, where he sat quietly.

Connor remained expressionless, but his eyes flared when he saw Val's condition. 'Hey, Val.'

Val said nothing, shifting to sit sideways on her chair with her back to Connor, pulling her hair down to hide her face.

'Here's the coffee.' Que served coffee and glasses of water for everyone as she tried to work out how to begin without falling into a wretched heap herself.

She dragged her chair to sit in front of Val with their knees almost touching, to gently brush the tangled hair free from Val's face, exposing the full impact of her many bruises. 'Who did this to you?'

'It's my fault …' Val stiffened defensively, fumbling with her glass of water. 'Gary's a good man. He just got upset I burnt dinner, that's all.'

Que frowned. 'I burn dinner all the time and play soccer with my home-made scones. That doesn't account for what he did to you.'

'Easy, babe,' warned Connor.

Que rubbed at her forehead to control her own anger. She needed to get a grip.

'Gary said he's sorry,' whimpered Val with a lisp of swollen lips and missing teeth. 'He loves me.'

'Of course, he does,' replied Que, hoping the bitterness was hidden from her voice. 'I'm not saying Gary doesn't love you. He's probably told you he'll never do it again.'

'Gary's under a lot of pressure. He lost his job on the mine, and the farm isn't working. He's ashamed he's failing and that people in this town will judge him. But he's a good father …'

'But he's failing as a husband.'

'Babe.' Again, Connor's tone was low and loaded, to help her rein in her anger.

Val sat there with silent tears dampening her dress, her breath raspy, her skin a mesh of bruising, displaying the physical abuse. But there was also the emotional abuse. Gary had stripped Val of all her pride and self-respect. Did the poor woman have any spirit left?

'Was Gary always like this?' Que asked.

'No. Never, just …'

'He lost his job, and with the farm not doing so well, he's lost control of the outside world, so he takes it out on you.'

'Yes—no. Gary is a good man. He never does this in front of the children.'

'But they can see their mother is hurting. They're so worried about you.'

'Gary's sorry.'

'And I bet he's the best husband in the world then, too. It's because Gary knows you love him so much, that you're willing to put up with this too.'

Val tilted her head, blinking at her tears, but listening.

Connor remained expressionless. Que couldn't read him at all.

'Do you ever say to yourself that you must try harder to never upset him, to please him, because that man is your entire world,' Que said. 'After all, he's the father of your children, the head of the family, trying to provide for you all. So, you'll walk around on eggshells and sit as if on thousands of razor blades, while sleeping on the edge of a bed that's filled with rusty nails, worried that something might trigger him, and start the nightmare again.'

'Gary doesn't do it all the time,' cried out Val.

'Once is too many!'

'You don't know what you're on about,' said Val, getting defensive.

'Val,' said Que, grabbing her friend's hands. 'I do know. I've felt the burning sensation you get when your hair is being pulled out in large chunks. I remember the hot throbbing pain in your jaw after a punch and the unmistakable feel of a shattering cheekbone from hitting the corner of a kitchen counter. I know how tender bruising across your legs makes it impossible to walk. Forget about chewing food because of the swollen gums and lost teeth.'

'But ...'

Que leaned forward, still holding both Val's hands. 'Has he held a gun to your head, yet?' Que shuddered, her nostrils pinching as she inhaled deeply, with closed eyes, forcing herself to continue because she had to get through to Val. 'How about a knife to the throat? Or is he still using his bare fists and his boots, huh? How many broken ribs have you had? I see he's done the nose and jawline, and I think he's got your collar bone too.'

Val pulled her hands free to hug herself, trying to hide her body, only wincing in pain. 'You know nothing.'

'I've been exactly where you are Val, but worse.'

Val's eyes widened at Que.

Connor's hand dropped to the table as his boots shuffled beneath his seat.

Que didn't want to face Connor, she could only re-grip Val's hands and talk to the woman. 'It started off with the open slap across the face that was followed by a tonne of sorrys. Only to get another backhander a month later, with more sorrys. It's the highs and lows, lady, this addictive cycle of the high when he's sorry and plays the perfect partner. Sadly, it never lasts because the lows get lower each time, working up to using closed fists. Then the boots kicked in, literally, and the hair pulling was more dragging around the house, which is where I suspect you're up to now.'

Val gasped with tears again welling in her bloodshot, swollen eyes.

'But I went and danced straight into the big leagues on so many levels. I got strangled and wore the finger marks around my throat for a week, eating soup because my windpipe was almost crushed. I got stabbed with a fork, knife, screwdriver ...' Que lifted her shirt to expose the scars along her ribs. 'I even had his stupid pistol pressed to my forehead or shoved into my mouth where my teeth cracked on the barrel. And every single freaking time he was so very *very* sorry.'

'Gary's not that bad.'

Que cupped her mouth as the tears squeezed from the corner of her eyes. How could Val say that? She was a mess?

Again, Que grabbed Val's hands, wriggling to the edge of her seat so their knees touched, and stared the poor women in the eye. 'It will get worse, much worse, believe me. I truly wish I could lie to you by filling you full of fairy-tale fantasies, but Gary will get worse if you don't do something today.'

'He won't.'

'Val, it's not just the physical, it's the mental abuse too, because you think that this is your fault. You believe the sorrys he says to you for what he's done. That's denial.' Especially when the woman was covered in countless injuries. 'I was there too, Val. Exactly where you are today.'

'I ... but ... Where ... how—I can't.'

'I get it,' said Que, squeezing Val's hands. 'I used to think that no one out there could possibly help or understand what I was going through. I also thought I didn't deserve help because it was all my fault. '

Val blinked with recognition.

'Honey, this isn't your fault. Trust me.'

'How did you ...'

'Get out?'

Val nodded, licking her swollen split lips.

'My friend found me. I was lucky he did. He refused to go away, taking me to the hospital when I truly thought I wasn't worth it. Billie was only six months old, and I was so scared about what might happen to her. But I was also scared to look after her alone, or to go to a shelter filled with strangers. I didn't want to leave what was meant to be my home, when I so desperately wanted that family. I didn't know how to get out.'

Val sat taller with her mouth open, listening, her breath rasping.

'The man who said he loved me had worn me down so much I believed I wasn't worth it, that I wasn't worthy of friends. That I was all alone.' She leaned down to stare Val in the eye and plead the truth to her. 'But you *are* worth it and you are not alone. You are an amazing person who doesn't deserve this treatment. No one has the right to hit you, especially your partner. And guess what?'

'What?'

'As your friend, I'll help you every step of the way. Because

I'm a survivor, and you can be one, too. You won't have to suffer in silence anymore because I won't let you. So, what do you say, Val? Let's get you the help you deserve.'

29

'**W**as all of that true?' Connor asked Que, leaning his back against the wall as Que paced along the wide hospital corridor.

She hadn't let him touch her since they'd found Val, when he so badly wanted to hold her, to drag her away from this nightmare of a day.

'What you told Val at the house, about what happened to you? Is it true?' It couldn't be. Sure, he'd seen the scars, even tracing over them with his tongue, exploring her curves, but never in his wildest dreams had he imagined this.

Que stopped pacing, hugging herself, and nodded.

She was a lot stronger than he'd realised.

'Billie's father?'

'Yeah. The freak got jealous of his own child, saying I was spending too much time on her and not him. It triggered him, not getting the attention from me. Before that, he treated me like a toy. Jeremy was, is, very possessive.'

Is? 'How so?'

'Um …' She peered down the corridor, avoiding his question.

'Hey, how possessive?'

She shrugged, holding herself tighter. 'Jeremy used to call me his cocaine. He loved knowing the power he had over me, knowing how desperately I wanted to be part of a family, to have a home …'

'You stayed because you wanted that family and home.' Which was understandable if Que never got that as a child. What a nightmare it must have been for her, to go from one form of family neglect to only end up in another.

'Sadly, it was nothing but lust and lies.'

'Hey, not all families are like that.' He reached for her, but she stepped away, pacing the corridor again. Who was he to talk about families? Not when he'd been living like a loner, shunning his own family for over fifteen years.

But as a kid, he'd had a happy childhood and he'd seen how hard Que was trying to provide the same for Billie, buying a house with a huge shed to skate in.

He leaned his back against the wall, flicking at the red band wrapped around his wrist, made by the little girl with pigtails, while the mother paced the tiles.

It then hit him in a barrage of fire, his throat thickened as his heart ka-thumped in hard heavy beats.

Billie had a bad father! Billie the amazing smiling, happy kid who was an angel of sunshine, never knew her father. She was a good kid, because of Que, despite her father's blood.

That's why Que never judged him!

That's why Que was so willing to believe in Connor, to help him understand that he wasn't bad because of his blood at all. Que truly understood more of his situation than he had ever realised.

Damn, he wanted to hold her so bad—but in her agitated state, she was fighting her own past.

No wonder she told him they could never have a long-term relationship. *No such thing as forever*, she'd said to him in the beginning. They weren't even dating, just having sleepovers until he went back to work, that was her rule. He now truly understood why she had those rules.

'Was it Mike who found you?' He asked.

'Yeah. I was lucky. We were living in Melbourne and he was on his way to New Zealand for a holiday and decided at the last minute to call in to visit.' She paced faster, frowning, head down. 'Some friend, huh? I've put Mike through hell.'

'What did Mike find, Que?'

She stopped pacing and stared at the floor tiles with no emotion. 'Me. Unconscious on the floor in a pool of blood. Billie sitting beside me, screaming.'

'Bloody hell—' He dragged his fingers through his hair, then pulled her to his chest, wrapping his arms around her. He never wanted to let her go.

'Mike took care of Billie while I was in hospital, and as soon as they discharged me, he moved us to Adelaide. Until ...'

'Until, what?'

'Jeremy found us ... so we ran.'

His eyes widened as his heart dropped. 'Are you and Billie —'

'Connor?' It was Marcus, removing his police cap, and for the first time Connor saw Marcus's weapons. Two Glocks, shoulder holstered over his bullet-proof vest with magazines clipped to his police belt, along with cuffs, baton, and taser. It was quite the contrast to the white coat of the blond doctor beside him. 'Hey, Que. This is

Dr Stewart Mannen, he's been treating Val.'

'How is she, doctor?' Que pushed away from Connor, wiping at her tears.

'She's got a lot of broken bones. We've reset her forearm and fractured shoulder blade, but we're more worried about her punctured lung. I'm in conversations with the city specialists now on whether to evac her or not.'

'You're kidding?' Connor said as Que stared with enormous eyes.

'Val is very lucky you found her when you did,' replied Doctor Mannen. 'Had it been much longer the internal bleeding might have been fatal.'

Connor gripped Que to his side, as his own guts recoiled in horror.

'Who found her?' Marcus asked.

'Me. Connor came with me.' She looked at him like he was some hero when he'd been stupid for not listening to Que earlier. His mother had told him to trust Que's instincts, that in this case were spot on.

'What made you go over?' Marcus asked.

Que said nothing, which was typical, but there was so much more to her story she wasn't telling him. He knew it.

'Que noticed things weren't right, spotting bruising on Val's arms earlier. Then it seemed okay until Val's son told Que that Val was attacked by bees and was having an allergic reaction to them that had her face all swollen. Que asked me what bees we had ...' *Days ago*. They could have easily turned the ute around in Que's driveway, then and there on Mother's Day, and gone to check on Val. But they hadn't.

'Native bees don't sting,' said Marcus, with the doctor nodding beside them. 'Did Val tell you who assaulted her?'

'Her husband.' Que spoke through clenched teeth.

'Right. Well, I'll need statements from you two.'

'What about Val?' Que demanded.

'She won't be going anywhere for a while,' replied the Doctor.

'What about her children? Her daughter is in the same class as mine? And her son.'

'Does Val have any family?'

Que shrugged, and Connor shook his head.

'Can I take them?' She asked Marcus. 'Please. I'm only across the road. The kids know me and my place. They skate there in the afternoons, they'll be safe there.'

'I'm with Que. Me and my parents will help her with the children. Just tell us what we can do, Marcus.'

'We'll need the mother's consent. A nod is all I'd need. Okay?'

'I'll get it. Where is she?' Que asked, looking determined.

'I can show you,' said the Doctor.

'Hey, Que …' Marcus pulled her to a stop. 'Would you mind sticking around?'

'What for?' With panicky wide eyes, she moved closer to Connor.

'I'd like someone to support Val while I ask her questions. Do you think you can handle it?'

Her whole demeanour softened as she nodded.

'Want me there?' Connor asked Que.

'No offence, mate, but I don't want too many people in Val's room,' said the doctor.

'Que, I'll be right here. I'm not going anywhere.' *Damn straight.*

She cupped his cheek, barely brushing her lips against his. 'Thank you. I mean that, thank you for everything.'

She walked away with Marcus by her side and never looked back.

That kiss felt like goodbye.

30

Que followed the doctor down the hospital corridors with the police sergeant at her side. Ahead, the green EXIT sign shone brightly, tempting her to run through that door, bundle up her baby into the Mighty T and not look back.

She rubbed at the scar on her arm, as the memory of her other scars burned across her skin. Her scalp tingled where hair had been ripped out in clumps. She touched the lump on her cheekbone that had been rebuilt with a fancy plate. She was lucky to still be alive.

But she should have gone to Val sooner.

'Here we are …' The doctor opened the door to Val's room.

Marcus stopped in front of Que, blocking her from going in. 'Que, I'll only ask the basics to begin with. If she's up to it, we'll just let her talk. It's best to get it out in one hit if we can.'

'To do what?'

'So I can act today.'

'Yeah, right?' She'd heard that before.

'Que, I'm serious. I don't know what your story is, but I'm guessing you don't like the police.'

'Let's say they didn't do what they promised.'

'Which was?'

'Keep people safe.'

'This is my town,' Marcus said, jabbing his thumb at his police vest. 'Now that I know of Val's situation, you bet I'll be doing my best. But first, I need Val to say it was her husband and to tell me what he did, then I'll kick down some doors.'

'I know you need proof, facts …' She understood that. 'I just should have done something sooner.'

'That's what I say to myself every time I show up to a job like this.'

'It might be just a job to you, but people are hurting.'

'I know …' Marcus narrowed his eyes at her as his tone softened. 'Que, are you a survivor?'

She didn't say a word, but her hot angry tears were enough for the cop to get the message.

'I promise you I'll do my best for Val and her kids, but we need Val to answer my questions. Can you help me with that, so I can do my job?'

Que nodded. 'I hope you do your job well, Marcus. Lives depend on it.'

Pressing the heels of her palms against her eyes to push back her tears, she took a deep breath. This wasn't about her anymore, she needed to help her friend.

Machines beeped in the sterile room where a large bed held the frail frame of a woman covered in bandages. Val's arm was in a restrictive sling that held up her collar bone, with drips and bottles running thin hoses to her arms like some science experiment.

Que didn't know where to look.

'Hey, there's my champion.' She tenderly held Val's hand, giving it a squeeze. 'The doctor said they're keeping you here for a bit.'

'My children?'

'I'll take care of them. I'll pick them up at school and I promise to spoil them rotten. You just have to say the word.'

'But will the school let you?'

'I'll call the principal and speak to her on your behalf, if you give your consent?' Marcus asked.

'Sure. My children would like that, they love visiting Que's place,' murmured Val.

Marcus nodded at Que as a flood of relief released the tension in her bones. 'Do you want me to bring them in and see you today?'

'Not today, tomorrow maybe?'

'Tomorrow sounds good. I like tomorrows ... You're going to be okay now. Marcus wants to help you if you're ready to talk?'

'Can you stay with me?'

'You bet.' Que sat by Val's bedside, holding her friend's hand, passing fresh tissues, holding the straw for water, anything and everything, as Marcus took down all the details ...

Leaving Val's hospital room, Que's every step was in slow motion, as if stuck in a see-through world of sludge. As the door swished shut behind her, she swayed on the spot, unsure where to go or what to do.

Marcus stepped up beside her with clipboard in hand. 'Are you okay?'

'Do you seriously expect me to answer that?'

Marcus shrugged.

'I couldn't do your job.'

'Yeah, days like this it sucks.' He adjusted his cap. 'I'll need some ID when you come in and sign the statements. I'll call the school principal now, for you to collect her kids. Now or after school?'

For a clock watcher it was the first time that day she took note of the time. 'School finishes soon. I'll get them then. What ID?'

'Licence,' Marcus replied, scrolling through his phone. 'Don't worry, I won't bother you with the other stuff. I'll be in touch shortly. I have Connor's number.' With a steady stride down the corridor, Marcus was a man in charge, giving orders over the radio.

But was Marcus a man of his word?

Or would Gary get away with it because he had some fancy lawyer who knew how to play the system. A system meant to protect the victims, instead of letting the guy walk free to nail the domestic violence orders on her front door with a brand-new hunting knife!

She knew very well that threats made great coffin nails.

'Hey.' Connor tenderly put his arm around her.

She burrowed into his shirt, gripping it in her fists as the tears fell. She howled, doubling over in pain.

Connor moved to a nearby seat and held her in his arms as she cried for Val, she cried for herself, and she cried for every other woman who was still suffering alone in the shadows. She cried for them all.

As the tears overwhelmed her, Connor kept hold of her like an anchor, as she struggled to breathe in a sea of overwhelming emotion, shipwrecked. She would have drowned if he wasn't there.

Que lifted her head from his chest, wiping her tears away. She had things to do. She had children to take care of. 'I want to stock up on some junk food before we collect the children. I'm in serious need of a sugar hit and buckets of ice cream.'

'Sounds good. I'm in the mood for spiders.'

'Huh?'

'My thing when I was a kid, soda and ice cream. My treat. Also, I told my parents what's going on, Mum's cooking tea for everyone.'

'That is so nice.' She cupped her mouth to prevent another sob. To have parents to help in situations like this was a blessing.

'Hey, come on, let's go home.'

Home? Was it really a home? With Connor only in town for a few more weeks, it was nice to dream of that home and family for just a split second.

But that desperate fantasy was what got her trapped inside her personal hell in the first place—trying to survive her past meant she wasn't living a life at all.

31

onnor paced up and down Que's front verandah, while old school 80s music blasted from the shed. The music had his parents dancing and singing in Que's kitchen, while three young children, Tommy, Maddy and Billie, rolled under disco lights in the shed up the back. It was like some party going on, while Que finished poking around her caravan and headed back inside the house.

Connor did not like that caravan. Not now that he knew what it represented.

What's worse was that he hadn't had a chance to talk one-on-one with Que, not since she cried in the hospital corridor after leaving Val's room earlier today. He'd never felt so helpless, unable to stop the tears that had dampened his shirt.

He had no idea how to cope with this emotional stuff, or how to fix this. Give him a gun and point him at an enemy — that he could deal with. But kids, puppies, and parents? Bah!

A twin-cab ute rolled up the drive.

'Bark, dog.' He growled at Princess, their so-called guard dog, who finally started barking, his body on alert.

'Get 'im.' Connor needed the dog to toughen the hell up. He

had a family to protect, like this military man who was on high alert until Gary was behind bars. He wasn't going to relax until Marcus called with the news.

Everyone stopped, as Princess barked down the driveway to meet the car.

'It's Uncle Mike!' Billie squealed. With her pig tails flapping, she rolled off the shed's concrete and onto the dust on her skates. She literally rolled in dust. Connor had never seen anything like it.

The Landcruiser ute, bearing a university emblem on its doors, pulled to a stop where the ginger stepped out to give the dog a hearty pat. That dog had to stop being so friendly with every goddamned male in this yard.

But Connor also had to remember, this wasn't his yard either.

Behind him, Que stepped out onto the verandah. 'Huh. Mike must have broken some land-speed record to get here so quick.'

'You knew he was coming?'

'I called him while we were waiting at the hospital. I couldn't have stopped him from coming if I'd tried. He does that.'

'When were you going to tell me?' She did that a lot, not telling him things, especially about her past. He knew, deep down to the marrow of his bones, there was so much more to Que's story. Didn't she trust him enough to share?

'Uncle Mike,' squealed Billie, hugging the ginger.

'Hey, munchkin.' Mike scooped up the little girl, holding her high in his arms. 'You've been eating too many of them magic veggies, the way you're growing.'

Connor wiped away his frown. He had no right to interfere. Not when Mike was the one who'd been there for Que.

So where did Connor stand in this family's picture, except to guard the house of adults, kids, and an overgrown puppy. This was meant to be a simple working holiday, indulging in a summer fling with the lady. He didn't sign up for this.

He watched Que with a sick knot of hot lead tightening his guts over what had happened to her. What sort of sick monster would callously hurt an amazing woman like Que? Would she dare trust a man again?

'Hey, it's the boy who never grew up, in a man's body,' said Que, all smiles. It was a relieved smile that Connor hadn't seen all day. How come Mike got that smile?

'Grown-ups are boring, and they do this thing called being responsible.' Mike gave Que a long, warm hug, lifting her off her feet.

This time, Connor didn't bother hiding the frown.

Why was that ginger here?

Billie, wearing a wide smile, waved at him. 'Connor, come and meet Uncle Mike. You'll like him, I promise.'

Did he dare join in and become a part of their world? A world he'd never thought he deserved to be a part of ...

Connor had never admitted it to anyone, but in those moments when loneliness weighed heavily, he was just like Que. He too wanted a family, to live in a home filled with happy memories. Did he dare dream big, or should he get back on his bike and report to base, where life was so much simpler?

32

'How're you doin' with all this, my sweet?' Mike asked Que, slinging his arm over her shoulders. 'I've been worried. I know how close this is for you.'

'Getting there. Thank you for coming.'

'Like I wouldn't show. So where do I crash?'

'Couch?'

'Cool. Considering I bought the thing.' Mike dragged his duffel bag from inside the ute and headed for the house. 'Got some company, I see?'

The house had that crowded feeling again, but this time Que didn't mind the company. Especially the tall, dark, brooding male, who was lean and muscular mean, being dragged down the front verandah steps by Billie in her skates. 'Mike, this is Connor.'

'Hey, it's the Sorry man,' said Mike, shaking Connor's hand.

'Behave, Mike,' warned Que.

'Chill, will ya, I know you're sleeping with him, my sweet,' Mike said cheekily to Que. 'How're you doin', Connor?'

'All right,' said Connor, warily.

Was Connor jealous of Mike? Why? It was just Mike.

'And these are Connor's parents, Bertha and Richard.' It was such a warm cosy feeling having them here with their parental wisdom, volunteering to do the cooking and laundry. All while the children roller-skated, excited to be having a sleepover. Que didn't know what to tell Maddy and Tommy about their mother, except that she wasn't well.

'Are you the neighbours? The bloke who grows those amazing tomatoes?' Mike asked.

'Yes, I am,' said Richard with a proud nod of his big cowboy hat, shaking Mike's hand.

'Hey, munchkin?'

'Yes, Uncle Mike?'

'Can you and your friends get the seedlings I've got stashed on the floor of the ute? We'll have a go at prettying up that boghole into the pond your mum wants, but full of stuff we can eat.'

'Better not be a vegetable garden?' Que asked with a raised eyebrow.

'No, my sweet, you'll have to graduate a few seasons for that. We'll start you slow, won't we munchkin? Let's get a little muddy, eh?'

'Absolutely, Uncle Mike.' Billie's pigtails bounced up and down, the excitement was infectious.

'Skates off, baby.' Que warned, 'No more rolling in the dirt after I spent ages fixing those wheels.'

The kid tore them off, running for the shed towards her friends. 'Tommy. Maddy. Get your shoes on to come and help.'

'Are you doing some gardening?' Richard asked, poking up the brim of his hat.

'I am …' Mike grabbed his Akubra from his duffel.

Should Que get one of those hats, now that she was living in the country? Except Connor wore his snug baseball cap backwards, watching everyone warily.

'Dad,' said Connor, 'Mike's a horticulturist, a lecturer at Darwin University.'

'It's just a fancy name for a student who never wants to leave school,' said Mike cheekily. 'Those tomatoes of yours, Richard, I'd love to learn how you grew them.'

'What are you planting out the back?' Richard asked as the keen farmer.

'I've got some sweet potato, watercress, water spinach, water chestnuts, and some taro. Don't worry, my sweet,' Mike said, tugging on Que's long ponytail, 'I'll share recipes on what to cook with them.'

'Do I have to water it?' Que asked.

'It's a boghole, because of your natural landscape's design, and with the irrigation on timers, no. All you have to do is keep that ribbon-wearing water buffalo out of there for at least six weeks.'

'All we can do is try,' said Billie, running up with her friends now all wearing boots, 'if Momma remembers to lock the gate.'

'I won't forget, baby.'

'I won't let her,' said Connor. With his wraparound shades on, she couldn't read his expression.

'Can we plant these now, Uncle Mike?' called out Billie, with Tommy and Maddy struggling to carry the punnets of seedlings.

'Sure. Care to supervise, Richard, while you tell me how you grow those tomatoes?'

Que followed from the verandah and smiled, watching Mike

play pied piper with almost everyone following him to the boghole of mud that was getting a makeover. For a moment all her stress was gone.

'Mike's a cheeky bloke,' said Connor, moving quietly to stand beside her in the verandah's deep shade with the view of the outback and her boghole.

He was so damned stealthy, sneaking up on her like that.

'Yeah, he can be. I'm surprised Mike hasn't got a punch in the mouth for it.'

Connor sniffed.

'Mike is harmless. He means well, and he's a wonderful friend,' she said, wrapping an arm around his strong bicep.

'Have you got some water up in that fancy bar of yours?' Mike asked, skipping up the back steps.

'Sure.' Que went to join him. 'Should I fill up the water cooler for everyone?'

'I think I left it under the sink.' Mike rummaged around in the outdoor kitchen area he'd built. 'Have you used the barbecue?'

Que dragged out a bag of ice from the nearby freezer. 'Connor does. He's brilliant at it.'

'Good to hear. You've told him about us, right?'

'What, that we're just friends. Sure.'

'Well, he doesn't believe you,' Mike said, as he filled up the water container. 'Want me to talk to him?'

'No.' Mike was right, Connor did seem jealous, when he had no reason to be. She'd never looked at Mike, or any other man, the way she did with Connor.

'How much does Connor know?' Mike asked as he put the lid

on the cooler and Que gathered some plastic cups.

'Only that day you found me.'

'And the rest?'

Que didn't know how to even start that sort of conversation. 'Connor's dealing with more than enough right now.'

'No, the man looks like he's stepping up to the plate to protect everyone. You need that.'

'No, I don't.'

'Who do you think you're talking to?'

A mobile rang, its shrilly sound echoed from the far corner of the verandah where Connor was watching the driveway, digging around in his cargo pockets for his phone. 'Yeah?'

Que watched his strong strides, the way his muscles in his shirt shifted.

Mike whispered in her ear, 'You really like him.'

'Connor is only here on temporary leave, then he'll go back to base or whatever it is he does in the military.' She couldn't afford to get attached to someone who could leave at any minute, especially when she was packed and ready to roll herself if it became necessary.

Connor strolled up, sliding his phone away. 'That was Marcus. He wants us to come in and sign our statements.'

'What? Why?'

'He needs them to raise a DVO.'

'Why hasn't he arrested this guy on assault, already? His wife is in hospital.'

'Shh, my sweet, calm down,' said Mike. 'There must be a perfectly reasonable explanation for this. Right, Connor?'

'Marcus has his officers looking for Gary now, and he wants

the entire file ready for the prosecutor to transport him straight to night court in the city. He wants Gary gone and out of this town today.'

'Can Marcus do that?' Que asked.

'If Marcus says he can, he will. That is why we need to sign statements now. So grab your ID and let's go.'

She looked at Mike. 'I can't.'

'Why not?' Connor asked. 'You want Gary arrested as much as I do.'

'I do, but I can't.'

Mike nudged Que 'Sweetness—'

'Stay out of this,' Connor said.

'No, mate, this is me getting in the middle. For the record, I'm on your side. It's this one,' Mike said, tossing his thumb at Que, 'who needs to fess up.'

'Hey, you're supposed to be my friend.'

'I am. And I'm helping you. Connor's here, *and* you've got a cop on call. Stop making excuses and tell Connor everything, or I will. I'll keep everyone occupied playing in the mud.' Mike jumped off the porch with the large watercooler swinging in one hand. 'Hey, kids, who wants some sunscreen and this thing they call water?'

That left Que and Connor alone on the verandah.

'Que, what is Mike talking about.'

'How well do you know Marcus?'

'Very well. Why?'

'Um ...' She gazed at the children, free from all adult burdens. She wanted to play with them.

'Hey ...' Connor gently stroked her hair, dragging her

attention back to his questioning eyes. 'I'm not going anywhere, Que, so you may as well tell me everything.'

'Only if you swear that you'll still go back to your job when your mum is better, just like you'd planned.'

33

For the first time in his life, Connor willingly entered the Elsie Creek Police Station through the front door, instead of being dragged from the back of a paddy wagon in handcuffs.

The place was the same, with a large front reception desk barring the outside world. Behind it was their muster room with chairs scattered around the old boardroom table. A silent television sat on top of the fridge, which stood next to the sinks and a bench, where a kettle rested beside assorted coffee and tea supplies.

The offices ran down the right, with the corridor leading to the cells and the police interview rooms out the back. Those areas he remembered well.

The front was where his parents used to wait for him.

'Hey, you made it,' said Marcus, coming out of the Sergeant's office. An office he had never in a million years expected Marcus to end up occupying.

'Here.' Connor plonked a bottle of bourbon on the counter. 'Have you got a minute.'

'Sure, step into my office.' Marcus booted his office door wide as Connor passed the bottle of bourbon to the man in uniform. 'Take a load off.'

Load, ha. Connor's shoulders had never felt so damned heavy, suffering from shell shock after the explosion let off by the little lady back at the house.

'Where's Que?'

'Not coming.'

'Why not? I need her statement more to seal the deal.'

'That's the thing, she can't have her name on anything.'

'Why not?'

'Que isn't Quentin Lawsten.'

'I know.'

'What do you mean, you know?' Connor scowled at the cop standing on the other side of the large desk.

'I did a check.'

'You always were a nosy prick.'

'Because she's hiding something. The woman has nothing in her name, not that house, the car or van. It's all some company name in Sydney.'

'She works for herself, maybe it's for business expenses.'

'A single mother who is linked to one of the most expensive legal firms in Sydney. And before you reach over and throttle me —'

'Don't say it's your job.'

'Que is on the run, isn't she?'

'Yeah.' Connor collapsed back in his chair.

'Who is she running from?'

'Her husband. She's been running from him for more than four years.'

This time, it was Marcus's turn to sit heavily in the chair, opening the bottom drawer of his large desk and pulling out two shot glasses. There was a sharp crack as he broke the bottle's seal, followed by the glug-glug-glug as he poured two nips of bourbon. He held one out to Connor.

Connor took his glass, tapped it against Marcus's in a silent salute, and they both took a swig.

'Que's got a restraining order against her husband that is valid in every state in Australia. Her brother's law firm manages them.'

'The same law firm for the house?' Marcus asked.

'Yeah. But those DVOs have never stopped her husband from going after Que.'

'So that's why she's in the van … and moved out here … And why she has no faith in the police.' Marcus rubbed his forehead.

'Que was hoping they'd be safe out here.' Connor had seen Que's genuine fear when she'd told him her story, her vulnerability exposed with none of her protective layers. He'd still be by her side if he weren't here for her protection. But he'd made a point of taking her car, so that she couldn't run on him in that damned van. 'Que won't sign the statements because she doesn't want her name to show up in the system.'

'That's why she freaked out about changing over her licence.'

'Que has a fake licence to protect herself. And I'm only telling you that as a friend.'

'I get it. I'm only after bad guys.'

They both snorted at the irony of two of the town's worst offenders now on the right side of the law. 'So, her name isn't Quentin Lawsten?'

'She was born Quentin Mornell.'

'Any relation to the high court Judge Mornell?'

'Yeah, that's her mother. And her father was a chief magistrate.'

'Huh …' Marcus's eyebrows rose as he took another sip of his bourbon.

'But the law hasn't protected Que, not when her husband put Que in hospital when Billie was six months old, and she's been running from him ever since. He should have been in jail.' And Que was ready to make a break for it, today. He could see it.

It all made sense. It's why Que never asked him questions or talked of long-term plans, because she was ready to run in a second. She was committing to no one and nothing but her daughter, for their own safety.

They were surviving—not living—just surviving.

It's how he chose to live, to not get emotionally involved, while Que was surviving for completely different reasons.

'Can you find out where this arsehole is?' Connor wanted this to end, he had to protect Que and Billie.

'Why hasn't Que divorced him?' Marcus asked.

Connor snorted over the rim of his glass, tossing back the last of the bourbon. 'I asked the same question. Believe me, she wants to. But he's refusing to divorce Que, trying to claim full custody of Billie, despite the domestic violence order against him. He's filed kidnapping charges against her. You know the law, officer …'

'Federal always trumps state or territory.'

'There's some legal irony for you.'

Marcus sat up in his chair, raking fingers through his dark hair. 'Does Que know where he is?'

'His last known address was in Esperance, WA, but he showed up in Tasmania when she was there. She barely got out.'

'Is Que's daughter aware of any of this?'

'No. Not a clue. The thing is, Que says Billie's father never had any interest in his daughter, that the violence started after she was born because the husband was jealous. Billie is an amazing kid any normal father would be proud of.'

'So, this man only wants Que, eh?'

Connor gripped his glass in his hand as if it was around this man's throat. 'Que says he's angry at her for leaving him. But Mike, her friend who just rocked up at the house, told me Que's husband is nuts and completely obsessed with her. Her husband believes Que is his property and loves her in some sick, twisted way. Last year, while Mike was working in Queensland, Que's husband approached him and threatened to blow his head off if he didn't say where Que was. The same gun he cracked Que's teeth with—' Connor was going to kill this bastard.

'Did this Mike give her up?'

'No.' Connor had to admire Mike for that. 'But for Mike's safety, Que ran in the opposite direction, and then Mike moved interstate to work here in the Territory. Que is terrified her husband will show up here. She's got that damn van of hers ready to run at a moment's notice.'

'And you're terrified she'll leave you behind. That's not a question, that's a fact, mate, I can see it. Here, make yourself useful. Go over your statement about Val's husband, Gary.' Marcus put a folder and pen in front of Connor.

Connor scrubbed a heavy hand over his ruddy face. With the

horror of poor Val this morning, then learning of the terror Que had been living with for years, it was the worst day ever for heartache. 'What's happening with Val? Have you arrested Gary yet?'

'I've got my entire team looking for him to execute the assault warrant. With your paperwork, I'll bump up the charges. I'd still need Que's signature to seal the case.'

'She can't. Believe me, Que is gutted that she can't defend her friend, but she can't risk herself either.'

'I get it.' Marcus nodded. 'While you read that, I'll see what we can find out about Que's husband. Do you think he's still looking for Que?'

'With how scared Que is, absolutely.'

'What's his name?'

'Jeremy Rawls.' A name Connor would never forget. 'If you can't find him, I will.'

34

Que jerked awake as the alarm clock went off on her bedside table, slamming on the button to silence it. She didn't want to get up, not with her body aching from stress and a poor night's sleep.

'I want to say something.' Connor slid his arm around her, holding her in place to look at him. Wide awake.

'Did you get any sleep?'

He shrugged, with worry crinkling the corners of his eyes.

'What's wrong, sweetheart?' She stroked the coarse stubble on his cheek, following his strong jawline. He tenderly grabbed her hand and kissed her fingertips.

'I love you, Que.'

She froze.

No. This could not be happening.

'I've got to get up. I've got stuff to do.' She jumped out of bed and hurried out to the kitchen.

Connor was never meant to say that. Telling him the horrors of her past should have scared him off. He couldn't mean that. It was purely a reaction to her horrible history.

The only problem was her heart wanted to believe it.

Why the hell did he have to go and say that for?

She flicked on the coffee machine and shoved bread into the toaster. With her thoughts shifting into overdrive, she struggled to focus.

'Are you upset with me?' Connor appeared behind her and grabbed the cups out of the cupboard to prepare their coffee as he did most mornings, while Que made breakfast.

It had become some unspoken routine between them that worked magically these past few weeks. Or month. Hold on, how long had Connor been sleeping over?

'What? No.'

'Yes, you are,' he said. 'You're working your way up to it. But what I said was true.'

'And I told you from the beginning that this thing between us—'

'I know what you said, and I wholeheartedly agreed at the time. But it happened. I can't help how I feel about you. Take this.' Connor passed her a cup of coffee.

'Thanks …' She paused to take a sip from the mug. 'Well, your timing's lousy.'

'I don't think so.'

'Oh, come on …' She pointed to Billie's room, where there was a slumber party for the neighbour's children.

'It's the perfect time, especially with what's been happening.'

'Hey, you're leaving soon.'

'I don't have to go anywhere. I'm on compassionate leave and can get discharged anytime with a full military pension. I have a choice in that, but I have no choice in how I feel about you. Que, I love you.'

'No, you don't.'

'Yes, I do. When I say I love you, I love you more than the bad days ahead. I love your more than any fight you'll try and pick with me. And I'll love you more than any distance you're trying to put between us, or any other obstacle you want to throw in our way, I will still love you.'

'It's just lust. This is just some convenient girl-next-door affair. We had a deal.'

'And I'm breaking all the rules by saying I love you, because this is much more than lust. We flipped that lid and climbed that mountain, babe, and we're now knee deep in love. Welcome to the big leagues, where I love you now, and will love you more and will love you the most. And that includes that little kid with pigtails and roller skates.'

'You're only saying that because you have this need to protect us.'

'Absolutely, I want to protect you both because I LOVE YOU.'

'Is this some pre-dawn lover's quarrel?' Mike sat up from the couch, scratching his head.

She'd forgotten he was there.

'No, we're not quarrelling,' said Que, raising her chin at Connor.

'Yes, we are.' Connor ignored Mike, narrowing his eyes at Que.

'Well, I hope the coffee's made.' Mike pushed off the couch and stretched lazily, then took a seat on a kitchen stool on the other side of the island bench. 'Do I need to play the part of a pre-marriage couple's counsellor before breakfast?'

Que frowned at her friend as Connor passed Mike a coffee.

'Or do you two usually debate everything first thing in the morning?' Mike leaned his elbow on the counter, resting his chin on his palm, while stirring his coffee.

'*No,*' Connor and Que replied in unison.

'It's none of your business, Mike,' said Que firmly.

'Fine, if that's how you feel.' Mike took a sip of his coffee while Connor and Que worked together getting breakfast and school lunches organised. 'But I have to say, you are game, Connor, in telling little Miss Loveless here you love her.'

Connor frowned at Mike.

'Que thinks she doesn't know how to love—'

'Bull,' Que said defensively.

'You do too.' Mike pointed his cup at her. 'You see, Connor, Que's parents didn't show our darling Que any form of love. Really, the only unconditional love she's ever had is from Billie. Then there's the best friend brotherly kind of love that Que and I share.'

'Bull,' exclaimed Que, again.

'For an intelligent woman, your vocabulary this morning is not that crash hot, my sweet,' said Mike. 'Que you love Connor, except it scares the crap out of you.'

Connor grinned at Que.

'Bull!' Honestly, Que didn't know what else to say.

'You do too, my sweet. You love the guy and I reckon you've been in love for a while now. At least Connor here's man enough to say it.'

Que opened her mouth to say something, but Mike put his hand up to stop her.

'Ah, no more bull. I've known you long enough to make my judgement on the matter. You just don't want to admit it, because I don't think you've ever truly been in love with anyone before, until Connor here.'

She wanted to hit Mike over the head with the frying pan. But what's worse was Connor was leaning back against the counter, gloating at her.

'You're also worried that what happened to you with Billie's father is going to happen again,' said Mike. 'And, well, I honestly believe Connor here would never hurt you.'

'Thanks, mate.' Connor nodded at Mike.

She couldn't believe it. The two men had just bromance-bonded over coffee.

'Bull!'

'Seriously, my sweet?' Mike grinned at her. 'Besides, you've been alone most of your life, moving on before getting attached to anyone. But you've been seeing Connor for almost two months?' Mike asked, looking at Connor.

'Yeah, just on seven weeks now,' replied Connor with a casual nod.

Her eyes widened at that revelation.

'And before Connor here, it's been nearly five years since you were with Billie's father, who you only married because you desperately wanted a family. We both know you never really loved Jeremy to begin with, and you certainly don't love him now. So why not give this new love a chance? Isn't that some song?'

Speechless, Que stood with her mouth wide open. Mike, her best friend, was siding with Connor, who was not supposed to confess his love for her, because he should be leaving soon. But now both men, wearing smug expressions, were ganging up on her like brothers.

'Aarrggghhh.' Que stormed off to the bathroom with both men chuckling behind her. This was not happening.

35

Connor cruised down the driveway in his dad's ute with Mike in the passenger seat, while Que and the children rode in the back tray for the quick trip from the house to the road. Chaos had new meaning for Connor, in the team effort it took to get three small children dressed, fed, and ready for school, which gave Que the perfect chance to avoid him.

Now that same tribe of children, with a pampered pooch and a water buffalo wearing ribbons for company, waited for the big yellow school bus to leave, with Que waving at the children from the side of the road.

Connor had told no one he loved them before. No one. Not even his adopted parents. Would Que ever say it back?

'Did that police friend of yours find Que's ex, Jeremy?' Mike asked from the passenger seat, while they waited on Que.

'Not yet.' But Connor now knew all about Jeremy Rawls and the long string of offences the idiot had racked up chasing after Que. He'd seen it all on Marcus's work PC, including the images of a battered Que that ripped his heart out. The man was an animal.

'What about the neighbour?'

'No sign of him yet. Marcus will call us as soon as he's got Gary in custody.' Then he'd relax a little. But, until then, Connor was not letting Que out of his sight. Cecil the water buffalo sniffed at Que's hair, making him grin at her smile. Damn, she was pretty.

He *loved her*—didn't that make his heart swell in his chest.

'You're riding shotgun, so you get to play gate keeper.'

'Yeah, right.' Mike opened the passenger door. 'You know she's ordered an automatic gate for this place.'

'Not a bad idea.' So would eight-foot-high fences topped with razor wire and 240 volts, with land mines set on the inner perimeter.

Now he understood why Que wanted those trees for privacy.

Connor scrubbed at his forehead and stared at the vision before him, the way the sun made her hair glisten, and her smile was radiant. It was still there. Only thing was she was smiling at the water buffalo wearing bright neon pink ribbons.

'Aw, sorry mate, I know,' Que said to the stumpy legged buffalo. 'Two days in a row we can't share our wise words with the world. But here, we've got some really cool green gunk that this horticulturist reckons you'll love. He's this greenie who's camping on my couch.'

'I paid for the couch. I like that couch,' Mike said, leaning on the gatepost as Connor drove past.

'Lock it, mate,' said Connor.

'No worries, mate.'

'Ugh, they're going to start mansplaining everything to me any second now,' she said to the buffalo with its mouth full. 'There's too much testosterone in my little house. It's not built for that much manliness under one roof, especially when they're ganging up on me like this.'

'Stop complaining, you love it,' called out Mike. 'Oh, look, there's that word again. L. O. V. E. I must find that love song.'

'Get in the car, the pair of you,' said Connor with humour in his voice.

Que sat between the men who'd become fast friends over bowls of cereal with conversations that went from sports to bikes, discovering they had a lot in common.

Most of all, Mike was on Connor's side over Que's feelings for him. They both understood why she wouldn't admit it. He just wished she did.

'So, what are we here for?' Mike asked as Connor drove them across the road to the neighbours' property.

'To feed the dogs and Que needs to get stuff.' Connor steered them down the small rocky laneway, with his eyes warily taking in the countryside.

'I want to get some personal things for Val for the hospital.'

'Ah, she speaks,' said Mike cheekily.

She glared at her best friend.

Both men chuckled at her. Connor patted her knee as they drove up to the house.

'Man, what a dump,' Mike said. 'Are they broke?'

'It never used to look like this,' Connor said. 'Mum was telling me Val's parents were houseproud farmers.'

'Do you think it's what tipped Gary over the edge?' Mike asked Que. 'You said Val was married to him for ten years.'

'No excuse,' said Connor coldly. 'No man should ever hurt a female.' Que might not say the L-word, but at least she gave him a soft smile.

'What does Val want to do with this place?' Mike asked.

'She wants to stay here,' replied Que. 'Her family has lived here for generations and she's hoping Tommy or Maddy will make it their home, too. The kids don't want to leave.'

'Val grew up in this house. She's lived across the road for as long as I can remember.' Connor had never expected the kid with brown curly hair to become the swollen, bruised mess he'd found with Que only yesterday morning. Yesterday felt like a week ago.

'A lot of work for one woman with two young children,' said Mike as they got out of the car and looked around.

'I'll help her if she needs it,' announced Que.

'You farm?' Connor arched his eyebrow at her. Que didn't even mow her lawn, she had Mike for that.

Que lifted that dainty chin of hers. 'Well, I'll learn.'

Mike chuckled. 'I'm on Connor's side. You know, him the farmer and me the horticultural guru of green.'

'If Val needs help, I'll do it. Isn't that what neighbours do?' The fire was stunning in her eyes, and with hands on hips, she was a force to be reckoned with. 'I'll be in the house.'

'She'll do it, you know,' said Mike.

'Do what?' Connor tilted his head watching Que head for the house. There were no other signs of life, except the dogs he'd chained up yesterday. Connor grabbed the bag of dog biscuits and dished up the dogs' meals while Mike refilled their water buckets.

'Que will probably spend all her time and energy helping Val,' said Mike.

'I notice Que gets quite determined once she puts her mind to something.' She was a very independent lady. He admired that about her.

'You see, before Que came here, she never got involved in people's lives, what with her travelling all the time.'

'Running you mean?

'Until she moved here, Que never got into the whole neighbourly thing. But look at what she did for your folks.'

'She did heaps for them, and never wanted anything out of it.'

'Well, not that our girl Que's a saint, but she chose for the first time to not only get involved with your parents, but with this Val, too, even if this whole incident is hitting pretty close to home for her.'

'Don't need to tell me.' Connor just wished there was a way he could make her nightmares stop.

'You don't get it. What happened to Que occurred in a block of apartments, smack bang in the middle of suburbia, where none of them idiot neighbours bothered to get involved to help Que when Jeremy started hurting her.'

Connor scowled. 'You're kidding?'

'Nope. Even when I was bashing down her door to find her on the floor, those neighbours poked their heads out, but they said nothing and did nothing.' Mike scowled with heated anger in his voice. 'If only one of them had bothered to make an anonymous phone call to the police, Que wouldn't have ended up as bad as she did.'

Connor remembered asking Que if she wanted to get involved with Val's business from the beginning. 'Well, we're here now, doing the neighbourly thing. Let's take a look at the place.'

'How long have you lived here?' Mike asked as they walked

towards the shed.

A whirly-whirly of red dust whooshed past the gaping shadow of the open shed only to fall like a red rain of dust by the deserted cattle yards, as if trying to put the ugly past to rest. 'Grew up here? Why?'

'How is it that Que, who'd only been here a few days, helped your folks out and no one else did? I thought country people were known for community spirit.'

They probably turned a blind eye because they didn't like Connor. 'It won't be long and they'll learn about Val.'

'Even though Que has commitment issues of the heart,' said Mike, 'she'll commit to helping Val first before anything else.'

That'd make her too busy for Connor. *Oi.* 'Have you got any ideas for what'd make for a good crop out here?'

'For you? Or for two single mothers about to break their backs on a place that needs a tonne of help?'

Connor frowned at the smart-arse, who was right. Que was a determined woman.

'There's plenty of infrastructure, and Val's parents did cattle and feed crops. Gary tried fruit trees but, in this soil ...' Connor kicked at the dusty paddock's soil, which wasn't nearly as rich as the soil on his parents' farm, or Que's. 'Any suggestions, guru of green?'

Mike's grin made his freckles blend. 'I'm sure I can come up with some ideas.'

'We should talk to my dad. He's quite knowledgeable, with his market gardening skills.'

'Your dad has skill and years of experience. I like him.'

'Let's see what else we can salvage ...' The men were walking around the sheds when Connor's phone rang. 'Morning, Sergeant.'

'Where are you? Is Que with you?'

'We're at the Cromwell's, feeding the dogs while Que gets some things for Val. Have you found Gary yet?'

'No. But, mate, the reason I'm calling is I've received word that Jeremy Rawls is in Darwin.'

'Jeremy is in the Territory?' Connor widened his eyes at Mike. The deeply tanned ginger went white behind his many freckles.

'He's transferred to work the mines up here,' continued Marcus over the phone to Connor.

'Which mine site?'

'The Ranger Mine in Jabiru.'

'Kakadu! That's too damned close.'

'I'm waiting on confirmation from Jabiru police, but I can't kick over too many rocks without giving away Que's position, you understand?'

'Yeah. I do.'

'Connor.' Mike thumped Connor on the shoulder. 'Look …'

Connor's scowl deepened and his grip tightened around the phone, as he stared at the hunk of metal hidden in the shadows of the tree line.

'What's going on?' Marcus demanded over the phone.

'Get over here now, Marcus. We've just found Gary's ute.'

36

Inside Val's house, Que made her way to the bedroom as the fridge hummed in the background and a clock chimed. Wallpaper peeled around holes dispersed along the corridor walls as her footsteps creaked on the floorboards.

In the lounge the photo frames held images with broken glass, the couch sat on bricks, and the curtains where so thin mere threads held them together.

Que only planned to get the basics because she was definitely going to pamper her friend with some new slippers, a nightgown, and a comfy but luxurious dressing gown.

In the bathroom, she packed creams and deodorant, and other items Val might require. The rest she'd score from the supermarket until the mail arrived with loads of online goodies, she'd helped buy with Val's children last night. Que was planning a Mother's Day surprise for her friend who was going to be stuck in hospital for at least ten days. They all needed something to cheer them up.

An exposed lightbulb shone in the bedroom, where the windows were boarded up. The bed was a mess. Linen was strewn across the floor, the mattress ripped with its metallic springs and coils poking out from open cavities, and the drawers tossed from a dresser that barely held up its smashed mirror.

Did someone break in? Or was it like this before, because Val was too sore to clean up the tantrums of her husband? A scene Que remembered all too well.

'Are you stealing from me?'

Que jumped and spun around to face the doorway. 'Gary!'

He wiped his nose with the back of a hand that gripped an almost empty bottle of rum. 'I know you. You're that nosy woman from across the road.'

'The neighbour, yes.' Que tried to remain calm, but inside her heart pounded in pure panic. 'Connor's here too, and Mike. Feeding your dogs.'

'My what? Who?' He peered back to the end of the hall. 'Yeah, right …' He scoffed at the silence. 'Where are my children?'

'At school.'

'What are you doing in my house, then?' Gary's eyes were bloodshot, and the ruddy stubble darkened his complexion, with his dirty shirt hanging over work jeans and boots.

'I'm just getting some things for Val. I'll get out of your way.' She tried to brush past him, but he blocked her exit.

'Where's my wife?' Gary's low voice made the hair on the back of her neck stand up. His rum-breath was like slime sliding across her cheek.

She was back in a place she never ever wanted to be, re-living her nightmare all over again.

'Answer me. Where. Is. My. Wife?' He poked her arm, and it rippled like a thousand blades beneath her skin.

'Don't you touch me.'

'This is my house. I can do what I want. *Thief.*' He stepped in so close, Que cringed against the wall.

Not again. Helping a neighbour and getting accused of stealing when trying to do good. 'I AM NOT A THIEF.' She shoved into Gary's left shoulder, it knocked him off balance, enabling her to scoot through the doorway.

'Where do you think you're going?' Gary's fingers tangled in Que's hair to yank her backwards.

She screamed and screamed as loud as she could and kept on screaming.

'SHUT UP.' Gary had his hands around her throat, cutting off her screams.

She couldn't breathe.

37

A scream carried on the breeze, chilling Connor to the absolute core. The screams of a woman. *'Que!'*

With his heart in his throat, Connor sprinted across the field, straight through the back doorway to find Que held against the kitchen wall, struggling for air. Tears and sweat trickled down her red face as she lashed out at Gary, scratching, kicking, fighting for her life as he lifted her off her feet by the throat.

'Let her GO!' Connor grabbed the animal and let his fists do the talking. He pummelled them into flesh, as his anger completely took over. Even as he felt bones break, he continued to punch. Punch after punch. Again, and again.

'Connor! STOP.' Que gripped his bloodied fist, blocking him from throwing another punch.

He didn't want to stop, pinning the animal to the wall as he tried to shake her off.

'Stop, Connor. Please, stop.' Her grip slipping, as tears streamed down her face, and with those angry red marks around her neck it only enraged him more. 'Please, Connor. Don't do this.'

He blinked at her, as the memory of that god-awful night, that left his brother a bloody mess and his mother on the floor, flashed in his mind.

'Connor, you can stop.'

Could he?

Inside, he wanted to kill. Purely. Simply. Kill. The man who'd hurt women—his wife, now Que. Gary didn't deserve to live, even with his face all smashed up and bloodied, wheezing for breath.

Just like his brother.

Except this time he let go …

Gary crumpled to the floor on hands and knees, gasping for air.

Connor had been so close to tripping over that edge of no return.

'Are you ok?' Que whispered, with her familiar fragrance enveloping him.

'Are you?' He checked her throat.

'I'm going to be fine, and so are you.'

Had he finally put his ghosts to rest?

Right now, all he could do was hold her tight. He'd come so close to losing her. Even though she hadn't said she loved him, he couldn't lose her. Ever.

38

'Do you think the doctor has forgotten about me?' Stuck in the hospital's examination room, Que was keen to go and visit Val.

'Be patient.' Connor shuffled closer beside her on the bed.

'I don't enjoy being a patient in a hospital.'

'*Impatience* should be the middle name for both Billie and her mother,' said Mike, leaning against the wall.

Marcus grinned, straightening up as he flipped over the pages of his clipboard. 'Right, Ms Quentin Mornell, I'd like you to read and sign this statement about what Gary did to you today, and you can sign-off on yesterday's statement as well.'

She looked at Connor because the policeman knew her real name. 'I can't.'

'Easy …' Marcus held up his palm. 'I've spoken to the prosecutors who are handling the case, and they're going to keep your name off the records under witness protection, without being in witness protection.'

'You can do that?'

'It's my town, I can and will do what is necessary to protect its people.' Marcus patted her arm and said, 'You live here, so that includes you and your little girl.'

'Thank you, Marcus. You're okay, for a cop.'

'Hey, don't ruin my reputation. People might mistake me for the good guy.' He chuckled. 'Now you two gentlemen, check over your statements and sign them if they're correct.'

A constable knocked on the door. 'Hey, Sarge, we're ready.'

'Please witness each other's signatures. I'll be right back.'

As they read, signed, and witnessed the statements, Marcus spoke with the doctor and two other officers in the hallway.

'What's going on?' Que asked Connor.

'I'd say they're getting ready to transport their prisoner.'

She went to move off the bed, but Connor stopped her.

'Where are you going?'

'To see Val.'

'Wait for the doctor, first. Please?' He slid his arm around her waist, holding her close to his side, and she rested her head on his shoulder. Why move when this was the safest place on the planet.

'Impatience, I tell ya,' said Mike with his cheesy grin.

'All done?' Marcus asked, returning to the room with the doctor.

'Yeah, here.' Connor handed Marcus the paperwork. 'You look busy.'

'Busier than normal.' Marcus scanned over the documents, then passed then onto the waiting officers, who disappeared down the corridor.

'Is Gary still here?' Que asked Marcus. Val would freak knowing they'd been attending to Gary's injuries at the same small hospital.

'Leaving for Darwin as we speak. I'm refusing his bail.'

'Gary wouldn't want to show his face near me again,' said Connor coldly.

'I doubt Gary will. Not in this town.' Marcus's phone rang. 'Excuse me.'

'Okay, now it's my turn,' said Doctor Mannen, approaching Que. 'Just to be on the safe side, I've ordered an ultrasound on your throat, just to check for any damage, as this has unfortunately happened before.'

She squinted at Mike, *big mouth.*

He responded with a silent, *up yours* grin that only a best friend could get away with.

'The nurse won't be too long to take you through,' continued the doctor. 'Then I'm suggesting you stay off solids for a few days.'

'Looks like I'm buying more ice cream for home, then,' said Connor, gently squeezing her shoulders.

'CRAP!'

Everyone looked at Marcus standing in the hall, staring at his phone.

'Marcus?' Connor approached his mate. 'What's wrong?'

Marcus removed his cap and brushed fingers through his hair. His boots clomped on the tiles, closing the door behind him. 'Connor, weren't you in bomb disposal?'

'Tactical disarmament for landmines and car bombs, yeah. Why?'

Marcus hesitated at those in the room.

'Marcus?' Connor stepped up to his mate with the doctor

beside him.

Que slid off the bed, with Mike coming to her side. 'What's going on?'

'A kid has taken a hand grenade to school,' said Marcus, speaking to Connor. 'He's lost the pin.'

'What kind of hand grenade?' Connor asked.

'I'm hoping you'll tell me.'

Que's skin crawled with goosebumps, holding a hand to her tender throat. 'What about the children?'

'The school principal is evacuating everyone now.'

'I'll alert the medical team and find our volunteer ambulance crews,' said the doctor.

'Thanks, Stewart.' Marcus nodded to the fast-exiting doctor. 'Connor, I could do with your help on this one, mate?'

Connor hesitated, looking back at Que.

Que squeezed his arm. 'Go, I'll get the kids.'

'No, I'll get them,' said Mike, stepping up to join the group. 'You stay here, my sweet.'

'Mike's right, the doctor hasn't given you the all-clear,' said Connor. He turned to Mike and handed him the ute keys. 'Mike, take the three children home. I'll call my parents to meet you there.'

Que noted that Connor said *home*. That's twice now he'd called her place home.

'You stay here. I'll come back,' he said to her quietly, 'so don't you go anywhere.' His lips pressed against hers in a kiss of confidence, with their lips flush and completely connected. She gripped his shoulders, hanging on for the ride from his all-consuming kiss. 'I love you, Que.' And then he was gone.

All of them, Marcus, Connor, the doctor, and Mike. Gone …

Just like she had wanted all along.

But was it what she truly wanted now?

With a heavy heart the eerie emptiness of the room pressed upon her, she finally found the courage to whisper, 'I love you, Connor.'

39

'You know, this is my first time in the front seat of a police car, Officer.' Connor grinned at his mate, who was driving with lights flashing as they sped towards the school. 'The old Sergeant took great pleasure in throwing me in the back.'

'Don't I know it, the old prick he was.' Marcus turned into the school, where fire trucks were flashing lights everywhere.

'Looks like the whole gang is here.'

'I'll need them, because I've just sent two of my best officers to Darwin on a prison escort.'

'Which is why you need me?' Both keeping the conversation light as they approached a heavy situation.

'No, you're the bloke I know who's been playing with ammo since we were kids, making trench art. You just never grew out of it, only to find a way to get paid for it.' The fire crews waved Marcus through to the main oval, where he parked. 'There's the principal, standing beside Jax in the fireman's outfit. He's the new fire chief. You'd like him, ex-air force, runs a gym from the fire station, which he calls the doll house.'

'The name suits it.'

'Yeah. Guess who his father-in-law is?'

Connor shrugged. 'Should I care?'

'The Station Hand.'

'Damn. So, this Jax …'

'Top bloke. He's got the station set up to sit back in these armchairs, drink coffee and watch the planes land after our work out. Jax is my sparring partner. Unless you want the challenge if you decide to stick around town.'

'I'd kill you in combat, cupcake.' They both chuckled only for their grins to disappear as they climbed out of the car where the tension hung thick in the air.

'Marcus, the boy is on the oval,' said Jax. 'I've got my team ready to create a perimeter, and the principal has the children getting on the bus now.'

'Excellent. How wide will the blast perimeter be, Connor?'

'We don't know what it is, so the bigger the better. Aim to clear a radius of five hundred metres for shrapnel. Marcus, I'd say the safest place for civvies is to have them gather at the sportsground.'

'Good call. You heard the man,' hollered Marcus to the many gathered around him. 'All non-essential personnel to the sportsground. Principal, have the buses take the children to the sportsground and tell the parents to collect them from there. Jax?'

'I'll have my team push back the traffic and block off the road and tell any parents where to collect their children,' said the fire chief. 'The Station Hand and his work crew are here to help.'

'Good.'

Sheesh, the Station Hand was the last man Connor needed to see.

'Sarge … Sarge …' An Indigenous woman in police uniform barrelled her way through the gathering crowds, dragging an enormous sack.

'Tanisha, thanks for doing this for me.'

'I grabbed everything I could think of from the storeroom, Sarge.' She opened the bag and dumped a range of police helmets and vests on the ground.

'Connor, have a look at it. We're not equipped for this sort of work,' said Marcus. 'The last time we used this riot gear was for a softball match.'

Amateurs. Connor had none of his usual webbing, no helmet, and no tools to do the job. His dad's tools were on the back of the ute Mike was using to collect the children.

He scoured the scenery for the old grey ute that had been following them from the hospital. It was now leading the parade of cars that followed the crowded school bus.

'You'll be wearing this.' Marcus pressed a vest to Connor's chest. 'That's an order.'

Connor slipped on the bullet-proof vest, bearing the word POLICE in big white letters. Securing the sides in place, he spotted the small child in the middle of the oval with a man in a black cowboy hat. 'Who's that out there?'

'My big brother, Ryder Riggs,' said another man in a fireman's outfit.

'Rigsy, meet Connor,' said Marcus, 'Rigsy, care to explain why your brother is out there?'

'He's ex-Army armament or something.'

'Are you saying your brother is a weapons fitter?' Connor

asked.

'Yeah, Ryder fixes up guns and stuff.'

'Good, he'll have the tools I need.' Connor grabbed a water bottle and stalked towards the field. 'See you on the other side, Sarge.'

'Not without me, you don't.' Marcus walked beside him as they aimed for the centre of the school oval.

The school was the same, with the one squat building and a big oval with a mixture of soccer and football goals on each end of the field. It even had the same cricket pitch in the centre. The only change was that the basketball-netball court was now undercover. 'It's smaller than I remember … fitting we're trying to save a school we both kept trying to avoid.'

Marcus gave a low chuckle beside him, both keeping it light considering the danger they were approaching.

'You could stay back and coordinate your crew, Marcus.'

'You haven't got a radio and if I give you one, you'll probably pull some karaoke crap that'll make us all tone deaf by the end of the day. Besides, I'm not letting you have all the fun.'

They approached the calm cowboy sitting with the trembling, pasty-faced child, covered in sweat. They sat facing each other holding the grenade between them.

'Mind if we join the party?' Connor squatted down on one side with Marcus circling them, checking the wider perimeter. 'I'm Connor, Sergeant Special Forces. You Ryder?'

'Yeah.' The man with a deep cowboy tan had a no-nonsense air to him 'You with the SOCs?'

'I am. And that's Marcus, he's a Sergeant too.'

'I know your brother, Rigsy.' Marcus nodded at Ryder.

'Everyone knows Rigsy in this town,' said Ryder, giving a nod of his black Akubra, while his hands remained steady on the boy's. 'This is Levi Kimble.'

'One of Supermom Karen's children?' Marcus squatted down next to the small boy and patted his shoulder. 'We'll get you back to you mother soon, mate.'

'So, what do we have, Ryder?' Connor knelt to check over the scene.

'It's an old grenade that Levi said the pin fell out of. I'm just here holding his hand waiting for you fellas to show up.'

'Glad to be of service. I hear you do armament.' Connor slid his cap backwards, then leaned down on two hands as if doing a press up. 'Got your tools handy, Ryder?'

'The zip case by my left boot. Good thing they were in the ute. We'd only come into town for supplies and have lunch at the pub, when we heard the news. It's an old grenade, but I didn't get a chance to touch it because Levi started getting a little weary and the whole safety catch collapsed on itself. If we let go …'

Connor nodded, getting the message. Ryder was holding the fuse down, if he let go, *boom*.

Connor flicked open the tiny toolkit and removed a small flathead screwdriver. 'Levi, you'll feel me touching you and the grenade. I'm just looking, so don't let go. Have you got him, Ryder?'

Ryder gave a firm fearless nod. 'We're solid.'

Connor peered around the grenade clutched in a sturdy set of working man's hands with the small boy's fingers underneath. With the screwdriver, he ever so gently scraped on the base for the identity marks on the rim.

'Do you recognise it, Connor?' Marcus asked.

'It's an Mk 2. A pineapple. I haven't seen one of these in a while. Hold him steady, Ryder.' Connor lay down on his side and peered underneath. 'Damn.'

'What?' Marcus asked.

Connor sat up and took a deep mouthful of water. 'The lugs have gone on the safety catch, which holds the entire fuse and full charge.'

'That's what I thought,' said Ryder. 'Do you know much about this grenade? I only know modern weaponry.'

'It was a World War II special, commonly used. But she'll be touchy. Over fifteen per cent never worked due to manufacturer error, or we can hope the humidity has stuffed the gun powder, or ...'

'In other words, don't let go,' said Ryder, with his hands covering those of the boy who looked like he was going to faint.

'We need to get Levi out,' said Marcus.

'Agreed.' Connor and Ryder replied in unison.

Connor sat back, wiping a hand over his mouth, then re-adjusted his cap. 'Here's the plan. Ryder, we'll hold the lever in place while you shift to the back of the boy. I want to be where you are. We'll move in a clockwise direction. Levi, Marcus will keep you in place covering the cap while Ryder gets behind you ...' And they slowly moved around like pieces on a sundial, all holding the bomb in between them.

'Ryder, you pull the kid's hands free. I'll take your place. Marcus, keep it steady.'

After what seemed like hours, Ryder pulled Levi away from the bomb. And they all sighed with relief.

'Get him to his mother,' said Marcus with his hands full.

Connor helped Marcus hold the grenade that was barely steady in one piece. He could feel its fragile state. 'Hey, Levi, tell your mother Connor says hello.'

The boy just trembled like a pale leaf, probably in shock.

'I'll buy you blokes a beer later.' Ryder scooped up the boy in his arms, rushing Levi across the oval to the waiting ambulance.

'So, what do we do now?' Marcus asked Connor, both holding the grenade between them.

'Remember when we used to find these pineapples and brass casings along the railway line?'

'The Triple Js have been scouring that district for years with their metal detectors. I thought they'd found them all.'

'This is too well maintained for something found in the scrub.' Connor looked at the grenade carefully. 'The safety clip is made of a different metal. It's aluminium when pineapples, or Frag grenades, were made from cast iron. And look at the area for where the pin sits, it's been stretched.'

Marcus narrowed his eyes at the metal work. 'Are you saying that the safety pin was meant to fall out?'

Connor shrugged. 'Or it could be a botched home restoration, because the lugs that hold the safety catch and pins are completely gone. There's no rusty remnants either for a piece this old.'

'What do you suggest.'

'You go stand by your fancy cop car and do your job, Sergeant.'

'While you do what?'

Connor grinned. 'How big a perimeter did you send them away?'

'Over five hundred metres. Are we far enough away?'

'Well, that depends on how far I can throw.'

'Think you can aim for that spot over there.' Marcus nodded at the sign poking up through the grass.

'I'll give it a shot. Look, nothing might happen at all, or the detonator could just go off in my hand.'

'My hand's in there too, so just do it.'

'You never did say no.' Connor grinned at the boy he'd known, now the man ready to ride along as always. 'On the count of three, you pull your hands away, I'll throw, and we both drop.'

Marcus nodded.

'One … Two … Three …'

40

Que stared at her phone, willing it to ring.

'Still no word?' Val asked, from her hospital bed. She had drips and splints on her arm, but her eyes were clearer today.

'Mike has the children at home, roller-skating. Connor's parents are there making afternoon tea.'

'Bertha makes the best banana bread,' said Val.

'Want me to bring you some with custard. It's easy on the throat.'

Val's lower lip quivered as her eyes watered. 'I'm so sorry Gary did that to you.'

'Hey, it'll be fine.' She squeezed her friend's hand. 'Do you want Mike to bring your children in?' Because Que urgently needed a decent hug from Billie. And Connor. She was desperately worried something had gone wrong. The man was working on a bomb.

Again, she jumped to her feet, chewing her thumbnail as she peeked out into the corridor. Nurses were milling around, and the doctor was nowhere in sight. From the window she could see the ambulance was still missing from its parking bay. If she were a St John's volunteer, she'd know exactly what was going on — this not knowing was the worst, because everyone knew about the grenade at the school, leaving the place a ghost town.

BOOM!

Que rushed to the window in Val's room with her heart aching. *Please let Connor be safe, please ...*

'What is it?' Val asked. 'Can you see?'

'Nothing, just smoke. A plume of black smoke, like those ...' She swallowed hard kicking herself for never telling him she loved him. Had she missed her chance?

Staff and patients ran down the corridor.

'I'm going to scout for a coffee. You get some rest.' Que followed the small crowd to the nurse's desk, where Jenny, the head nursing sister, was in charge.

'Calm down, everyone!' Jenny called to the gathered crowd of staff and patients. 'The children are safe at the sportsground and are being collected by their parents as we speak. So please, everyone, back to your rooms. Nurses ...' Jenny lowered her tone and said, 'we have an incoming ambulance bringing a small child, clear the area *now.*'

Que hung back. 'Jenny, can I leave.'

'No. Doctor Mannen will get to your paperwork soon, he's just a little busy.'

'I understand, but I'm fine.' Que wanted to play with the children, to banter with Mike, to laugh with Richard's fatherly assurances and indulge in Bertha's motherly warmth. But most of all she wanted to hug Connor, to squeeze him tight as they watched over them all. She wanted to go *home!*

'I'd love to let you go,' said Jenny, 'but as it's part of a police investigation, they need to be thorough. You understand.'

'Yeah.' Sadly, Que did understand the technicalities, all too well.

For the umpteenth time, she sent a text message to Connor. *Are you okay? Please answer. Please let me know.*

When a shadow fell over her phone while she waited for Connor to text her back, she glanced up, only to do a double take and for her jaw to drop.

It was him.

'Hello, beautiful.'

Que swallowed, blinked, then bolted for the nearest exit.

'QUE! GET BACK HERE!'

It was Jeremy. A voice she'd never forget. A voice that made her skin crawl.

And in a sheer blind panic, she ran down one corridor, twisted down another and spotted the green Emergency Exit sign. Dead ahead.

She wasn't stopping for anyone.

41

BOOM!

It was an impressive display of smoke and dirt exploding high into the sapphire sky, only to rain down as the aroma of gunpowder filled the air. It left a gaping hole in the dirt with a charred sign that read: *The Site for Elsie Creek's New Pool.*

'Looks like we've given the school a head start in digging their new pool,' said Marcus. Both men lay on the lawn, laughing, watching the smoke clear.

'It's good to have you back in town, brother.' Marcus playfully punched Connor on the shoulder.

'Glad to help, brother.' And they were brothers.

A tall shadow from a man with an enormous hat, blocked the sun. 'I could never split you pair up, now could I?'

Damn, it was the Station Hand.

'Ron.' Marcus got to his feet, helping Connor up. 'You remember …'

'Connor Symes, I do. Your partner in crime, who helped steal my ute.'

Connor looked at Marcus. He'd never rat out a mate, especially one in Marcus's position.

'Ron, build a bridge and get over it, already. I told you Connor had nothing to do with it.'

Oi? Connor arched his eyebrow at Marcus. Could he still be charged for a crime that happened over fifteen years ago? 'Brother ...'

'You be quiet,' snapped Marcus sternly at Connor who then faced the legend. 'Ron, there was no proof. And you know it. You got your ute back in one piece and, really, under Northern Territory law you could've been booked for leaving your keys lying around as temptation for juveniles to go for a joyride.'

'Still sticking up for each other, eh?' Ron squinted at them, his leathery skin crinkling around his hard eyes. Poking back the rim of his Akubra, exposing the flecks of grey in his dark hair.

'If you don't mind, Ron, this is not the time or place. I'm sure once it's all settled, we can have a sit down,' said Marcus.

'No need. I only came out to say boys do things, but I know now you two were meant for more. Look at what you did here, for this town. Ryder told me what you do in the military, Connor, he says it's hardcore. What you did here, today, you two men are heroes in my books.' Ron even gave a nod, then held out his large working hand.

Connor shook the hand of the legend, feeling a change in the wind, where the other people watching on were no longer scowling at him.

'Welcome back to town, Connor.' Ron patted Connor's shoulder. 'Well done, both of you.'

'Thanks.' Connor shrugged at Marcus.

'Now let's get back to work. Ron, can you and your road crew check this rubble for shrapnel, we wouldn't want any of the children getting hurt.' Marcus pointed to the hole they'd made.

'Sure thing, Sarge, I'll get my men on to it.'

'Who can give me a lift back to the hospital?' Connor wanted to get back to Que.

'I'll take you,' replied Marcus. 'I want to talk to Levi about where he got that grenade from, if he hasn't gone into shock.

'I thought he was bigger,' said Connor, as they crossed the oval with Ron going in the other direction. The Station Hand was smaller, greyer, older, just like his parents.

'We just grew up, mate.' Marcus gave him a sly grin. 'For the record, it was my plan, I drove the ute. And I told Ron it was all me over a bottle of rum ages ago. I had to if I was to take this town's posting. I told him that you had nothing to do with it. You were just made guilty by association.'

'I stole the keys and helped you push that ute. Why did you boot me out of the car that night?' In the dark well beyond the town's limits, Marcus had shoved a hand full of cash into his pocket and pushed his friend out.

'We had to split up while they were chasing us. You needed to get out of this town, especially when you were being blamed for things you didn't do. Off the record, they never caught me, so we were never there ...' Marcus patted Connor's back as they headed across the oval. 'I'll always have your back, brother, because you've always had mine.'

'Thanks, but I'm shouting you another bottle of bourbon for us to drink together.'

'Sounds like a plan.

Connor's phone beeped and he smiled at Que's message. *Are you okay? Please answer. Please let me know.*

'Days like this, I'd love to have something like that.' Marcus nodded at Connor's phone. 'Messages from a loved one telling me they're worried about me.'

Connor's grin grew as he scrolled through the many messages. He didn't think people cared.

'How many did you get?'

'Twenty-four.' From his parents, Mike, but most of them were from Que.

'If you stick around, I might have the perfect part-time job for a man of your skills.'

'Doing what?'

'Well, you could run a women's self-defence class for starters.'

Connor slowed down his step, thinking of Que and Val straight away.

'I've also been looking for someone to manage the local firing range a few days a week,' said Marcus, as they resumed their stride back to the car. 'It needs some work done to the place, but I have a budget for my crew to do regular firearms training. I also need someone to educate the locals applying and reapplying for their firearms licences. You've trained men in your outfit; this should be easy?'

'I didn't say I was staying.' Yet it was so very tempting.

'You're staying.'

'But I might be busy helping the neighbours with their farm.'

'Who, Que's?'

'I wish. No, Que wants to help at Val's place.'

'Que doesn't strike me as a lady who farms.'

'She doesn't.' He shook his head. 'But Val needs help.'

'Well, mate, have you ever heard of the Outback Sisterhood?'

'No.'

'Now there's a town secret I don't mind sharing with you. You should talk to your mother about the Outback Sisterhood and Karen Kimble—considering you just saved her son.'

Ryder approached, handing out water bottles. 'Hell of a blast, fellas.'

'Here, thanks for the loan of your tools.' Connor swapped the tools for water.

'Did Levi say how he ended up with a grenade at school?' Marcus asked.

'From a father at the school,' replied Ryder, poking back the brim of his hat. 'Not his own father. Levi told me he was supposed to pass it to another child for show and tell. He was told the grenade was a fake. When the teacher saw it, she raised the alarm.'

'What was the child's name?' Marcus asked.

'Billie.'

'The boy?'

'Billie, the new girl with the roller skates.'

Connor's blood turned to liquid ice. 'He's here! He's going for Que.' Connor and Marcus ran for the police car. With doors slamming, siren blaring, and tyres screeching, they tore out of the school and raced for the hospital.

42

Que's throat burned, aching for air, as she slammed her shoulder against the heavy EXIT door. It triggered an alarm as it opened. *Whoop-Whoop-Whoop.*

The sound was deafening.

But she wasn't expecting anyone to show up, as they were all too busy focusing on the school.

With arm raised over her head to shield her from the bright sunlight, she tried to get her bearings. She was on the helipad.

'Get back here, Que!' Jeremy called out behind her.

She sprinted across the helipad, heading for the airstrip.

Mickey, in his grey coveralls, drove his fancy golf cart towards the airstrip, towing a plane. With a scowl of his leathery wrinkles, he twirled his grey cloth in the air like a short stock whip. 'Hey, get, lady! This is restricted airspace!'

But Que couldn't stop. Jeremy was her worst nightmare she didn't want to share with anyone. The man had tried to kill her best friend and wouldn't blink at destroying an old man like Mickey if they got in his way.

She tore across the tarmac towards the hangar. Maybe she could hide in there because the police and fire station stood empty.

She was on her own!

In the distance Cecil, the water buffalo, grazed on the far edges of the airstrip's tarmac, eating the wildflowers. Nearby lay a pile of star pickets and other fencing materials, glinting in the sun.

Cecil was her friend. And this was her town. Wasn't it?

She leaped over the fencing poles and wire, rolled in the dust, then sprang to her feet. She was done running.

Jeremy was never going to leave her alone. It was time to fight for her family, for her home, and for her freedom to live.

She picked up the nearest star picket and turned to face her greatest fear. Her past.

'What do you think you're going to do with that?' Jeremy chuckled, resting his hands on his knees, catching his breath.

'You come any closer and you'll find out.' Determined, with her heart hammering in her chest, she raised the picket like a lance, ready to spear the enemy. It was heavy, and hot from lying in the sun, but it was time to take charge and be her own knight without a horse or shining armour.

Jeremy looked the same as the day they'd met, six years ago. The handsome man she'd met over a croupier table, dated, then proposed to her when she'd told him she was pregnant. The man who'd handfed her cake on their wedding day. The man everyone liked, who had a dark side that had scared her from ever loving anyone again.

'This ends today, Jeremy. It's over. We're done. This is my house.' She was playing for the house and the house always won — she was fighting for her *home*.

'We're done when I say we're done,' Jeremy said. 'Did you

honestly think you could hide from me? Out here?'

'How did you find me?'

'Mike. Hightailing it out here in a panic yesterday, straight to your front door. I see you still have that van.' He then scowled at her in a black vicious look that scared her to the core. 'But I wasn't expecting you to be shacked up with some other man. He looks like a soldier. Do you sleep with him for protection?'

'Leave me and my family *alone.*'

'You are *my* family. No one else's. You are my wife and you belong to me.'

She backed up with the star picket aimed and ready. 'What do I have to do for you to leave me alone?'

He pulled out a pistol from an ankle holster and aimed it at her. 'Drop the pole and come with me, because I'm not going anywhere without you, wife.'

She trembled under the outback sun, as a bead of sweat trickled down her face, but tightened her grip on the pole. 'NO.'

'You can't say no to me, after all you've done. You owe me. But that's okay,' he said, flipping from anger to an eerie serene calmness. 'We'll be a happy family again, you, me, and maybe even Billie, if she survived that blast.'

'YOU STAY AWAY FROM BILLIE!' Her voice echoed over the tarmac as her hatred fired the adrenalin through her system. This ended today.

An almighty deep grunty-growl rumbled behind her, as if from the belly of hell itself.

'What is that?' Jeremy waved his gun to the one side.

Que peeked over her shoulder.

It was Cecil. The tame, ribbon-wearing, stumpy-legged water buffalo, with flowers drawn over his sides in chalk. But with his big black head down and his blunt horns wrapped in neon pink ribbon. His large heavy hooves pawed at the dirt, snorting with fury, keeping his angry dark eyes and scowl aimed at Jeremy.

'Go on, get!' Jeremy fired a shot in the air.

Que flinched.

But Cecil didn't hesitate. His hooves kicked up a trail of red dust behind him as he charged with head low and ribbons flying. The ground shook beneath Que's boots as the buffalo charged right past her and straight for Jeremy.

Jeremy pointed his gun, and another loud shot rang out.

Cecil didn't stop, slamming headfirst into Jeremy's stomach, with the full weight of half a tonne of charging water buffalo.

Jeremy's harrowing screams echoed as he was tossed into the air, landing with a thud, only to be rolled in the dust by those horns.

The large beast skidded to a stop, galloped in a half circle, then pawed at the dirt with head down, putting his body directly between Jeremy and Que. Cecil gave a loud snort, anger showing on his normally gentle face, as his front hoof angrily slammed hard at the dirt. Then he charged again, straight for Jeremy.

Again, the ground rumbled under his heavy weight.

On his knees, covered in dirt and blood, Jeremy struggled to lift the gun to aim at the buffalo.

BANG-BANG-BANG. Three shots exploded in the air, from different directions.

Jeremy dropped to the ground.

Cecil stumbled.

Que screamed as her ears rang from the gunshots.

The water buffalo crashed on his side in the dirt, unleashing a heart wrenching cry of pain. Blood splashed his ribbons as he bleated on his side.

'Cecil!' Que dropped the pole and ran for the animal who'd come to her rescue. She tore off her jacket and pressed it against the gaping hole in his chest.

Further along, Jeremy lay motionless in the dirt.

On the edge of the tarmac stood Marcus and Connor. Elsie Creek's notorious bad boys, now men, wearing matching POLICE vests, holding identical pistols steadily pointed at Jeremy.

Mickey was the first at her side. 'Cecil, you'll be right, old fella. You'll be right, mate.'

'Que, are you, okay?' Connor demanded. Both men kept their arms steady with weapons aimed as they approached Jeremy, lying still in the dirt.

'I'm okay, but Cecil's been shot.' Adrenalin pounded in her ears, as tears and perspiration fell freely. This shouldn't be happening.

Cecil was her friend, visiting her every morning, bringing her joy when she didn't want to smile. He'd helped her to forget her fears, helping her share words of hope and wisdom. But now the waddling black mass of fur and horns lay on his side as she pressed against the bullet wound with blood seeping through her fingers. She did not want Cecil to die.

43

People came from all over to crowd the outback airstrip. The fire truck arrived with a long flatbed trailer, using a winch to drag the wounded buffalo onboard. A doctor arrived in surgical scrubs, along with nurses and the vet, as they transferred Cecil to the nearby hangar, where its large doors shut out the world.

Outside, the crowd grew as the sun sank lower, all keeping a vigil, waiting for the hangar doors to open with news.

Que sat with the grey-haired Mickey and his brother Billy, with the Triple Js nearby. They all sat along the hangar's edge and waited.

'He's gonna be all right, missy,' said Mickey, gripping Que's hand. 'He's got the doctor and that fancy vet who can fix anything. Cecil's a tough bugger, he is.'

'I'm so sorry …' Crippling guilt burned her chest. She'd caused all of this. She should never have come to Elsie Creek, for the sake of all those around her. 'I didn't mean for anyone to get hurt.'

'Cecil was bein' a hero, he was. Even if he is a flamin' pain in the posterior, I'd never seen Cecil do that. He protected you, missy. I never knew that overfed pet had it in him to defend anyone like that, so he sure must love you, which means you must be a good sort.'

Connor and Marcus were at the Police Station, while Jeremy lay in the hospital's morgue. Connor had filled her in on what had happened at the school. Just the thought of how Jeremy had endangered all those children added another layer to the heavy burden of guilt she carried.

But all the children were safe, with the school silent. Relieved that Billie, Tommy, and Maddie were with Connor's parents and Mike.

Poor Mike would be so guilt-ridden for leading Jeremy straight to her, but she'd never hold that against him. They'd been through hell together, and would survive as best friends forever.

Kat showed up with Lucy, providing coffee and blankets. Kat put a blanket around Que's shoulders. 'Do you want me to get you a clean shirt?'

Que shook her head, trying to hide the blood on her shirt as much as she could. 'How's Karen's boy, Levi?'

'Levi's going to be fine, lapping up the attention from his siblings. Karen's a mess, but she's going to be fine, too, and told me to tell you to hang in there. She's sitting with Val.' Kat put an arm around Que's shoulder, giving her a tender squeeze 'Hey, we know about your husband ...'

Probably half of Elsie Creek knew by now. There were few secrets in this town.

As the last of the orange fire in the sky disappeared, the first stars of twilight sprinkled like diamonds, to become one giant chandelier. The hangar's outdoor lights attracted a swirling display of night bugs, while she looked to the stars and prayed for the water buffalo to survive.

More people arrived, gathering for the animal, asking if she was okay. Strangers, all willing to help her, the woman who'd brought all this trouble to their tiny outback town. But she also heard many fine things being said about Connor and Marcus, who were the true heroes in this town.

Finally, the hangar door slid open and a robust woman with purple-grey hair and red rimmed glasses approached. 'Are you Que?'

'I am.'

'I'm Esther, Cecil's owner.'

Que jumped to her feet. 'How is he? I never meant for Cecil to get hurt. I'm so, so sorry.'

'Cecil is going to be fine.' Esther shared a gracious smile, stroking Que's upper arms in a grandmotherly fashion.

'What's his injury?' Mickey asked as Billy and the Triple Js crowded around.

'The bullet hit the meat in his shoulder, but they were able to remove it,' replied Esther. 'He'll be grounded for a few weeks, but he'll be fine. I heard my baby boy was quite the hero.'

'Ya should've seen the buff charging at that fella aiming to shoot at this girl here, Esther,' Mickey said, pointing at Que. 'He put his big black heinie in the way to protect her, takin' that bullet for her the way the secret service would for the president.'

'Cecil's my hero,' said Que. But not the only hero of her day. As news of Cecil spread among the crowd, cheers rose around her. She wiped her tears of relief, crossing the airstrip and headed for the roof painted with The Strong Arm of the Law, highlighted by bright spotlights.

'Que?' Connor met her at the Police Station's rear perimeter fence and opened the mesh gate.

'What are you doing out here? I thought you'd be inside.'

'We finished what we could in our reports. I was just coming to find you. We're going to have a drink.' He pointed back to Marcus, giving her a nod from his armchair. There was a row of armchairs, with a cowboy in black beside a fireman, who was pouring coffee from a flask.

'Who's that with Marcus?'

'Jax, the new fire chief, and Ryder Riggs, who helped me out today. How is Cecil?'

'He's going to be okay.' And then she realised. 'It's all over, isn't it?'

'What?'

'Jeremy's gone.'

'Yes.'

'Are you in much trouble?'

'No. But there's a tonne of paperwork, and Marcus is ticked at me because I stole a handgun from him. We broke so many rules today, but I'd do it all over again to save you.'

'Will Marcus get into trouble?'

'Doubt it. As kids, we broke enough rules to know the difference. This was purely justifiable. But he's gone, Que. Jeremy will never bother you again.'

'He's gone.' As she gripped his hands, she smiled through the happy tears streaming down her cheeks. 'My nightmare is over. I don't have to run anymore …'

'I know. So, what are you going to do? Move closer to Mike?'

In that moment, all the pieces came together—just the way it should. It all made sense. Everything about Connor made sense to her.

She pulled him close, and her lips meshed with his, finding that undeniable bliss of love within a kiss that could make time stop. She had crashed into something soft and warm when she didn't deserve it, for she had found love. True love.

'I love you, Connor,' she whispered. 'I love you in the way where love is not damaging, it's nurturing. I love you the way our chemistry is stronger than communication and common sense. I love you in a way that's messily and unapologetically a roof-top shouting kind of love. You and me, it's us.'

'Are you saying the kind of love that we can grow into?'

'The kind of love that will heal our jaded broken souls because we're both worthy of love for each other. I love you,' she said, gripping the sides of his face, 'so you'd better not skip out on me now, sailor, or I will hunt you down.'

'Good thing I'm trained to follow orders, and I like your kisses.'

'Me too.' They grinned against each other's lips as their kiss intensified. It wasn't punishing or cruel, it was loving, and beautiful, for this was the kind of love that truly healed the broken-hearted.

44

'You can stay at my place for a few days, if you want,' Que said, as she drove down the red dirt road with dust pluming high behind them. Val was in the passenger seat, finally free from the hospital.

'No, I want to go home,' replied Val, adjusting her arm splint. 'Don't worry, Jenny has a nurse and a carer coming to help me with things around the home until I get this splint off.'

'Are you sure you're ready?' Que hadn't been back to Val's place, not since her confrontation with Gary ten days ago.

'I miss not being home, especially my children,' said Val. 'Gary won't be around, so I need to get things in order.'

'Well, if you ever need me …'

'I know you're right across the road.' Val gently patted Que's hand. 'Thank you for everything.'

'That's what neighbours are for.'

'More like good friends,' said Val as they turned into the driveway, which had been freshly graded, now smooth and free from rocks and ruts, with its trimmed natives exposing a large lane way. 'Who's been looking after the place?'

'Connor, Mike, and Marcus too. Mike has taken leave to stick around for a while. He sleeps in the Mighty T, claims it's his now.' Que rolled her eyes. The trio of men had become best mates, hanging out by the bar on her back verandah. They'd take turns manning the barbecue, in between taking swings at golf balls, aiming across her pretty new pond. They were training Princess to retrieve them, which finally wore out the hyper dog.

Then, when the children were sleeping, the grown-ups would settle at her amazing gift from Connor, a large card table with proper clay chips. While she learnt their tells in poker, Marcus and Connor talked about the new firing range, taking turns trying to convince Que to become a paramedic-in-training for the local bush hospital.

But she couldn't, not until she knew Val was back on her feet.

Que was also involved in conversations with Marcus and Jenny, the nursing sister, to help run a support group for women in their region. But she'd put it all on hold for Val. Val needed the support today and for who knows how many tomorrows.

'And how are my children?' Val asked.

'The best. I can keep them, you know.' Que grinned at Val. 'Tommy's been helping the men out after school.' She was so proud Tommy had some positive male role models in Mike, Connor, and Marcus. 'They said they've brought your children here ...'

Around the bend, the drive opened wide to the homestead, Que slowed right down to lean over the steering wheel.

'Oh, my word ...' Val covered her mouth, staring wide-eyed through the front windscreen. 'What's happened?'

'I don't know.' Que stopped the car and stared at the many cars parked where there had once been a rundown junkyard. It had now been miraculously transformed.

'Do you know all these people?' Que recognised some of their faces. Once strangers, now people with names she remembered.

Billy, in his snappy suspenders, carried a sheet of corrugated iron with the help of his brother, Mickey, in grey coveralls. They held up the tin sheet for the Triple Js to screw it into place on the side of the hay shed.

'Why is my van here?' Her caravan stood by the shed's corner, which had been repaired, with men on the roof also replacing sheeting panels. Connor's father, Richard, along with a group of men she didn't recognise, were fixing the rails in the cattle yards, with more people spread out fixing fences and irrigation lines.

Jenny and her team of off-duty nurses were painting the outside walls of the house. Farmers she'd spoken to at the Mother's Day fundraiser were on the roof of the house, putting in a solar system. There were volunteer fire crews on tractors, moving the firebreaks. School teachers and children were working on the gardens around the house, and she spotted Kat with Karen inside the house, hanging new curtains over the newly repaired bedroom windows.

'I think the entire town ... everyone is here,' said Val. 'What are they doing?'

'I don't know.' Que blinked as happy tears erupted at a familiar sight. 'Cecil.' She unclipped her seatbelt and grabbed a muesli bar from the stash she kept under her car seat and approached her wounded hero. 'Hello, Cecil.'

He snorted in recognition, sniffing at her hair, fluttering those lush thick lashes that highlighted his big black eyes. She giggled as he clumsily ate at his muesli bar. No chalk on his back, but ribbons of white gauze bandage over his shoulder. It hurt to see him wounded, but she was so happy to see him, she eagerly hugged the beast.

'Well, it's about time you got here,' said Mike with hands on hips, his eyes shaded by his sweaty Akubra. In boots and cargo shorts, he looked like he was working.

'What is going on, Mike?' Que pointed to the miraculous change of the place.

'Farmhouse makeover, we like to call it. Hi, you must be Val,' he leaned past Que to shake Val's hand. 'We've never been formally introduced, I'm Mike the guru of green.'

'Hi,' said Val, shyly. 'What's happening to my house?'

'Momma, you're here!' cried out Billie. 'Tommy, Maddy, your mummy is here!' It was a family reunion, as mothers hugged their children in a place that had once radiated sadness was now filled with joy.

'Welcome home, Val,' called out Connor, as he came up behind the children.

'Can someone tell us what's going on here?' Que asked Connor.

'Well, hello to you too, honey,' Connor cupped her cheeks and kissed her on the lips, rendering her speechless.

Until Billie tugged at her shirt. 'This was a surprise, Momma.'

'Were all of you children in on this?' Que asked.

'Yep.' Tommy hoisted up his little jeans, his proud smile shining wide. 'We didn't tell the girls, until today.' His little sister was as jumpy as Billie.

'Who, what, how?'

'It was all Connor and Mike's idea. Come on, Mum, let's show you what everyone's done.' Tommy grabbed Val's good hand leading her to their house, with Billie, Maddy and Mike joining them to explain.

'How?' Que asked Connor, as she took in the amazing transformation.

'Well, Mike and I got talking.'

Que raised her eyebrow. 'A-huh?' Because the pair of men never stopped talking.

'And then we talked to Mum and Dad. Mum spoke to Karen Kimble, who called in the Outback Sisterhood. Dad talked to other people, and we talked to the men you play cards with in the hardware store and the girls you drink coffee with and they ...'

'Are you saying you gossiped? You hate gossip.'

'This time we used the gossip for good. People showed up donating stuff. There's a new washing machine, fridge, beds, and all of those goods you managed at the silent auction ended up here.'

'But that was to raise funds for the school pool.' She looked to where Kat and Karen were pulling across heavy drapes. Que recognised them as the curtains Karen had her eye on. 'Everything from that silent auction is here?'

'Except for your graphic design thing. There's furniture, car repairs, mowing, electrical, plasterwork, woodwork. All those people *paid it forward* to Val, as well as volunteering their time to give us a hand. We've repainted the inside and out of her house. Mum's making curtains for the children's rooms, and they even got a new lounge suite and wide-screen television.'

'It's a total house makeover.'

'Think bigger, babe.'

'Really?' Was she dreaming all of this?

'Mike has worked out an amazing deal for Val, too.'

'Doing what?'

'Mike wants to lease Val's land to the university and the agriculture college in a combined project, where the students can gain real-world experience.' Connor waved his arm towards the paddocks. 'The students will work on this farm in a rotation, so Val doesn't have to worry about it. The two schools will also pay her power and water bills and even offer Val a wage as the caretaker of her own property, until she's ready to take over. I'd like you to donate your caravan as a place for those students to stay.'

'What?' She blinked at her security blanket, The Mighty T, which had been her home for years.

'It's time to cut those ties, honey, and let it be home for someone else.' He squeezed her shoulders.

Connor was right.

'Where did you get the idea to do this? Why …?'

'I did this for you.'

'Me?'

'Yes. I'm very selfish about the time I get to spend with both you and Billie. Especially you. So when I realised you were going to sacrifice everything to help Val, I didn't want that for you. I want you to start living your life the way you've always dreamed of, Que. Maybe be that paramed—'

She grabbed the sides of his face and pulled him close, pressing her lips against his, and kissed him like an explorer discovering the treasures of the outback. She kissed him. Fully. Completely. And undeniably with every bit of experience she could muster.

But it went so much deeper …

It was the type of kiss that tasted so sweet and warm it came with loaded layers of luscious love.

He wrapped an arm around her waist, pulling her into his chest, gathering her silky hair in one hand, and they dived deeper into that kiss. It was a kiss she'd never dreamed of ever giving, and one she never wanted to end. It was a kiss that meant everything, that said …

'I love you, Connor.' Once she'd admitted it, she felt their love grow stronger every single day. 'I didn't think the boy-next-door was my type.'

'I didn't think I was the boy-next-door type,' he said, gently stroking her hair. 'But I'm glad the old neighbourhood's picking up, since I came back to town.'

On a red sunburnt carpet, the once derelict homestead seemed to rise like a phoenix from the ashes. It was the foreground of an incredible endless blend of cornflower-blue sky.

Que's neck ached at the impossibly endless sight of the altitude. Yes, the gravity was crushing, but it was also glorious, with the sun shining like a lightbulb in the big blue ceiling.

And with it, the wind whispered a dusty promise of a fresh new start.

'Will we stay here forever, in Elsie Creek, Connor?' She looked back to the red dusty road that led to her home, then to the people who once were strangers, now friends. She loved this town.

'Forever isn't long enough, but I look forward to spending every minute of forever with you, in this town.' He kissed her forehead and whispered, 'Welcome home, baby, welcome home.'

THE END

For now …

I have a gift for YOU!

Learn the secrets of

ELSIE CREEK

Exclusive to Elsie Creek Readers!

Simply go to:

https://melarowe.com/elsie-creeks-secrets/

Did you like the story?

If so, *your opinion* matters to me!

I'd love to read your review on
GOODREADS, or BOOKBUB.

I'd also be doing my own *dance-in-the-dust* if you shared the cover of this book on social media for me to see how far this story has travelled!

Please add *#Escape2HEA* for me to find you.

With much gratitude,

mel
A . R O W E

ACKNOWLEDGEMENTS

Thank you

Thank you for reading this story of the fictitious town of *Elsie Creek*. She may not exist, yet there is a part of her found in the Northern Territory townships, roadhouses, dusty sports grounds, crocodile-crowded boat ramps, and even in the rural pubs sparsely scattered across northern Australia.

Thank you to the amazing Handbrake for not disowning me whenever I burrow down into a new story and for the technical military terms. I'd also like to thank the rest of my family who have never read a word I've written, so again, I'm putting this right here in case they do dare to indulge. As always, a big thanks to Snr ACPO Glen Coonan, Aunty, and Tony 'Duwun' Lee of Larrakia Nation for your cultural assistance. To the amazing Detective Senior Sergeant, and friend, Vanessa Barton for helping me remember the SOPs when I was all about shoot first ask questions later.

Thank you to my online writer friends who've helped me so much when I live in a world where finding decent wi-fi is like discovering gold. Thank you to the amazing editing Deb team at DNP, Kristen Woolgar for having a sharp eye, and the Fabulous First Readers team, I am truly blessed to have you all join me on my writing journey.

I'd also like to thank the quirky, colourful, and exceptionally extraordinary people I've met while working and living throughout northern Australia. The experience has been—and continues to be—priceless.

Most all, thank you to you, dear reader, I am so grateful to you for taking the time to read my story and for supporting this outback Oz author. It means the world to me.

Until next time,

A. ROWE

ABOUT THE AUTHOR

Australian bestselling author, Mel A ROWE, creates escapes for today's busy women to enjoy from the comfort of their home.

Delivered with a dash of drama, witty humour and quirky family units, Mel is known for reinventing romantic versions of home, taking her common characters on uncommon journeys that lead from boardrooms to billabongs as they try to find their own HAPPILY EVER AFTER.

Living in Australia's Northern Territory, Mel enjoys random outback road trips, fumbling with her camera, annoying her family with her bad singing, and making new friends in the middle of nowhere—except for water buffalos. She's been chased by a few.

Feel free to contact Mel, as her word journey continues, at...

MelAROWE.com

Also by Mel A ROWE

***Australian Bestselling* ELSIE CREEK SERIES**

The ART of DUST

DIAMOND in the DUST

CAKED in DUST

XMAS DUST

MUSTER in the DUST

ROLLED in DUST

WRITTEN in DUST

Standalone Stories

Avoiding the Pity Party

Unplanned Party

The Football Whisperer

USA Bestseller—Winter's Walk

Watch for more at Mel A Rowe's site.

www.ingramcontent.com/pod-product-compliance
Lightning Source LLC
Chambersburg PA
CBHW050140120726
47903CB00002B/431